A NEW DAWN

A STONEWALL CHRONICLES NOVEL

HERBERT GROSSHANS

A NEW DAWN
Copyright © 2019 by Herbert Grosshans

ISBN: 978-1-68046-745-1

Melange Books, LLC
White Bear Lake, MN 55110
www.melange-books.com

Published in the United States of America.

Cover Design by Ashley Redbird Designs

THE STONEWALL CHRONICLES NOVELS

[1]

TERREX STONEWALL EXPERIENCED A FEELING OF DÉJÀ VU AS HE stepped out of the shuttle. Almost everything looked the same. In many ways not much had changed. The mushrooms were still as huge and intimidating and the air as humid and hot. Standing still for a moment, he took a few shallow breaths, letting his system get used to the stifling heat.

Outpost Epsilon had been his first assignment as a Scout for the Solar Union. As he stood looking around, he could hardly believe that fifteen years had passed since then.

He swallowed hard as suppressed memories rushed into his conscious mind. It was here on Epsilon where he fell in love with a Tangari girl.

Sheera. He never really forgot her.

Shrugging, he studied his surroundings. The original dome, which protected the outpost, was still there, but he saw three more domes, one of them larger than the others. All four domes were connected by tunnels.

The area around the domes had been cleared of vegetation and a large number of the giant mushrooms, allowing a good view of the sky overhead. Even the landing pads for the shuttles had been enlarged and paved.

1

A Builder-ship was parked near the largest dome. Construction robots were busy cleaning up the site. As far as Stonewall knew, the habitat was finished. The ship might move on to another part of Epsilon and begin building another settlement or it might possibly travel to a different planet. He didn't know its schedule and didn't really care.

This time, nobody came to greet him. He wondered how many members of the original crew were still around.

They had changed the entrance to the dome. Instead of a door, he saw a small building, like a guardhouse. His assumption proved correct. When he approached the dome, a door opened and a man wearing the brown uniform of the Scouts appeared. He carried a flash rifle, but he didn't act hostile.

Stonewall wore the same uniform, except his was adorned with a small bar on his left sleeve, proclaiming his rank as Master Scout.

"Welcome, sir," the guard said, saluting stiffly. "You've been expected."

Stonewall returned the salute and smiled. "I hope there's a cold beer waiting for me."

The guard gave him a strange look, his posture still rigid. "I'm not sure what you mean, sir."

Suppressing a chuckle, Stonewall said, "I have a feeling things have changed a lot. Relax. I'm not going to shoot you for not rolling out the red carpet as soon as I stepped off the shuttle."

"I still don't understand, sir."

Stonewall sighed. "Forget it, son. Just let me get out of this friggen greenhouse. I'm dying here."

"Sorry, sir." The guard didn't move. "I need to see your papers, sir."

"My papers?" It was Stonewall's turn to stare. "Didn't they brief you about me?"

"They did, but I still need to see your identification papers, sir."

Stonewall glared at him, irritated. "I am Master Scout Terrex Stonewall. I didn't come here for a vacation because I love it here so much. We used to call this place *Shithole* and I was happy when I finally left it after spending two friggen years evading oversized lizards and other hungry beasties. So be a good boy and step aside!"

Stonewall noticed the tightening of the young man's jaw muscles and the flickering in the brown eyes. He had to give him credit, because the man didn't flinch otherwise.

"I am aware of your name, sir, but it is my job to insure that you are really Master Scout Stonewall. I can do that only after looking at your papers and taking a retina scan."

Sighing again, Stonewall reached into his breast pocket. "You are a stubborn young man, but I guess you're only doing your job. I hope this is not an indication of the way things are run here now. I don't need any more aggravation." He pulled out his ID card and handed it to the guard.

The guard ran his wrist scanner over it and gave it back to Stonewall. Holding the scanner in front of Stonewall's face, he said, "Please, look into the screen." Satisfied, he nodded. "Go ahead, sir. Sorry for the inconvenience, sir." He saluted again and stepped aside.

Stonewall tipped his helmet and shook his head. "Welcome back to Epsilon," he murmured. Then he walked into the guardhouse and through the door on the other end.

He stepped into cool air and breathed deeply.

At least that hadn't changed.

When he looked up, he saw the sky above him as clearly as if the dome didn't exist, even though it looked solid from the outside. *Just a matter of bending the light.* He still remembered William Peters explaining it to him the first time he entered the protection of the dome. Since then he had been in similar habitats on other planets, but it didn't diminish his admiration for the brilliant minds that had invented and designed these marvels of engineering.

Walking toward the Administration building, he wasn't sure how he would be greeted. He surely hoped that the incident with the guard was not an indication of what he could expect. The new chief of the outpost may not be as lax as Chief Farmer had been. He could still hear the Chief's words the first time they met.

Call me Chief. We are not that formal around here.

Entering the building, he walked down the familiar corridor toward the office at the end. The man behind the desk looked up when Stonewall walked through the door.

First impressions are usually the most important. Stonewall didn't get much of an impression from the man. Of average height and weight, in his early forties, his dark hair cut in the usual fashion of the Scouts, he didn't look imposing. Neither did he emanate any power or anything that set him apart from the regular Scouts.

"You must be Chief Wallace," Stonewall said, holding out a hand.

Wallace ignored the outstretched hand. He looked at Stonewall with expressionless eyes. "And you must be Master Scout Terrex Stonewall," he said, his voice as expressionless as his face and eyes. "I was informed of your arrival."

Stonewall smiled thinly. Taking back his outstretched hand, he said, "I expected a warmer welcome, Chief Wallace. After all, I came here to investigate alleged violations of treaty agreements with the indigenous population. Why the hostility?" He was surprised at Wallace's apparent resentment. Even though they had briefed him about the new chief, he suspected they hadn't told him everything.

To Stonewall's surprise, Wallace actually allowed himself a small chuckle, but it didn't sound friendly. "How would you feel if they'd send someone to undermine your authority, Stonewall?"

"So that's what you assume the purpose for my visit is. Let me assure you...I'm not here to undermine your authority, Chief Wallace. And if for some reason you are afraid I might be looking for your job, relax. I have no such intentions. The two years I spent in *Hell*, one of the nicer labels we gave this planet, will last me a lifetime. I'm here only because I am an experienced tracker, I know this planet and I had a good relationship with the Uur queen." He put his duffle bag onto the floor and began rummaging in it. Pulling out a bottle, he handed it to Wallace. "I brought you a present. This is from Earth. Authentic too. It is over forty years old. I was told you appreciate good Scotch."

Wallace glanced at the bottle and then at Stonewall. His face and posture seemed to relax somewhat. "It's been a while since I had a glass of good Scotch. Alcohol is not allowed on the outposts. You are aware of that, aren't you? How did you manage to smuggle a bottle through controls?"

Stonewall grinned. "Did you forget that I am a Master Scout? I'm not only good at finding things. I'm also good at hiding them. Take a look at the label."

"Dinosaur repellant," Wallace read. He shook his head and

chuckled. "Maybe you're not such a bad sort after all, Stonewall. Will you share a drink with me?"

Stonewall sank into the only chair in the room and sighed. "I thought you'd never ask. I don't mind a good stiff drink once in a while myself." He removed his helmet and wiped his forehead. "There was a time when I didn't drink alcohol, but time changes a man."

"Yes, it does," Wallace agreed.

Looking around the office, Stonewall said, "This office hasn't changed much since I was here last. You haven't even removed Chief Farmer's pictures."

Wallace sighed heavily. "I haven't had a chance to do much of anything since I took over Farmer's position. Too bad about him. He was a good man."

"He did have his good qualities." Stonewall watched Wallace take two glasses and a corkscrew from a drawer. It seemed that alcohol did make its way into the outpost at times.

Wallace took his time removing the cork from the bottle. He sniffed it and smiled. "Reminds me of the time I spent with my grandfather in Scotland. He taught me how to drink this stuff." Carefully, he poured two glasses and handed one to Stonewall. "Slainte Mhath."

"Slainte Mhor," Stonewall said solemnly. He downed his glass, tried not to flinch when the potent liquid ran down his throat.

Wallace closed his eyes for a moment. When he opened them, he regarded Stonewall silently. "Thank you, Master Scout. Maybe I misjudged you."

"It wouldn't be the first time someone read me wrong." Stonewall smiled, leaning back into his chair. "I'm curious, Chief Wallace. What exactly happened to Chief Farmer?"

Wallace shrugged. "I think he just got tired of this place." He squeezed the cork back into the bottle and got up to put the bottle into a small cabinet in the corner. Then he picked up a blue-shimmering many-faceted sphere from his desk. "You know what this is, don't you?"

Stonewall nodded. "A sapphire. You could buy yourself a small space ship with that one."

"Anywhere else but on Epsilon. This precious stone and others are found in abundance on this planet. The Uur mine them and shape them. They are masters when it comes to cutting gems. Of course, there are plenty of prospectors now on Epsilon who spend most of their time in the jungle digging for precious stones. The Union controls the export of these gems. Anyone smuggling them off planet is severely punished." Wallace stared at Stonewall. "There are some people out there who dispute the Union's right to control the gems and the drugs. Some very powerful people. It's all politics, you know. Farmer tried to interfere in the politics and he was caught in the crossfire. Pirates and drug dealers are another problem. We haven't been able to prevent every ship from landing in the remote regions and trying to make deals with the Uur. Some of those deals end up badly...for the Uur."

"Where is Farmer now?"

"I don't know. Maybe he's rotting on some prison planet. They took him away in chains." Wallace lowered his voice. "His reward for being a faithful servant of the Union for twenty years. I wonder what they have planned for me."

"You are certain it was a Union ship that took Farmer away?" Stonewall asked.

"It had no markings, except for its black color. The soldiers who picked him up wore the black uniforms of the Solar Union Special Forces."

"Nobody asked any questions?"

"You don't argue with members of the SUSF." Wallace chuckled grimly.

"Where were you when it happened?" Stonewall asked.

"In the office next to this one. I was Chief Farmer's assistant, in my second month of my one-year contract. That was two years ago. They told me if I wanted to rise in the hierarchy of the Scouts, I would accept the position of Chief of the outpost. By the way, I'm also the Governor of Epsilon."

"Governor? Hmm."

"Don't let the title fool you. I have very little powers. I'm just a representative of Earth."

"Well, it's a title, but I detect some reluctance on your part," Stonewall said.

"I have a problem with being forced into doing something that may never have been my ambition. Besides, anywhere else would have been acceptable but not on this forsaken hellhole."

"You could have declined."

Wallace shrugged. "I could have but then what? I'm forty-two. Too old to start another career. They would have stashed me away on some other frontier world, worse than this one."

Stonewall shuddered a little, remembering the four months he spent on Snowball, a world of ragged mountains, ice storms, and continuous volcanic eruptions. "I know what you're talking about," he said. "As hard as it is to imagine, but there are actually worse places out there than Epsilon."

"You are right, it is hard to imagine." Wallace smiled.

Stonewall rubbed his chin. "If you are so unhappy with your job why would my arrival worry you? I might want to undermine your authority? I don't quite understand that."

"Actually, it is not my authority I'm worried about. I resent the fact that they presume I am not capable of handling the situation with the natives."

"I don't believe that is the case, Chief Wallace." Stonewall leaned forward, dropped his voice to a confidential level, as if afraid someone might hear his next words. "We have a problem. The Spiders have a battleship at the edge of this system."

Wallace's eyes widened. "This is the first time I hear of it. Why haven't we detected it?"

"The ship's been there for a month. It is just beyond reach of Epsilon's detection net."

"What do they want?"

"Epsilon."

"Epsilon?" Wallace almost shouted it, his voice echoed from the walls of his office. When he saw Stonewall's brows lift, he continued almost in a whisper, "Are they insane? Why would they send a battleship to a system that has nothing they ever wanted?"

Stonewall smiled at the other man's short outburst. "It is true Epsilon had nothing to offer them...until now."

"Like what?"

"Ancient ruins."

"Those ruins are evidence that a reptilian race once inhabited this planet." Wallace searched Stonewall's face. "Is there something you are not telling me?"

"Apparently, one of the mining companies unearthed ruins older than the ones of the reptilian races. Much older. Epsilon may be one of the birthplaces of the Spider race."

"I thought the Spiders originated in the Arcturus System?"

"Possibly not. The race of the Spiders is far older than humanity. Arcturus is probably just one of the systems they colonized long before Humans climbed out of the trees and began walking erect." Stonewall laughed. "We are newcomers to the denizens of Space. Even the dinosaurs are older than Humans. Much older."

Wallace shook his head. "Assuming Epsilon is a planet the Spiders originated from, what would they want with ancient ruins? Are they saying we are desecrating the bones of their ancestors? Even if there were any, they became dust a long time ago." He chuckled. "We've had that problem with many indigenous people on Earth. Maybe we should watch out for angry Spider spirits?"

Stonewall didn't find any humor in Wallace's remark, remembering the disappearance of the holy burial grounds of his own Iroquois ancestors. "We don't know anything about the Spider's spiritual beliefs," he said. "They gave no reason. My real mission here is to find out why they are risking an interstellar war with the Humans over a planet that is not hospitable to their kind."

"What is the Union doing about it in the meantime?"

"A Union Battle Cruiser is on its way to Epsilon. They're also sending two hundred Union Troopers."

"I'm afraid to ask where they'll be stationed." Wallace stared. "But I'm asking anyway."

Stonewall chuckled. "I understand you have a brand new bubble just waiting to be filled."

"Not with soldiers. It was supposed to be training facilities for rookie Scouts." Wallace rose and walked over to his cabinet in the corner. Taking out the bottle of Scotch, he said, "I need another drink. How about you?"

Stonewall nodded. "Maybe a small one."

———

STONEWALL RECEIVED A STARTLING SURPRISE AFTER CHIEF Wallace said, "I'll have someone take you to your quarters."

The man who walked in was older than the last time he'd seen him, fifteen years to be exact, and his presence did come unexpectedly, but Stonewall would have recognized his lanky form anywhere.

"Peters?" He peered into the man's face. "What the hell are you doing here?"

Peters grinned. "I could ask you the same question. I thought you married that Tangari girl and by now you'd have at least half a dozen children."

A cloud settled over Stonewall's features momentarily. "Things didn't happen the way I hoped. Her father did not approve of his daughter's marriage to a Human." He smirked. "In the eyes of the Tangari, Humans are physically handicapped because we don't have wings."

"At least our children are beautiful and not homely like theirs." Peters shook himself. "I still remember the ugly humps on the backs of those girls." He smiled. "Of course, that didn't seem to bother you."

"You have to admit those girls were beautiful after their metamorphosis." Stonewall chuckled ruefully. "I really did love Sheera."

"I guess your ambition of becoming an ambassador didn't work out either?"

"It was never my ambition. The whole idea came from Sheera. It would have given me a chance to be near her and things could have developed from there." Stonewall smiled. "That is all in the past. It wasn't meant to be." He scrutinized the other man. "Enough of me. How about you? Why are you here and not with your wife and children? As I remember, you left the Scouts two months after I arrived here."

"Yes, I did." Peters nodded. "We left Earth to settle on *Kolibri*...to start a new life. A year later our settlement was hit by raiders. They murdered nearly half the population. My wife and son were among those killed." A twitch ran through his face. "I couldn't protect my own family. I was on the other side of the planet surveying land designated for a new colony."

"I'm sorry about your wife and son. Did they ever get those responsible?"

Peters worked his jaws in a visible effort to control his emotions. "I joined the Enforcement Patrol for a couple of years to give me an excuse to rid the universe of vermin like that. A few of us survivors from *Kolibri* formed a special unit and we searched for the raiders."

"Did you find them?"

"We did. We destroyed the whole fucking asteroid they used as their base and killed every last one of them, including their families," Peters said grimly. "I'm not proud of what we did, but their sons and daughters would have grown up to become pirates like their parents. It was justified." He gave Stonewall a sad smile. "Unfortunately, it didn't make much of a difference, did it? There are still plenty of criminals roaming the space ways."

Stonewall shrugged. "At least you got your revenge. That is something."

"Yes, it is." Peters looked at Wallace. "Sorry, Chief, to bore you again with my past. It's just..."

Wallace waved his hand in dismissal. "I understand. Seems you and Master Scout Stonewall are old acquaintances. I wasn't aware of that."

"We knew each other only for two months," Stonewall said, glancing at Peters. "But we became good friends during that short time."

"Good to hear that." Wallace heaved a sigh. "It means you two will get along. Peters happens to be the liaison officer between the Uur nation and the Humans. He can be your guide if you so wish."

"I have no objections." Stonewall smiled at Peters. "A friendly face will make my job much easier."

"I'm looking forward to working with you again. At least this time you're not the greenhorn you were back then." Peters turned to walk out of the door. "Come on, I'll show you to your executive suite." He laughed. "I believe I used the exact same words the last time, but don't worry, it won't be the dormitory. We have made some progress since then and as I understand a room has been prepared for you."

"Anything will be better than my last assignment," Stonewall said as he walked beside Peters. "Three months of traveling on the hard back of a giant worm and sleeping in a tent at night listening to howling, screeching, and the flapping of winged horrors reminded me how comfortable and safe it is in a domed habitat like this one."

Peters chuckled. "In that case it will be a picnic when you travel again on the surface of Epsilon."

"As long as it is inside a rover," Stonewall said, smiling. He knew Peters was kidding. Traveling on Epsilon was anything but a picnic. The two years he spent here had seemed like a lifetime. When he finally left, he vowed never to return. But thirteen years away from this place had softened the memories. Besides, his superiors did not give him a choice when they handed him the assignment.

Peters took him through the connecting tunnel to the next bubble. They stepped onto a street paved with molten and fused rocks. Two-story buildings lined the street on either side. The umbrellas of nearby mushrooms loomed over the buildings and the invisible shell gave the illusion of a small town nestled in a fairy tale setting.

Stonewall stopped for a moment to take in the peaceful scene. "Like a picture out of a children's storybook," he said.

"I never looked at it that way," Peters said. "This is where the enlisted men live with their families. The unmarried men still live in a common room in the first bubble. Not all of the apartments are occupied. One of them has been reserved for you."

When Stonewall looked to the end of the street, he saw the entrance to another tunnel. Beyond that, the opaque rounded surface of the third habitat rose out of the ground.

"That is our latest addition," Peters explained when he noticed Stonewall's object of interest. "You've probably seen the Builder-ship outside. They sure didn't take much time with this one. A human construction crew wouldn't be able to build something like this in such a short time. And without mishaps. So far, this last shell is unoccupied."

"Not for long," Stonewall said. "Expect two hundred Union soldiers. They should be arriving within days."

"Why would the Union send soldiers to Epsilon? Are we at war with someone?"

"Not yet." Stonewall's expression was grim. "The Spiders have expressed a sudden interest in Epsilon."

"The reason?"

"Ruins. Let me fill you in over dinner. I am thirsty and hungry. Is Tommy, the cook, still around?"

"No. He took his lover Garth and left Epsilon about four years ago. We haven't heard from either of them since. The new chef is a woman. She is quite capable, and so is her kitchen staff. All females." He winked. "I understand they do more than cook meals for the men. Anyway, those are only rumors."

"Rumors again? Like the ones about Tommy and Garth?" Stonewall laughed.

"The ones about Tommy and Garth were true," Peters protested.

"What about the kitchen staff? You're not sure about them?"

Peters shrugged. "Never felt the need for their services. After my wife died, I lost all interest in women. My career is all I'm thinking of." He glanced at Stonewall. "And you?"

"I have needs and I have no problem with searching out female companionship. I never say no to a willing woman." Stonewall smiled. "There is only one condition. She has to be beautiful."

"Of course," Peters said dryly. "Beautiful women are better lovers than ugly ones, I suppose."

"I'm not saying that. The way I look at it, making love is like eating. A good-looking plate of food enhances the appetite. Does the food taste better?" Stonewall shrugged. "Maybe."

"How about closing your eyes when you eat?"

Stonewall punched Peters on the arm and laughed. "And rob myself of one of my senses? Never!"

"You are a demanding man, my friend. I hope your expectations are always met."

Stonewall grinned. "Not always. Maybe that is the reason I haven't had much luck lately."

"I'm afraid your luck won't change greatly here." Peters stopped in front of one of the buildings. "Here we are. Your quarters are on the first floor."

They entered the building through the main entrance. Each building contained four apartments. Peters pointed to the door on the left. "That one is yours." He opened it and made a motion for Stonewall to go through the door. "There are no locks." He smiled. "No privacy, either."

Stonewall looked around in the apartment. It was surprisingly spacious, considering space was at prime inside the bubbles. "It seems a shame that one man should occupy this much room," he commented.

"It wasn't meant for only one man. We just happen to have a few still empty. All of these buildings are fairly new. Not all the families have arrived yet. In a few months from now these will all be occupied."

Stonewall shook his head. "Much has surely changed since I left. I still remember the cramped quarters we lived in, sharing one room with a dozen other guys. I suppose some of the families have children?"

"They do."

Stonewall didn't really have to ask the next question. He could guess, but he was curious anyway. "What about their education?"

"Oh, that is taken care of. We have a classroom and a teacher. There are only nine children here, but we are expecting six more. She'll have her hands full."

"She?"

"Yes. The teacher is a woman. Miss Leroux. Simona Leroux."

Stonewall threw his duffle bag onto the small couch. Looking at his watch, he shrugged. "I'll have to get my watch adjusted to local time." He searched for the computer readout on the screen beside the door. It showed five zero three. Pressing his watch against the screen, he said, "Synchronize time."

It took only a moment. "Time synchronized." The computer advised him with a pleasant female voice.

He glanced at the watch, satisfied when he saw the numbers matched the ones on the screen. Then he looked at Peters. "What time does the kitchen open?"

"It is open now. Meals are usually served between five and seven."

"Well, let's go then. I'm starving."

They walked back into the first bubble and headed for a building Stonewall hadn't seen before. It turned out to be the kitchen and mess hall. Some of the tables were already occupied. Peters waved to a group of men sitting at the second table.

Stonewall studied the two women behind the serving counter and had to agree with Peters. They would never win any beauty contests, but they seemed capable of doing their job as they efficiently and with a smile heaped food onto the trays. The counter looked nice and clean and the food steaming hot.

"You're new here," the first woman said to Stonewall.

He nodded and gave her a friendly smile. "How did you know?"

She smiled back. "I know every guy on this base." She bent forward and whispered. "If you ever feel lonely, come to the women's quarters and ask for Orina. That's me. I'll keep you company for a while. And believe me, it does lonely here." She looked at Peters. "You too. My door is always open."

Peters grinned. "So I've heard."

She made a face. "Don't believe everything you've heard, smart guy." Then she chuckled. "But on the other hand, maybe you should."

"Thanks for the invitation," Stonewall said. "I'll think about it."

The second woman winked at him. "Hi. I'm Melina. What do they call you?"

"Stonewall." He studied her casually. She wasn't bad-looking, he decided.

Nice figure. I guess in a pinch I could overlook her thick, wide lips and overbite.

"Stonewall?" she repeated. "I like it. Nice, strong name." Her teeth flashed white in her freckled face. "Don't be a stranger. I'd like to welcome you properly. Make your stay on this hellhole a bit more pleasant."

"Thank you," he said. Shaking his head and chuckling quietly, he followed Peters. *Things have changed more than I thought since my last tour of duty.*

The four men at the table Peters headed for looked up and gave Stonewall a nod.

"Watch out for that one. Her pussy has more teeth than a carnosaur," one of them said, laughing. Then he noticed the bar on Stonewall's sleeve. He stiffened in his seat. "Sorry, sir, I didn't mean to

14

sound...chummy, Master Scout." He threw a glance at Peters. "You could have warned me," he said with an accusing tone.

Stonewall smiled. "Forget about my rank. I've never been one for rules and regulations. Think of me as one of the guys."

"Thank you, Master Scout."

"And don't call me Master Scout, please. I'm Stonewall." He took his seat and looked at his plate. "I hope it tastes as good as it smells and looks. I've been eating too much gruel for these last few months."

"They may not be the best looking women, but they know how to cook. Among other things." The man chuckled. "By the way, I'm Barry Sanchez." Then he pointed at the other three men. "The guy with the mousy mustache is Felix Morano. The short one is Paul Tsang, and last but not least I'd like to present Greg Erickson. We've nicknamed him 'The Giant' because of his size."

Erickson laughed good-humoredly. His blue eyes twinkled. "I'm barely seven feet tall. There are bigger men out there," he said with a rumbling voice.

Stonewall, who stood six-one, grinned. "There are but I haven't met many with shoulders as wide as yours. I feel like a dwarf against you."

"We all do," Tsang said. "Don't feel bad." He chuckled. "Of course, I always feel like a dwarf."

The other men laughed.

Stonewall felt an instant liking to these men. Maybe his stay would turn out pleasant after all. He dug into his food and found it delivered what it promised. "This is good," he commented. "Too bad we have to drink water instead of beer."

"Beer?" Peters asked. "I was under the impression you didn't drink alcohol. Well, well...it seems there is hope for you yet." He looked around the table. "We're about to get company. Stonewall tells me the Union is sending two hundred soldiers to Epsilon."

"Really?" Morano raised his eyebrows. "Can't say I'm surprised. On my last visit to Star City, I spoke to a couple of miners. They told me that the *Uur* have been attacking spore-miners. Maybe they're getting frustrated and asked for protection." His dark eyes rested on Stonewall. "Am I getting warm?"

"Not really." Stonewall looked at the men. "I shouldn't be

discussing this with you, but I see no harm in it. You'll find out sooner or later. A Spider battleship is sitting at the edge of this system. The Spiders are disputing our claim on Epsilon. They want us gone."

"Are they mad?" Sanchez asked. "We've been here for over twenty years. We've barely begun colonizing the planet. They can't demand and expect everyone leave. We won't take that lying down!"

"We won't," Stonewall said. "That's why the Union sends its own warship. The *Jupiter*, a Class seven Dreadnought, is already on its way."

"That should put some fear into those *Webspinners*," Sanchez said.

"Let's hope. We know very little about them and what they're capable of," Stonewall warned. "The reptilian races keep their distance from the Spiders. So do the Crows. Maybe they have reason to fear them. We are relative newcomers to the Space Community, the new kids on the block. We don't want our noses bloodied by messing with the wrong people."

"By people you mean the Spiders?" Peters chuckled. "I wouldn't exactly call them *people*."

"What would you call them?"

"Pumpkins with hairy legs. How dangerous can they be?"

Everyone laughed again.

"I ran into them on *Fortune*, an unexplored planet in the *Silica System*. One of their exploration shuttles went down in the desert. The Union sent me to lead a rescue team and check for survivors. We did find the stranded shuttle, but the Spiders didn't even let us come close. Two of them met us with weapons in their hands and told us to leave the area immediately. They had not requested our help and wouldn't need it. If you ask me, they looked pretty intimidating. I wouldn't call them pumpkins on legs." Stonewall sipped from his glass. Putting it down, he smiled thinly. "I think we need to tread carefully around them and not rattle our sabers too much. Nobody wants a war with the Spiders."

[2]

The Union troop transporter landed without much fanfare on the cleared area the Builder-ship had vacated. It sat there like a huge black, ugly bug. Under the giant mushrooms it looked almost as if it belonged. Stonewall stood beside Chief Wallace to welcome the troops.

The first man to step onto the hard-packed soil was big and imposing. His black uniform was snug, almost too small for his large frame. He appeared unarmed but Stonewall spotted the big gun hanging from the man's wide belt.

Two more black-clad soldiers climbed down the steps and positioned themselves on either side of the big man, large flash rifles at the ready.

"That's Commodore Chelzic," the Chief said. He allowed himself a small chuckle. "Did he expect to be attacked the moment he jumped out of the transporter?"

"I imagine he is only cautious," Stonewall said, not wanting to make any derogatory remarks. One never knew what kind of listening devices the Military used. It wouldn't do to be on the bad side of Commodore Chelzic. He didn't know the man personally, but he had heard rumors. Chelzic was not a man to be crossed.

The Commodore seemed to have seen them because he began walking toward the spot where Chief Wallace and Stonewall waited for him.

Behind him more soldiers began spilling out of the ship.

Chelzic reached them and saluted. "Chief Wallace, I presume?"

"You presume correctly." Wallace returned the salute.

Chelzic looked at Stonewall. "And who might you be?"

"Master Scout Stonewall, Commodore." He also saluted but didn't put much enthusiasm into it.

Chelzic scowled, obviously disapproving of Stonewall's behavior. "I was told of your presence, Master Scout. I expect a report of conditions on Epsilon on my desk first thing in the morning." His eyes flicked to Wallace. "I hope our accommodations are ready, Chief Wallace."

"They are ready," Wallace said. "The Builder-ship left two days ago."

"Good. Now, if you don't mind, have someone take me to my command post."

Wallace cleared his throat. "We don't really have an actual command post ready for you, Commodore. You must remember this is not a military base but an observation post. The new bubble was constructed to house rookie scouts, not soldiers."

Chelzic gave him a hard stare. "My orders are to make this outpost my base of operations. I expect to get you and your staff's full co-operation. Starting now, Planet Epsilon is under Marshall Law until further notice. Is that understood?"

"Fully understood," Wallace said.

Stonewall suppressed a chuckle as he became aware of the Chief's irritation. And he had been worried Stonewall might undermine his authority.

Wallace turned to the two men behind him. "Take the Commodore into Bubble four and show him his quarters."

"Yes, sir."

Stonewall recognized Erickson's deep voice. He turned to look at the *Giant* and winked, but Erickson looked straight ahead. If he had seen Stonewall's gesture, he didn't acknowledge it; however, the other scout smirked.

The Scouts had no love for the soldiers of the Solar Union, but neither did soldiers have much respect for the Scouts. In their eyes, Scouts were only glorified watchdogs, who did nothing but stand guard or do some tracking once in a while. The real men joined the Military, not the Scouts.

Stonewall watched Chelzic and his two Troopers follow Erickson to the new bubble. He was glad they had their separate entrance. The soldiers would keep to themselves in their habitat and would not mingle with the outpost's crew.

The only pain in the ass will be Chelzic. He looked at Chief Wallace, not envying his position. This was his post and he didn't need a blockheaded military officer giving him orders.

"What a pompous ass," Wallace cursed under his breath when he thought Chelzic was out of earshot.

"I couldn't agree more," Stonewall said, watching the soldiers assemble in front of their transporter. All wore black uniforms; all were heavily armed. It made him wonder what lay ahead. He didn't have a good feeling about it.

"Let's get back to my office," Wallace said. "I'm ready for another Scotch. I fear we are in for some unpleasant times. There is only one thing I'm curious about."

"What's that, Chief?"

"How in hell is he going to impose Marshall Law on this whole damned planet with only two hundred men?"

"Beats me, Chief." Stonewall had been thinking about that same thing. He lifted his head to look into the sky where dark clouds were beginning to gather. Rain or possibly a storm was on its way.

Epsilon seemed angry about something. As if to underline Stonewall's feelings, the challenging roar of a carnosaur echoed from the nearby jungle.

He followed Chief Wallace back into the habitat.

"Do you mind if I skip that Scotch, Chief? You heard the Commodore. He wants to see me in the morning. I have to get some stuff ready. Nobody advised me about any reports." That was only partially the reason Stonewall didn't want to join Wallace for a drink. He had made a date with Orina, the Kitchen helper. He needed something more than a Scotch.

She waited for him by the women's quarters. Smiling, she slipped her arm into his. "I wasn't sure if you would follow up on my invitation," she said.

"Why not?"

She shrugged. "You don't seem like that kind of guy. I hear you're a Master Scout. That true?"

"It's true, but don't let that impress or intimidate you. Deep down I'm only another guy with needs and a few dreams."

"I can satisfy your needs, but I don't know about your dreams." She laughed. "Maybe you should tell me about them."

"Let's get to my place first," he said, steering her toward the entrance of the tunnel that led to the next bubble.

As they entered the short tunnel, a couple of men came out of it. They glanced at Stonewall and Orina and chuckled, but they didn't say anything. Stonewall felt self-conscious about being seen with the woman. Obviously, everybody knew the reason she kept him company.

She seemed to sense his uneasiness but misread the cause. She laughed and pinched him in the side. "Are you that anxious to get me into your bed? How long has it been since you've been with a woman?"

"Too long," he murmured, hurrying her along.

"Look at the dark clouds," Orina exclaimed. "I think we're in for a big storm. I wouldn't want to be outside now."

Stonewall agreed. Even though he knew that a protective shield covered the habitat, it was still disconcerting to see black clouds swirling and rolling across an angry looking sky. He couldn't hear any sound, but he knew that a fierce wind was beginning to blow across the artificial barrier and that soon it would turn into a howling storm.

They arrived at the building he lived in. He opened the door for her and let her enter the main entrance.

"I've never been in one of these buildings," she said, doing a little dance on the polished floor.

"Well, then it is about time," he said, opening the door to his apartment.

When she walked into the large living room, she exclaimed loudly. "Wow! I surely call this living. I believe I like it here. Maybe I'll move in with you." When she saw his expression, she laughed. "Don't worry, Master Scout. I could never belong to only one man. Now, where is the bed?"

"In the other room, but I was hoping we could just talk for a while. Or do you have another appointment tonight?"

"No other appointment." She sat down on the couch and studied him. "You are a strange one. Most men don't want to talk, not with their mouth anyway. All they want is get me naked and themselves between my spread thighs. What do you want to talk about?"

"Nothing in particular. Whatever comes up."

Orina's teeth flashed white in her black face. "Whatever comes up? I like that kind of talk. Come join me on the couch. I'll sit in your lap and we'll see what comes up." Then she became serious. "Maybe some talking will do me good too. I mean...talking with a man about other things than male and female anatomies and how they fit together so well." She patted the seat beside her. "Come, sit and let's talk."

He joined her on the couch, wondering if it had been such a good idea to invite her to his apartment. What was there to talk about with her? They had nothing in common.

"How long have you been here?" he asked.

"About three years."

"Do you like it here?"

She stared at him. "Does anyone like it on a planet where you can't walk around without worrying if you'll be the next meal of a giant lizard? Where you need a facemask and an oxygen tank strapped to your back for fear of inhaling poisonous spores?"

"What then made you come here?"

"Money. I grew up in old New York. In the slums. My two brothers are in jail for killing someone. My oldest sister got murdered by a customer. I don't need to tell you how she made a living." She shrugged. "There was no future there for me, so I left Hell behind and came here."

He chuckled. "From one hell to another. I'm not sure if you made such a good trade."

"Believe me, I did. Maybe when my contract is over they'll transfer me to another outpost or perhaps to another planet that is more pleasant and more people-friendly." She looked at him, a dreamy look in her eyes. "Maybe I'll meet some nice man, get married, have children, live in a house with a large yard, have a garden where I can grow my own vegetables, lie naked under the sun and go swimming in a lake with clear, clean water."

"That sounds nice."

"It's a dream that I have. How about you? You are a handsome guy. Have you ever been married?"

"No."

"Engaged?"

He shook his head, thinking of Lucinda. They had been lovers for a while until she started fooling around with her own cousin. She was the reason he joined the Scouts in the first place.

Orinda's dark eyes were full of questions. "How old are you?"

"I'm thirty-eight."

"Thirty-eight? There must have been some woman in your life? Ever been in love?"

"Yes, I have. A long time ago. Her name was Sheera. She was not human."

"What was she?"

"Tangari." *Oh Sheera, beautiful, lovely Sheera. Why couldn't you have been human? Things would have been so different.*

"I've heard of the Tangari. They have wings, right?"

"Yes, and that was the problem. Her father didn't think she should marry a Human. As far as the Tangari are concerned, Humans are crippled. Earthbound." He chuckled. "I loved her with all my heart, but I might as well have loved a dream-persona. That's all she is now, only a memory out of a beautiful dream."

"At least you have that. I've never loved anyone." Orina reached for his hand and stroked it. "I don't know if I ever will." She moved into his lap and kissed him. "Let's go into your bedroom. I'm good at making a man forget the things that haunt him. And if I'm lucky I forget about mine."

They lay on the wide bed and began undressing each other. When she was naked, she turned onto her back and opened her legs wide. Staring at the black curls that covered her swollen vulva, he touched it, trailed his fingers down to her pink slit and inserted one finger. She moaned and grabbed his wrist. "I need more than a finger," she whispered.

He moved on top of her and looked into her large, brown eyes. The dark skin of her face shone like soft satin and he bent to put his lips on hers. Her hand snaked between them and grabbed his erection. "Put it in," she moaned into his mouth.

He chuckled and pushed forward, enjoying the wonderful feeling of her soft walls closing around his hard shaft.

"There is no hurry," she gasped as he began to move in and out of her. "I'm prepared to spend the night with you. I hope you can last long."

"Get ready for a long night," he groaned, closing her mouth with his.

―――――

THE STORM WAS A BAD ONE. AS STONEWALL WALKED ACROSS THE hard floor toward the building where Commodore Chelzic had set up his headquarters, he glanced at the artificial suns lighting up the inside of the dome. There was nothing to see past the shield but angry and rapidly moving black clouds blocking the light of the primary sun from reaching the surface of this part of Epsilon.

He felt tired. Orina had kept him up half the night talking to him with her body. She had not disappointed him and made him forget his troubles for a while. For that he was grateful. She was a woman with great passion and she hadn't held back when she lay in his arms.

Of course, he was fully aware that her passion was not reserved for him alone. She had told him about her dream of getting married, but he knew that may never happen. Orina was not a woman who would be happy with just one man. He could be wrong about that. People have a way of changing, of adapting to conditions around them.

He sighed. She had given him what he needed, but this was probably only a one-time thing. He didn't know if he would ever seek her out again.

Saluting the two Troopers standing guard in front of the entrance to the building, he suppressed a grin and walked past them. *Talk about being paranoid! What kind of dangers is he expecting here in the safety of the bubble?*

Chelzic looked up when Stonewall walked through the door. He sat behind a massive desk and Stonewall wondered briefly if Chelzic had brought it with him. He saluted and waited for the Commodore to say the first words.

"You're late, Master Scout." Chelzic scowled. "I expected you here at seven hundred hours."

"You said in the morning," Stonewall said, irritated. He didn't like to be criticized.

"That's right...in the morning. Early morning! It is now past nine hundred hours. That is not early morning." He glared at Stonewall, but then he shrugged. "I should know better than to expect anything different from a Scout. You are not military and lack the discipline of one trained in the art of war where a man's discipline is part of his survival skills."

I may not be trained in the art of war, but I can handle a gun, and if I had one, I might just shoot you arrogant bastard! Stonewall was beginning to fume, wondering how long it would take until he forgot about *his* discipline and lose his temper. As far as he knew, it was not his duty to report to Commodore Chelzic. Then again, he had to tread carefully. He didn't want to end up in front of a firing squad. Declaring Marshall Law was serious business. "I believe if there would ever be a war, I would be able to defend myself. So would any of the other Scouts. However, we are not at war right now."

The Commodore's gray eyes almost spewed bolts of lightning as he regarded Stonewall with a look of disgust. "There is a Spider battleship on our doorstep laying claim on a planet we have owned for over twenty years. Make no mistake, Master Scout. We are at the brink of war. It is imminent."

"We may be at the brink of war, but it isn't imminent, sir. Nothing ever is. There is always a way out. We should not be making hasty decisions we might regret later. We know very little about the Spider race and engaging them in a stellar conflict might end up disastrous."

"You're damn right it will end up disastrous!" Chelzic growled. "We'll blow them out of existence."

"I meant for Humans, sir. I advise extreme caution."

"You advise extreme caution?" Chelzic's expression was almost one of pity. "I wasn't aware that you are a professional strategist. What military academy did you attend, Master Scout Stonewall?" His words dripped with sarcasm.

"None, sir. I'm only trying to use common sense, sir. The Spiders are an unknown factor and may well be our superiors when it comes to advanced weaponry and warfare. Their race is much older than ours." Stonewall found it difficult to stay calm.

"Let the experts be the judge of that, Master Scout. I suggest you just stick with what you've been trained to do. By the way, what is your actual assignment on Epsilon?"

"To find out the real reason the Spiders are here, sir."

Chelzic chuckled. "We know why they are here. They want Epsilon."

Stonewall swallowed, determined not to let this man upset him. "But why do they want Epsilon? My mission is to find out."

"Well, mine is to protect what belongs to us. Whatever their reason, it doesn't matter. Epsilon is ours and it will stay ours. If they want to fight us over it, then we will oblige them." He chuckled again. It sounded like the rumbling of a carnosaur. "We have developed some new weapons which we are dying to try out."

"I hope you are using those words hypothetically, Commodore. I don't want to sound like a pessimistic prophet, but I have a feeling your way will have catastrophic consequences."

Chelzic laughed. "As I said...for the Spiders. Show some backbone, man. We have to stand up for what is ours. We can't let a bunch of oversized, eight-legged, hairy arachnids, who happen to display a certain level of intelligence, dictate terms to us. We have to show all of those non-Humans that we are a superior race. They need to know that they can't mess with us. Today it is Epsilon, tomorrow...?" He shrugged. "Maybe Earth herself. We have to make sure that never happens."

"We'll see," Stonewall said. He didn't find any reason to argue the issue any further. "You said yesterday you wanted a progress report? Well, I've arrived here only a few days ago. There is nothing I can report to you."

"According to my files you've spent two years on Epsilon and are an expert on conditions on this planet."

"My knowledge is thirteen years old. Much has changed since then."

"That may be so, but there are things that are still the same. I understand you've made sort of a connection with those giant ants?"

"With the Uur nation. I had a good relationship with their Queen. She trusted me. But I don't know if she is still around. If you want to communicate with the Queen, you should have a talk with William Peters. He is the liaison officer between Humans and the Uur."

"There is no need for me to talk to the indigenous population. I suppose we don't have any jurisdiction over them...yet. Some day that will change. They will have to be indexed and brought under Human control. If they want our protection, they'll have to contribute to the cost of giving it to them."

"They haven't asked for our protection, sir. And as for indexing them, well, good luck. This is still their planet, you know." Stonewall couldn't help but commenting on the Commodore's remarks.

Chelzic let out a rumbling chuckle. "Somehow I expected you to say something to that effect." He bent forward. "Listen, the Galaxy is a violent place, populated by violent life forms. It's has always been like that, dog eat dog. Unless you work your way up to be at the top you will always be the underdog. Hell, from what I've heard, this planet is one of the worst ones when it comes to violence. These ants are used to that system. As soon as they recognize that we are the top dogs, they'll accept that."

Stonewall smiled grimly. "They are not dogs, sir. They may not know about that rule. Their society is different from ours, different from many other races. They may just put up a fight."

"It doesn't matter, Stonewall. How can they stand up against *our* superior weapons? Besides, if we don't defend Epsilon, the Spiders surely will claim it. What do you think they'll do to your precious friends?"

"I don't know what the Spiders will do, sir. We know less about them than we know about the Uur."

Chelzic shook his head. "You know, Stonewall, you are the most pessimistic person I ever ran across. You'd never cut it in the Military. How did you ever make Master Scout?"

"By doing my job well, sir." Stonewall drew himself erect. "If you think that soldiers are the only ones facing danger, I would like to correct that assumption. Scouts may not have to confront enemy soldiers, but we don't live a peaceful existence. Our hazards are different from yours but just as real and possibly even more treacherous. I challenge you to go alone into the jungle with only a scooter and a flash rifle. Then we'll see how much help your warfare training really is."

"That was quite some speech, Master Scout, but I've heard all that before. Scouts whining about their harsh life." He pointed out of the window. "You live in a protected environment most of the time. Soldiers hardly do. We are used to hardship and we never whine about it. So spare me yours. You'll get no pity from me."

"I wasn't asking for any. Is there anything else I can do for you, Commodore Chelzic?"

"You suggest I should venture into that mushroom jungle out there? Well, as it happens, I've been planning exactly that, but not on a scooter. My sources tell me, that the raging storm out there is slowly abating. Tomorrow at dawn, if conditions permit, we will take a ground-vehicle and you can introduce me to the wildlife on Epsilon. Just you and me. And a couple of Troopers."

"What is the purpose of that exercise?"

"I want to pay Epsilon City a visit."

"In a ground-vehicle? Do you have any idea how far Epsilon City is?"

"I'm familiar with the cities and the location of most of the larger settlements on Epsilon. And their distances from each other." Chelzic sounded condescending. "It is roughly one hundred miles from here to the City. Why? Is that a problem?"

"One hundred miles of thick jungle, infested with carnosaurs, dragons, poisonous plants, and insects, small and large. It is not advisable."

Chelzic laughed. "Didn't you tell me you do this kind of stuff all the time? Traveling through jungle teeming with hostile wildlife?"

"If I'm forced to, yes, alone, when I don't have to baby-sit a bunch of inexperienced men who have never even seen a carnosaur or a viper that spits acid into your face. Acid so strong it will eat through your facemask and clothing in moments. Or a beautiful flowering plant that looks harmless until you come close and it wraps its tendrils around your body so fast you can't escape its crushing embrace."

"Come on now. Don't make it sound so glamorous. We'll wear protective armor and carry detonation-rifles and flamethrowers. You scouts always like to over-dramatize." Chelzic made a dismissing motion. "Report at dawn tomorrow. And make sure you're not late again."

Stonewall sighed. "I'll be here. One request though. I'd like to have William Peters accompany us. He'll be a great asset."

"All right. Let him tag along. I'm sure we won't need his presence, but I'll let you have that little whim if you feel more secure. Dismissed."

Stonewall saluted and walked out of the office.

It's your funeral, Chelzic. I won't make a special effort to save your hide should the opportunity present itself.

As luck would have it, he ran into Peters on his way to the mess hall.

"You're late for breakfast," Peters said.

Stonewall grinned sourly. "You're the second person today who tells me I'm late."

"Who was the first?"

"Commodore Chelzic."

"Ah, the man who is here to protect us from the evil Spiders."

"Yeah, right. I have a feeling we need protection from him. He's an extremist. A man with delusions of grandeur. Maybe Epsilon will teach him some humility. By the way, you are going to join us tomorrow on an expedition to Epsilon City. Through the jungle. In a tank."

"I am? Who's going?"

"The great Commodore and two of his Super-troopers. You and I will have to keep them out of trouble."

"Great! Why in a tank? Why not use one of the armored jets?"

"Because he wants to experience the perils of the jungle. After all, he and his Troopers are invincible."

"All those Union soldiers seem to think that. I really hope that Epsilon will cut him down to size." Peters grinned and punched Stonewall on the shoulder. "Rumor has it you had a visitor last night."

"There are a lot of rumors going around. I wonder where they originate."

"This is a small community, Stonewall. There are no secrets. People see and hear things and they talk about them." Peters gave Stonewall a somewhat puzzled look. "I'm a bit surprised, though. Are you that desperate that you have to seek out the company of a...a whore?"

"Is that what Orina is? A whore?" Stonewall asked, not keeping his irritation out of his voice.

"What would you call her?"

"A woman who has needs like everyone else. A lonely woman. She doesn't take money. I wouldn't call her a whore." Stonewall shook his head. "Why is everybody always so concerned with what certain people do?"

"Maybe they're bored. Anything that breaks the monotony is welcome entertainment."

"And me spending a night with Orina is entertainment?" Stonewall chuckled humorlessly. "That's what I call desperate."

"I suppose it is." Peters shrugged. "This conversation has gone way past what I intended to say. So let's drop it. I don't really care how you spend your free time." He lifted his gaze and studied the dark clouds above them. "I hope he doesn't want to go into that."

"He believes the storm will be over by tomorrow morning."

"I'm curious. Why does he want me to come along?" Peters asked.

"I requested your presence."

"Thank you, my friend. Why?" Peters didn't look happy.

"Because I need someone I can trust and rely on. And because you are much more familiar with present conditions on Epsilon than I am. I just got here, remember? There have been many changes since my last stay here." Stonewall's eyes were grave. "Commodore Chelzic is a dangerous man. A fanatic. He'll destroy Epsilon if we let him."

Peters smiled grimly. "We can't let that happen, can we now?" He tipped his cap with his finger. "Well, enjoy your breakfast. I gotta run. Have to look over some reports. Apparently, a group of worker ants raided one of the spore miner camps and helped themselves to a lot of tools and supplies. The mining company wants me to file a complaint with the Uur queen." He sighed. "This job is getting to me."

Stonewall watched him walk away. Shrugging, he made his way to the mess hall.

I haven't even started mine and already I'm apprehensive and tired of it. No job is easy on this friggen planet. And it will only get worse.

[3]

AT EXACTLY SEVEN A.M. STONEWALL ARRIVED IN FRONT OF THE building Chelzic used as his headquarters. The two guards stood already on each side of the entrance. This time he didn't salute.

"Commodore Chelzic is expecting me," he told them curtly.

"We know. Go right in," one of them said, favoring him with a condescending look.

Stonewall shook his head and walked past them into the building.

Idiots!

There would never be any camaraderie between Union Soldiers and Scouts. Not until Hell froze over. And that would not happen, at least not for an eternity. He grimaced as his thoughts drifted briefly to that hot and dry ball of dust they had named *Hell* circling much too close to its primary. A planet Humans should never have tried to colonize. Perhaps Epsilon should be put on the list of unsuitable planets.

Commodore Chelzic was already in his office. He was dressed in a shiny new camouflage battle uniform. Two huge energy pistols hung from a wide belt strapped around his waist, their holsters tied at the bottom to his thighs. A flash rifle slung across his shoulders made him look like a greenhorn ready to go on a supervised hunt in one of the animal reserves on Earth.

Stonewall suppressed a grin when he saw the Commodore. He couldn't help himself and said, "Are you planning to walk through the jungle?"

"What do you mean by that?" Chelzic's eyes narrowed dangerously.

"I'm only wondering about the arsenal you carry, that's all."

"Standard equipment when entering enemy territory." Chelzic slapped the guns on his side. "These babies will stop anything this planet can throw at me," he said proudly.

"Have you ever seen a fully grown Tyrannosaurs Rex, sir?" Stonewall asked.

"Not in real life, but I've studied the holograms."

"Watching holograms and seeing one in the flesh are not the same, as you may have the opportunity to find out. Besides, not all dangers on Epsilon can be defeated with a gun."

"It can't be that bad." Chelzic waved it off with a careless move of his hand. "If a Scout can survive out there, a soldier should have no problem." He gave Stonewall a questioning look. "Didn't you tell me another Scout would be accompanying us? Where is he?"

"William Peters, sir. He'll be here," Stonewall assured him. He turned when he heard footsteps coming down the corridor. Moments later, Peters walked in. Stonewall smiled. "Well, speaking of the devil, there he is."

Peters saluted sloppily. "I hope I'm not too late to join the party," he said.

Chelzic frowned. Then he barked, "This is not a party, Scout Peters. And you are late. Why weren't you here the same time Stonewall arrived?"

Peters shrugged. "No real reason. Around here we are not that strict." He grinned. "I'm here now. That's what counts."

Chelzic shook his head in apparent disbelief. "I can see this post needs some discipline. How can anything be run with such inefficiency? I will have to have a talk with Chief Wallace. This is unbelievable." He gave Peters and Stonewall a piercing stare. "As long as you are under my command you will treat an officer of higher rank with respect and you will display discipline in your actions at all times. Is that understood and clear?"

32

"Yes, sir." Stonewall and Peters said in unison.

"As clear as mud," Peters added, which earned him a reprimanding look from Chelzic.

"Scouts," he murmured under his breath. Then he proceeded out the door. "Follow me," he said. "We might as well get an early start."

When they stepped outside the habitat, Stonewall became aware that the storm had calmed down considerably. The wind blew still strong from the north, but at least the rain had stopped. He inhaled the humid air, found it laden with strong scents of newly sprouting mushrooms.

They boarded an armored vehicle that looked large enough to provide a comfortable ride and, once inside, Stonewall did find it quite roomy. Two rows of seats behind the driver and the co-driver, divided by a narrow isle, allowed room for ten passengers. One of the two Troopers accompanying them took the driver's seat. Stonewall and Peters sat behind him, while the second Trooper climbed into the seat in the far back. It faced the rear of the vehicle. His job was to guard them from dangers threatening from that direction.

Chelzic noticed Stonewall's curious expression. "Don't worry about our safety, Stonewall. If you will check out the back panel, you'll see the controls for the large flash-cannon mounted on top of the rear hood." He chuckled. "Trooper Mendez will blast anything coming at us into tiny atoms."

"I hope Trooper Mendez has fast reactions," Peters commented.

Chelzic ignored him and slapped his hand against the invisible dome over their heads. "This is made out of the same material that is used to build the habitats. Not even a direct hit from a projectile weapon or energy rifle will be able to penetrate it. Since it is opaque from the outside and sealed, no predator can see or smell us. We are completely safe inside this vehicle."

"I never feel safe inside a vehicle," Stonewall said. "I don't believe you have any idea how large these carnosaurs are. One could pick up this tank and drop it again or roll it around on the ground. We would be tossed about like marbles in a boy's pocket."

"Should that happen, and I don't believe it ever will, we'll be held in place by powerful magnetic fields." Chelzic shook his head. "As I've said, you two would never last in the Military. Fear is something a soldier doesn't have."

"I'm not scared, just concerned," Stonewall mumbled.

"Same thing," Chelzic said with contempt. Then he gave the driver his orders, "Let's go, Trooper Cromwell. We don't have time to waste."

The tank began to roll on its tracks and Stonewall grudgingly admitted that it promised to be a smooth ride. Epsilon City lay west of the outpost. At least they didn't have to cross Dragon's Gap. Even though Chelzic seemed confident that they were safe inside the tank, Stonewall wasn't so sure. Those giant reptiles sailing the air currents above Dragon's Gap wouldn't hesitate to take a crack at anything that might provide them with a quick meal.

He remembered the first time he and Peters crossed that stretch of bare rock on a scooter. Some of the scouts had christened it Death Valley because nothing existed there but hot granite and huge boulders. The wide cracks in the ground were populated with Anteaters, giant Rocksnails, Dustserpents, and other ferocious predators. Not a place he'd want to visit too often.

That didn't mean that Dragon's Gap was the only dangerous place on Epsilon. Stonewall had come across many even more treacherous in the two years he spent on this world of giant mushrooms and oversized lizards.

He sighed and leaned back into his seat.

I was hoping I'd never see this place again, he thought, yet, here I am. Sometimes I think the Universe hates me.

He threw a glance at Chelzic, who sat beside the driver in the front seat. The big man didn't seem to have a worry in the world. He believed in his gadgets and his own abilities to fight his enemies. Maybe he had never met one he couldn't defeat. Perhaps this time he might not be so lucky. Maybe Epsilon would teach him a lesson and bestow on him a measure of humility and respect. Unfortunately, Stonewall would be there to keep him company.

What have I ever done to deserve this?

Taking a deep breath, he rejected the thoughts of self-pity and watched the landscape go by. Giant mushrooms rose into the sky, shutting out part of the sunlight. The ground was covered with the blue-shimmering moss found all over the planet. The wide tracks of the tank rolled over the tiny mushrooms growing everywhere, crushing them into soft pulp, but it wouldn't be long before others replaced them. Things decayed and grew fast on Epsilon.

Stonewall couldn't smell anything inside the airtight bubble of the tank but artificial air, but he knew that the forest outside exuded a cacophony of scents and odors, some pleasant and some repugnant to a Human's sense of smell.

The sudden appearance of a group of small lizards interrupted his thoughts. They stood in the path of the tank and eyed the intruder who dared to invade their territory. Behind them lay a large valley covered with tall ferns, a few mushroom trees, and huge mounds of brown matter.

Dinosaur dung.

Looking past the huddling lizards, Stonewall spied a herd of plant-eating dinosaurs grazing among the ferns. Their long necks weaved between the smaller mushroom trees trying to reach the gills that contained seeds and parasitical vegetation.

Trooper Cromwell slowed the tank and brought it to a halt.

"Should I take them out, sir?" Mendez asked from the back.

"Don't waste any energy on those," Chelzic growled. "Just drive through them," he said, addressing Cromwell.

"I wouldn't advise that," Stonewall said.

"Why not?"

Stonewall pointed. "Because their mother wouldn't be too kindly disposed if you flattened her offspring. An enraged dinosaur is no laughing matter."

A colossal bulk appeared from the direction Stonewall had pointed. It came at them with surprising speed. Behind the first behemoth two more emerged. Over the external microphones the angry bellowing of the charging beasts filled the interior of the tank's canopy.

"What the hell are those?"

"They're the equivalent of the Apatosaurus from Earth's distant past, only larger and a bit more belligerent," Peters explained. "I suggest you make a speedy but careful retreat, unless you want the whole herd on top of us."

"I never retreat from anyone or anything," Chelzic blustered.

"This might be a good time to change your tactics," Stonewall said hastily. "These beasts are usually quite peaceful, unless they feel threatened. And they feel threatened right now."

Something in Stonewall's voice must have convinced the Commodore to heed the warning. Perhaps it was the wall of huge scaled bodies rising threateningly up in front of them. It didn't matter to Stonewall what caused Chelszic to bark, "Retreat full speed, Cromwell. Get us the hell out of here." He was only too happy to feel the tank moving out of the danger zone.

When they were safely backed into the thicket of the jungle, he breathed a sigh of relief. He knew the beasts wouldn't follow. They were, as he had told Chelzic, peaceful when left alone.

"How will we get to the other side of that valley?" Chelzic asked, obviously annoyed at running into a roadblock he couldn't forcefully remove.

"We'll have to go around it," Peters said. "In fact, that is the route we should have taken in the first place."

"Why didn't you suggest that before we left?"

Peters shrugged. "Nobody asked me. You seemed to know where you were going."

Stonewall suppressed a grin when he saw the Commodore's expression. This was another peg into deflating the man's overblown ego.

"Why exactly are you here, Peters?" Chelzic asked.

"I don't know, sir. I guess because Stonewall asked for my company."

Chelzic threw an angry look at Stonewall. "I went along with your request because I thought Peters might be of some use. It seems I was wrong."

Stonewall cleared his throat. "I'm sure the reason he didn't speak up is simple. He didn't want to undermine your authority. I felt the same way. Maybe next time you need information you should consult us, sir."

"Next time I want you to speak up without being asked. Don't you Scouts have a backbone or a mind of your own? Think for yourself, man!"

Skirting the valley also meant to drive around a large swamp. They didn't run into any other problems. Swamps usually were a good hiding place for all kinds of critters. Bullfish especially loved to lurk beneath the surface among the tall reeds. The moment a suitable prey came close they rose out of the murky water and pounced on the unlucky victim. They made no distinction. Anything with a heartbeat was edible.

Bullfish were not exactly fish. They possessed long, sinewy bodies with grotesque, huge heads. They could spend hours under water, their breathing tube barely visible above the surface. Covered with a hard, scaly skin and huge bony plates they were not easily killed. Their toothy mouths were large enough to swallow the tank with one bite. The tank might get stuck inside their gullet, but that would be no consolation to the people inside.

Stonewall kept watching the swamp for any signs of Bullfish and other predators that might be hiding among the reeds and under the water. He breathed a sigh of relief when they finally left the swamp behind but didn't stop watching the terrain. Danger lurked everywhere and could confront them anytime.

He didn't trust Chelzic's belief that they were safe inside the tank. Nothing was ever safe on Epsilon. The predators were large, and the flora was equally dangerous. A solid looking surface might be only a thin membrane covering a deep hole filled with *Acidwool*, a fungus that swallowed up its victims and coated them with acid. The metal of the tank might be impervious to the acid, something Stonewall questioned, but there would be no way for the occupants to escape. They would starve to death inside the safe cocoon of the tank and die an excruciating slow death.

I'm getting paranoid, Stonewall thought. He had spent two years traveling across the surface of Epsilon and survived. Not all of the many planets he had visited in the last fifteen years had been peaceful and safe. But Epsilon was different. The beasts and plants seemed to be more ferocious, more aggressive than on any other planet he'd seen.

A rumbling sound and someone cursing ripped him out of his contemplation and brought him back to the present. He hadn't realized that he had drifted off. His eyes flew open and when he looked up, he stared into a double row of dagger-like teeth.

A Tyrannosaurus Rex. He had forgotten how huge they actually were.

Still cursing, Cromwell tried to increase the speed of their vehicle, but a mountain of dung blocked the trail.

"Blast the damn lizard," Chelzic bellowed.

"He's huge," Cromwell said.

He can speak, Stonewall thought after hearing the blond Trooper uttering his first words since they left the outpost. "I've seen bigger ones," he commented.

"So have I," Peters said.

The Rex rumbled again and poked the tank with its nose. Mendez fiddled with the controls in the rear. Stonewall had to give the Trooper credit. He seemed unshaken by the huge predator looming above them.

"What are you waiting for?" Chelzic shouted.

"We're too close. I can't seem to see the target on my screen," Mendez said. "All I see is a bright pattern."

"That's his belly," Peters said.

Mendez pushed the firing stud of the flash-cannon. Something exploded on the screen. Then a deafening roar echoed through the cabin over the speakers. The Rex reared up and staggered away; its huge tail struck the side of the tank with a loud thump. The tank lurched sideways and began to roll until it smashed into the stem of a nearby mushroom tree.

Stonewall was grateful for the magnetic field that pulled him into his seat and kept him and the others from being tossed around. When the tank stopped rolling, he discovered the side of the tank was now the bottom. Hanging in his seat, he searched for the dinosaur and found it lying not far away, its limbs and tail thrashing the vegetation and mushrooms.

A gaping hole in the huge belly testified to the power of the flash-cannon.

Beside him, Peters moaned. "How the hell do you release this pressure?" he groaned. "I can barely breathe."

"We'll have to put the tank in the upright position first," Chelzic said. "Don't be such a whiner."

"How are you going to do that? We can't get out of this traveling coffin."

Chelzic snorted. "No need to get out. Cromwell will apply a gravity field to one side of the tank which will put us back in position."

A slight vibration ran through the tank. Stonewall felt it move and after a few moments it sat upright again. The pressure from his chest lifted and he took a deep breath.

Perhaps I was wrong worrying about our safety. Seems Chelzic knows what he's doing after all.

The body of the great carnosaur was still convulsing. The beast tried to rise but was unsuccessful.

"I believe you fried its spine," Chelzic said. "Good job, Mendez." He turned to look at Stonewall. "As you can see, we can deal with anything. There is nothing to worry about."

"As long as we stay inside this tank," Stonewall said dryly.

Chelzic shook his head. "Always the worrier. Is that a Scout trait or some kind of motto?"

"Always be on guard and expect the worst," Stonewall said. "That is a Scout's motto. It keeps us alive."

"How about *Everybody is your enemy. Keep your weapon loaded and ready to fire.* That guarantees a soldier's survival." Chelzic couldn't keep the contempt out of his voice.

"That motto explains a lot," Peters commented.

"What do you mean?"

"It explains why every soldier appears so uptight. Must be hard to live with that. Do you have any friends?"

"A soldier cannot afford friends. Not outside his unit, anyway," Chelzic said sharply. "A soldier is trained to shoot and kill. He cannot allow his emotions to get in the way."

"Yeah, well, you can have that." Peters glanced at Stonewall. "I'd rather cultivate my friendships than carry any hatred inside me. I went through that after my wife and son were murdered and I didn't like the man I became."

It was silent inside the tank after that. Stonewall brought his attention back to the environment outside and watched the trunks of the mushroom trees go by as the tank made its way through the thick vegetation. Tall reeds and swampy ground replaced the trees and mushrooms after a while. Stonewall grudgingly admitted that traveling in the tank was far easier and safer than trying to brave the hostile jungle on a scooter.

The tank stopped rolling when a wide expanse of water blocked further travel.

"Is there a way around this?" Chelzic asked.

"Yes, there is, but this lake stretches for miles. If we travel south we will come to a wide river, which empties itself into this lake. The only way to cross here is by boat, which we don't have." Peters gave a little chuckle. "Even if we had one, I wouldn't advise it. Many dangers lurk under the surface. If you think that Rex was huge, wait until you see the critters in the water."

Chelzic sounded like a father who found out his son had run home crying after a girl threatened to beat him up. "Peters, Peters. How you managed to survive this long is a mystery to me. You can't give up every time you run across an obstacle. You say we don't have a boat? Well, you are wrong. This tank is amphibious. It can travel across water as easily as across land."

"Your orders, sir?" Cromwell asked.

"Full steam ahead." Chelzic laughed cheerfully. "Sometimes even a soldier needs to display a sense of humor. We are not always *uptight*, Peters."

The tank slid into the gently splashing waves. It bounced for a moment then it leveled out as Cromwell worked the controls.

"What will we find on the other side?" Chelzic asked as they headed north.

"More jungle, what else?" Peters said curtly.

Stonewall knew how Peters felt. When the tank slid into the water, he had experienced a momentary tightening of his stomach muscles. He couldn't shrug off a feeling of dread when he looked across the rolling water surface. They might be safe inside the tank, but that safety was worth nothing inside the belly of one of the giant denizens of the lake.

"There is something large ahead of us," Cromwell said suddenly.

"Where?" Chelzic sounded annoyed but not worried.

"Under the water." Cromwell studied his scanner. "It doesn't appear to be biological. Some kind of metal artifact."

"Maybe it's a crashed spaceship. Go around it. We don't have time to investigate it."

Cromwell steered the tank to the right.

"No good, sir. It...it's following us."

"What the hell do you mean by that?" Chelzic barked.

Stonewall stared at the dark shape rising out of the water in front of them. Cromwell had been correct by calling it a metal artifact. No question about that. The part visible above the water was round like the bubble of a habitat, but it was studded with turrets and other objects. None of them inspiring or conveying a friendly welcome.

"Does anyone else have the feeling we are trespassing on someone's property?" Peters asked.

Stonewall could only agree with Peters. This lake had been claimed by someone else and the Humans were trespassing.

The dark shape had risen higher out of the water, revealing the black metallic surface of an artifact; something that was not a natural part of this lake or this planet. Stonewall recognized it for what it was.

"That's an *Anorian* spaceship," he said.

"I know what it is," Chelzic bellowed. "I want to know what the hell it is doing here. They have no business even being on Epsilon."

"You want me to take it out?" Mendez asked from the rear seat.

"You can't shoot at everything you see, what's more, I believe they have us outgunned. I suggest we refrain from taking any rash action," Stonewall said.

"You have no idea what our weapons are capable of, Stonewall," Chelzic growled. "But in this case, I will listen to your recommendation. Stand down, Trooper Mendez. Let's wait and see what they are planning."

An opening appeared in the side of the ship and a figure stepped out and onto a small ledge.

"An Anorian all right," Chelzic said. "I've never trusted them."

"They are not usually aggressive," Stonewall said. "I've had dealings with them before."

Chelzic snorted with contempt. "So have I. They are cunning and sly, like most females. I'd be much happier if we'd be dealing with a species where the men wear the pants."

"The Anorians don't wear pants," Peters remarked.

"Just a figure of speech, Scout Peters." Chelzic sounded annoyed.

"If they'd at least wear something. I've never felt comfortable dealing with naked women."

"I've never had problems with that," Peters said, chuckling.

The figure on the ledge of the ship waved. There was no mistaking the meaning of the signal.

"I believe we've been invited to come aboard their ship," Stonewall said.

"An invitation we will accept." Chelzic turned to Cromwell. "Open up. We'll go visiting."

"Are you sure it is safe, sir?"

Stonewall was surprised to hear Cromwell questioning Chelzic's decision. He was also surprised when Chelzic didn't reprimand the Trooper. "They wouldn't dare harm us, Cromwell. The Anorians have never shown aggression toward us. I don't believe they'll be starting now."

The door in the side of the tank slid open. Stonewall inhaled the sudden hot, humid air and let out a small curse. He wasn't the only one who felt uncomfortable.

"I've forgotten how hot this damn place is," Chelzic grumbled. "Cromwell, get us as close as you can so we can step across onto that ledge."

Cromwell maneuvered the tank slowly closer to the alien ship. The Anorian on the ledge threw them a rope ladder. Mendez caught it and swung himself onto the first rung. He climbed the ladder with great agility. As soon as he stood on the ledge, Chelzic followed him. Stonewall came next and then Peters. Cromwell stayed behind in the tank. He closed the door the moment Peters reached the ledge and took the tank away from the ship.

The Anorian stood silent until the Humans were assembled on the ledge. As Chelzic had observed already, the alien was naked. There was no mistaking the alien's gender.

A female. Her breasts stood away from her ribcage like two perfectly round apples. They were not large but Stonewall registered their lovely shape. Anorian females were known for their extreme beauty and shapely bodies. Her sex organ was hidden behind a thin flap of skin between her muscular legs. Tiny, silvery shimmering scales covered her slim body.

She carried a number of tools on a belt around her waist. Stonewall didn't recognize any weapons, but that didn't mean she didn't have any.

The alien female smiled, revealing a row of pointy teeth. "Please, follow me. My Captain is anxiously waiting for you." She spoke the language of the Humans with a slight lisp, mainly because of her split tongue, but with barely an accent.

"Lead the way," Chelzic said his manner civil and polite.

Stonewall breathed a sigh of relief. He had expected Chelzic to be belligerent and pompous. But then again, the day wasn't over yet.

They followed the female into the interior of the ship. Stonewall stumbled into Mendez as his eyes adjusted to the dim light inside the corridor they entered.

"Sorry," he mumbled. The air inside the ship was not much different from the air outside. Reptilians liked it hot and humid. Epsilon was an ideal planet for them.

Walking down the corridor, they didn't meet any crewmembers, but Stonewall knew that a ship like this held at least thirty, possibly forty.

They halted in front of a circular door. It irised open and they stepped through. The room they entered was large and furnished with low cushions strewn across the floor. Another female stood in front of an oval window on the opposite wall. Her body was sharply outlined against the diffused light falling through the window. She was taller than the one who had brought them.

She had her back turned toward them and Stonewall admired her shapely form, mainly her round buttocks.

When she turned around to face them, Stonewall was not disappointed by what the silhouette of her figure had promised. She was quite muscular, like most Anorians, but still feminine enough to be considered beautiful. Her golden eyes looked at them out of a delicate face.

She waited until they were close before she dismissed the one who had brought them with a wave of her slim hand.

"I am Captain Norgana. Please accept my hospitality. Feel free to sit. We are not formal here in this room." She spoke with the same lisping voice as the other one, but her accent was strong. Stonewall found it quite attractive.

She looked at him and smiled. He remembered that her species had a limited ability of reading minds. It was mostly intuitive, but some had developed that ability to a high degree.

Her split tongue played across her lips as she looked at him. "You are not a stranger to our species, are you?"

"No," Stonewall said. "I've had dealings with members of your kind before."

"You are not a soldier, like the others in your party." It was a statement, not a question.

"That is correct. I am a Scout."

Her golden eyes flickered to Chelzic. "You are the leader and a soldier. You command many soldiers. You do not trust us." She gave a silvery laugh. "We did not come here to start a conflict."

"Why are you here?" Chelzic asked.

"To observe."

"Observe what?"

"The impending conflict between Humans and the Spiders."

"And the Anorians? Which side are they on?"

She laughed again. "Neither side. We are not getting involved."

"No? Then why have a ship full of soldiers hiding on a planet the Humans have claimed?"

"This is not a warship."

"Yet it bristles with weapons."

"To defend against aggressive enemies." She walked to one of the large cushions and sank into it with graceful movements. "Let us not talk politics. Be comfortable and enjoy the hospitality we Anorians are known for."

The men waited for Chelzic to sit down before they joined him on the cushions. Stonewall crossed his legs the way the Anorian captain did. He noticed with some satisfaction that Chelzic struggled to make his knees touch the ground.

I guess being a soldier and being supple don't go hand in hand.

Captain Norgana chuckled softly. *There is not much you can hide from an empath.* Her golden eyes seemed to study him. When he looked at her, she smiled. *I am not fond of soldiers either.*

Stonewall stared at her, startled. The voice had sounded clear and without an accent, yet he had not seen her lips move.

She put a finger against her lips. *Let that be our secret. I am a true telepath. Not even my crew knows that.*

When he wanted to speak, she shook her head. *Don't react.*

He nodded, his mind reeling. How could he respond to that? Should he be loyal to his commanding officer or to an alien woman he didn't know anything about?

Follow your heart. I mean you no harm, but your superior is a dangerous man. Do not trust him.

He knew she was right. There was nothing to be gained by telling Chelzic about Captain Norgana's ability. "How long have you been here?" he asked aloud to cover his thoughts and to break the silence that seemed to have lasted for an eternity.

"Not long," she said, still looking at him. He understood what she meant. She had answered his spoken question and the one in the back of his mind. The silent conversation between them had lasted only a moment, not an eternity.

He became aware of a soft whispering sound as the door behind him opened. Turning around, he watched two of the females walking in. They carried trays laden with fruit and vegetables, which they put down in front of the men.

Norgana picked up a piece of fruit and put it into her mouth. "Anorian's have a metabolism similar to Humans. You can eat anything we do. These are vegetables and fruit found on this planet. We have been eating them without ill effects. They are delicious and nourishing."

"You don't eat meat?" Peters asked.

She shook her head. "We are vegetarians. Our species has stopped eating meat a long time ago."

"But you could eat meat?"

"I suppose we could, but we have no desire to do so."

"Humans eat meat," Chelzic said. It sounded like a casual remark but Stonewall detected the sarcasm in the man's voice.

Obviously, Norgana didn't miss it either. Stonewall envied her ability to read Chelzic's thoughts.

"I know. We believe that it is barbaric to kill and eat other living beings."

"They are only dumb animals."

"Even dumb animals are aware of being alive and mourn the loss of a partner or offspring. They feel pain and sorrow." She spoke softly but Stonewall could not miss the scorn in her voice.

"There are many Humans who share your views. It is not a new idea. As far as I'm concerned it is only natural to eat meat. Some animals are carnivores...hunters. Others are victims...food. That is the way of nature, the way it was designed. One sustains the other. Humans are carnivores by nature."

Chelzic spoke like a lecturer. He laughed congenially and reached for a smooth-skinned fruit. "I am a tolerant person when it comes to people's beliefs. Whatever makes you happy. As long as you don't try to push your beliefs on me, we'll be friends."

Stonewall nearly choked listening to Chelzic. *What a hypocrite! And an idiot.*

He glanced at Peters, became aware of Norgana's silvery laughter. "I'm not trying to influence what you believe," she said, addressing Chelzic. She smiled. "I guess that means we are friends, right?"

Chelzic didn't answer. He studied the plate in front of him and removed a green, root-like vegetable. Biting into it, he said, "This tastes actually quite good. Reminds me of a carrot. I used to hate those when I was a kid." He took off his helmet and scratched his scalp.

"Why do Humans cover their bodies with so much clothing?" Norgana asked.

"To keep warm in cold climates and cool when it is hot." His eyes lingered on her breasts. "And to keep certain parts of our bodies hidden from view."

She was aware of his scrutiny and laughed. "You are uncomfortable in the presence of a naked female?"

"To be truthful? Yes, I am. Unless I am naked, too."

"Then take off your clothes. It is warm in our ship."

"It would not be appropriate. Our customs are different from yours."

"I know. Quite different, actually. In your society the males are the dominant sex. Anorian males are weak. They are the ones taking care

46

of the children and the home." She leaned back into her cushion, pushing out her breasts.

Stonewall suppressed a chuckle. She knew quite well the effect her nude body had on the Humans.

Chelzic grunted something and took another piece of fruit from the plate. "Our women tried to muscle their way into the men's territory by taking all the good jobs, by putting women into key positions, by believing that they are as good as men, better even, but in the end, they did a worse job than we ever did. Women are not good when it comes to warfare, for instance. They don't have enough balls to get the job done."

Peters chuckled beside Stonewall. "I prefer women without any balls," he snickered.

"That is very funny, Scout Peters," Chelzic growled. "I would put you into the brig for a remark like that. You Scouts lack discipline."

The two females who had brought the plates filled with fruit came back and handed each man a round container with a spout on top.

"Fruit juice," Norgana explained. "You must be thirsty." She put her container down after sucking on it. "It is safe to drink. We didn't put any poison into it."

Stonewall took a drag from the spout and found the liquid cool but a bit too sweet. "It quenches the thirst," he commented. "Thank you."

She inclined her head. "Your comfort and wellbeing is my wish."

She lay back into the cushion and opened her legs wide. He stared at her suddenly exposed sex-organ. Beckoning with her hands, she said, "Come and join your body with mine. I've been without a male for a long time and I need to feel your organ inside me."

Startled by her invitation, he turned his head and looked at his companions. They sat on their cushions, eating, and drinking from their gourds, seemingly oblivious of their surroundings.

Her silvery laughter teased him. "Don't worry about them."

He rose almost without conscious thought and crossed the short distance between him and the alien woman. With shaky fingers he removed his clothing until he stood naked in front of her. She reached up and pulled him down on top of her. Putting her hand behind his head, she drew his face close and kissed him hungrily.

Her split tongue probed the cavity of his mouth. Warm fingers circled his manhood. Moaning, he moved between her spread legs. She guided him into the heat of her feminine organ, engulfed his manhood with the soft walls of her sheath, moved against him with forceful thrusts. A wave of ecstasy rushed through his body. He lost all sense of time. Tirelessly he moved between her clutching thighs, his ears and mind filled with her moans of pleasure. Crying out hoarsely, he spilled his seed into her, rapture consuming his mind and body...

Blinking, he looked around. He felt suddenly tired, exhausted. Norgana sat cross-legged on her pillow, watching him with lidded eyes. She smiled when his eyes met hers.

He became aware of Chelzic speaking. "We have to protect our interests. Epsilon is a strategic piece of property in this region of space. Suddenly, everybody wants it. Until now, we've had enough problems just to keep smugglers and pirates away."

"Maybe I can help you with part of your problem. We know of a pirate base not far from here. I could give you its location," Norgana said. "That is the least I can do for you."

"I would appreciate that." Chelzic rubbed his hands over his legs. "It seems I've been in this position for hours. I'm not used to sitting on the floor."

"Time can sometimes play tricks with your senses," Norgana said, glancing at Stonewall. "I am happy we have met. Perhaps in the near future you can come and visit us again."

Chelzic cleared his throat. "Is your ship the only Anorian ship on Epsilon?"

"Yes, it is. We are no threat to you."

"If there is a war between Humans and the Spiders it might be wise if you move your ship to another planet. You may not be safe here."

"We will deal with that situation when it happens," Norgana said. She rose with a fluid motion. "You seem tired," she said to Stonewall. "You could remain on my ship for the night and leave in the morning. We have room for guests."

"We wouldn't want to impose on your hospitality," Chelzic said, rising to his feet.

She shrugged. "It would be no problem. We are capable hosts. You wouldn't have to sleep alone."

"I am not familiar with what etiquette requires of us, but I believe we have to decline your invitation, as tempting as it may be." Chelzic's voice had suddenly gone hoarse. "If I read your proposition correctly."

"You are reading it correctly." Her eyes glistened with a smoldering golden fire. "You would not be disappointed."

Chelzic laughed darkly. "That may be so, but I believe it is time for us to leave."

"That is regrettable. I would have liked to know you better. I don't even know your names," Norgana said.

Liar. You know more about us than we do.

Her eyes flickered. *I know more than I care to know. Being a telepath is not always a blessing, Stonewall. Your leader is a complicated man with many issues. That is the reason why I made the offer. I hoped I could put a few suggestions into his mind.*

You can do that?

She curled her lips into a smile. *You have experienced what I am capable of. Another secret you will share with me. Was it real? Perhaps it was. Perhaps it only happened in your imagination.*

The others didn't seem to be aware of the silent mental exchange. She read his thoughts.

Communication between us is instantaneous. No measurable time passes.

He didn't understand the concept, but he knew she was right. *You are a remarkable being. I wish you good fortune.*

And I you, Human Stonewall.

Chelzic's voice brought him back to reality. "I am Commodore Chelzic. This is Trooper Mendez and these two are Scouts Stonewall and Peters."

"I will remember your names. Perhaps our paths will cross again." She inclined her head and walked back to her place under the window.

Stonewall threw one last look at her slim form outlined against the dim light and then he followed his companions with a feeling of deep regret, his thoughts in turmoil. Had he imagined the sexual encounter with Norgana or did it happen? The memory seemed real but was it?

Trooper Cromwell must have been watching the ship. The tank

came closer the moment the four men stepped out of the exit and onto the ledge that circled the spaceship.

"How long have we been in there?" Peters asked.

Stonewall looked at the darkening sky. He remembered looking at his watch only a short time before they encountered the alien space vessel. It had been a few minutes past two o'clock. Now his watch displayed five twenty.

It meant they had spent nearly three hours on the ship.

The dark slit of her split pupils was wide as she stared into his eyes. Her forked tongue licked her open lips as she churned lazily above him. His hands reached up to cup her small breasts, kneaded them gently. When he clamped his fingers around her narrow waist, her silvery skin felt soft and warm. He couldn't take his eyes away from hers. They seemed to hold him in a hypnotic grip.

He shook his head to clear it. Had he been daydreaming? How long had he sat there not hearing any of the conversation going on around him?

Her silvery laughter chimed in his head. *What you experienced was real, but what is reality? What is memory? Did what your mind remembers really happen or is it just wishful thinking?* A ghostly feeling like the touch of a feather passed across his forehead. *I will keep you in my memory. Live well, Stonewall.*

He climbed into the tank and sank into his seat, more confused than ever. This was something he needed to sort out. He had encountered telepathic beings before, but never one like Norgana.

He remembered the Accilla. Intelligent giant slugs that could mimic other life forms. They communicated through telepathy, but they didn't have the ability to influence the minds of others.

The Uur, the giant ants of Epsilon, had limited abilities to cloud minds, to make other beings see them in different forms, but they didn't have vocal cords to talk and make audible suggestions. Even though they could communicate telepathically, they could not force their will on other minds. At least that was the common belief. It may turn out to be false.

Norgana seemed to be able to manipulate time and possibly even space. She could be a dangerous individual. Should he tell Chelzic about her and about what may have taken place on the ship?

He decided to keep his secret. Would Chelzic believe him? Probably not. He would most likely wonder about Stonewall's state of mind. He didn't have a high opinion of the Scouts or of Stonewall. This would only add to the contempt he felt.

"I was beginning to think something happened to you," Cromwell said.

Chelzic chuckled. He seemed to be in a good mood. "We dined on fruit and vegetables. Even had a good tasting refreshing drink. The Anorians wouldn't dare to harm us, Cromwell. As expected, we only found a ship full of weak females. If the Anorian men would be more aggressive, I would have said you had reason to worry, but Anorian men do not run the ships. In fact, they run nothing. They stay home cleaning house and doing stuff women should be doing."

Stonewall could hear Peters snicker beside him. "I knew a few women who might take offense hearing that," he murmured.

"Did you say something, Peters?" Chelzic growled.

"No, sir. Just thinking out loud."

"Well, keep it to yourself, unless you have something important to tell us." He touched his hand to his forehead. "Dammit! Didn't that Captain say she knew of a smuggler camp? She didn't supply us with any more information."

"I know where it is," Mendez said.

"How can you know it? She never told us."

Mendez shrugged. "I have the coordinates in my head, sir. I can give them to you."

Chelzic stared at him. "How is that possible? When did she tell you?"

"Don't you remember? One of the crew came in and asked me to come with her? She took me to the bridge where she showed me the location."

"What the hell! I don't remember that. Are you certain?"

"Of course I am, sir. I didn't imagine it. My memory is quite clear."

"So is mine. I don't remember that happening."

"I might be able to shed some light on that," Stonewall ventured. "According to my information, the Anorians have limited empathic abilities. They could have put that information into Trooper Mendez's mind without him realizing it."

"I remember clearly what happened," Mendez said. "I was on that bridge."

"Maybe you were...in your mind, Mendez. What Stonewall says makes sense. I've heard similar stories about the Anorians." Chelzic seemed satisfied with that explanation. "Feed the information into the tank's navigation system and let's get away from here."

The alien vessel sank under the surface of the lake and the Humans headed for the other shore. Stonewall was happy when the tank finally rumbled across dry land.

Her slim arms kept him in a tight embrace and her strong legs encircled his body as she writhed under him. He dug his fingers into her solid buttocks, pushed deep into her...

He couldn't get her image out of his mind. When he concentrated, he could still feel the heat of her body, the softness of her skin, the sweet taste of her lips. He knew it would be a long time before the memory of her passionate embrace would leave his mind.

"How far is that base?" Chelzic asked.

"About twenty miles," Mendez answered.

"It is getting dark. Maybe we should hunker down and wait until morning," Chelzic suggested.

"We should have taken the Anorians up on their offer and stayed in the protection of their ship," Peters said.

Chelzic shook his head. "I've never trusted those Anorian females. You saw what they did to Mendez. I don't even want to think about what might have happened had we stayed a whole night and given them time to work on our minds."

Stonewall sighed. "And our bodies," he murmured, more to himself than so the others could hear. "They might have tortured us."

Peters chuckled. "I must admit, looking at that body of Captain Norgana made me think of other things than the task at hand. I wouldn't mind being tortured by her."

Chelzic let out a snort of disgust. "Somehow, I'm not surprised by your remark, Peters. Nothing surprises me when it comes to you Scouts. As I've said many times before...no discipline. Not in body and not in mind."

[4]

AN ARMORED TANK WAS NOT MEANT FOR SLEEPING. STONEWALL didn't sleep well, although the seats were comfortable enough. His dreams were filled with the women he had known in his life.

Lucinda. His first great love. He thought she loved him, until he found out that she played house with her own cousin. She was the reason he left Earth to come to Epsilon fifteen years ago.

On Epsilon he had fallen in love with an alien girl.

Sheera.

Her butterfly-wings shimmered in the sun as she circled above him. She landed on soft feet and, laughing gaily, she came into his arms, pressing her nude body against his.

"Come, make love to me."

She pulled him down, on top of her. He moved between her soft, opening thighs.

As he looked into her purple eyes they changed, turned yellow. Her pupils became dark slits, reptilian.

"Join your body with mine." Norgana pressed her strong thighs against his burning hips and kissed him with great passion. He let out a deep moan as he entered her slippery sex-organ and slid deep into her. Her slim body moved snake-like beneath him...

He awoke, covered with perspiration. Beside him, Peters rubbed his eyes and stretched. "For a moment I thought I was back in my own bed. I guess I was wrong."

Chelzic sat like an idol in his seat. He seemed comfortable. Opening his eyes, he cleared his throat and looked at the brightening sky above them. "It looks like a promising day. Time to move."

"I wouldn't mind stretching my legs and..." Stonewall hesitated. "You know...the call of nature..."

"All right," Chelzic growled. "I'm not exactly immune to the natural urges. I guess we can spare a few minutes."

Cromwell scanned the surrounding area for any possible danger lurking somewhere nearby, waiting for the Humans to climb out of their protective shell and then pounce to devour the delectable morsels. "All clear," he reported and opened the door.

Even this early in the morning the air was hot and humid. There was no escaping it. The men climbed out and walked around, trying to get the kinks out of their limbs. Stonewall knew better than to relax. He kept careful watch as he walked a short distance away from the tank.

He stayed clear of a cluster of red low-growing shrubs. Not only did the branches have razor-sharp thorns, the dense foliage hid many dangerous creatures, the Fire-spitters among them. He didn't feel like having his face burnt by a wad of acid.

He knew the dangers, as did Peters. Chelzic and his troopers were not as careful. Stonewall was not surprised when he heard Cromwell uttering a string of loud curses. The crackling of a discharging flash rifle made him grab his own weapon and run in the direction where he knew Cromwell had searched for a private spot.

Cromwell crouched in the knee-high vegetation, his rifle aimed at something on the ground. Stonewall approached carefully, not knowing what it was that held Cromwell's attention. What he found was not an animal but a plant or what was left of it. Half of the main body was a mess of charred tissue. A couple of its thick tentacles had been sheared off by the burst of energy from Cromwell's rifle. They were still kicking on the ground, their sucker tips opening and closing like the hungry beaks of nesting birds, waiting to be fed.

"What the hell is that?" Cromwell asked when Stonewall arrived.

"That, my friend, is a Tentacle-tree. You could have been its breakfast."

"What do you mean?"

"This is a flesh-eating plant."

"It looked so beautiful. I mean...those lovely red flowers... who would assume it could be dangerous? I thought it was a harmless plant."

Stonewall chuckled. "Nothing on Epsilon is harmless. The more beautiful it is, the more deadly it can be. Like I told Commodore Chelzic, Scouts may not have to face enemy soldiers, but the challenges we deal with are just as real and perilous as an enemy with a weapon in his hands."

Cromwell gave Stonewall a thoughtful look. "I would rather know the face of my enemy than cope with unknown dangers like this every day. How do you handle that?"

Stonewall shrugged. "You get used to it. If you want to know the truth, I'd rather do this than what you do."

"What is all the commotion about?"

Stonewall turned around to look at Commodore Chelzic. "Just one of the insignificant dangers we sometimes run across in the jungle, that's all. Trooper Cromwell dealt with it in a professional manner."

Chelzic let out a satisfied chuckle. "I didn't expect anything else. Now, if you gentlemen are done with your chatting, I suggest we get back into the tank and move on."

They managed to travel without being accosted by any of the larger carnosaurs for the rest of the way. Once in a while a pack of smaller reptiles crossed their path, but none of them seemed interested in the ugly bug that crushed vegetation and the abundant small mushrooms under its wide tracks.

"We are close," Cromwell said. "According to the computer we are within a mile of the target."

"I would advise caution. I'm sure they have sentries," Chelzic suggested.

Cromwell had been correct in his estimation. They could see two small habitats inside a cleared area, connected by a narrow tunnel. A shuttle was also parked nearby.

"I don't think we have to announce our presence," Chelzic said.

"Luck seems to be in our favor. I can hardly believe they haven't detected us yet, but let's not take a chance. We are close enough to take them out. Surprise is still on our side."

"You only have the word of the Anorians that this is a smuggler base," Peters said. "Shouldn't we give them the opportunity to explain their presence first?"

"I don't believe there is anything to explain. Who else would erect a habitat in the middle of nowhere on this planet? If they are not smugglers, they are outlaws of some kind or other. No question about that." Chelzic spoke with authority.

Stonewall was watching the habitat. Peters had voiced his own concerns. As he watched, a door opened in the side of one of the domes and a couple of figures stepped out. One was a man, the other a woman. Both carried flash rifles. They began walking toward the tank.

"It seems we've been spotted," Mendez said from the backseat. "What do you want me to do, sir?"

"Take out the shuttle first," Chelzic said.

"Aye, aye, sir."

A slight vibration ran through the tank as Mendez released the destructive beam from the cannon in the rear of the tank.

Stonewall watched with mixed feelings as the shuttle exploded.

The two people, who had covered about half the distance between the tank and the two domes, fell to the ground from the force of the detonation. They lay for only a few moments and then they rose and ran back to the habitat.

"So much for our surprise attack," Peters said laconically.

The tank shuddered as the ground exploded in front of them.

"Retreat," Chelzic bellowed. "They must have waited for us to come close enough."

Cromwell took the tank away out of the danger zone. Twice more the ground exploded nearby, but the shots fell short.

"They have only a short-range cannon," Mendez said. "What are you planning to do, Commodore?"

"We'll attack on the ground," Chelzic said, his voice crisp. "This is war." He looked at Peters. "Are you still questioning my decision, Peters? Our hesitation may have cost us victory."

"I wouldn't exactly call this a war," Peters said.

"Any hostile engagement is an act of war. But not being a soldier, you wouldn't understand that, Scout." He fastened the straps of his helmet under his chin. "Move it, men! They won't expect us to act this fast. Surprise is still on our side."

The door in the tank slid open and the five men jumped out, weapons ready.

"Cromwell, Mendez, you two men go around and attack from the opposite side," Chelzic ordered. "Stonewall, you take the east side and Peters the west. I will move in from here as soon as I get the signal that you are in place."

"Aye, aye, sir." Cromwell and Mendes ran away, crouching in the vegetation that was high enough to cover their movements.

Stonewall moved in the direction Chelzic had given him. He felt a heavy pit in his stomach. This whole thing didn't seem right, yet he had no choice but to follow Chelzic's orders. He was the commanding officer of this operation. In fact, he was the self-appointed War Lord of Epsilon. His word was law. Chelzic had every right to have him executed if he disobeyed.

He had no intentions to fire his weapon unless he was forced to do so by circumstances beyond his control.

Cromwell and Mendez would be the ones doing all the shooting. They were the soldiers, trained to kill. Stonewall was only a Scout. He wasn't a killer.

"We're in position." The voice of Cromwell rang loud in his speaker. "We're moving in."

Stonewall didn't see them. Everything seemed peaceful around the two domes. The vegetation around the destroyed shuttle was still burning. Plumes of smoke billowed into the sky and Stonewall smelled the smoldering plants as they turned into charcoal.

Suddenly, a door opened again in the dome nearest to him. Three men, holding weapons, stepped into the open.

Stonewall wanted to shout *watch out*, but his vocal cords didn't obey his impulse. Frozen, he watched as a man in a battle uniform rose out of the high vegetation and began firing.

None of the three men had a chance. They fell before they even knew a killer had appeared among them.

Stonewall recognized Cromwell as the shooter. Moments later,

Mendez joined Cromwell. Both men walked through the opening in the dome. He walked slowly toward the dome, his thoughts only on the job at hand.

He saw Chelzic coming from his left, flash rifle ready. Stonewall knew, neither of them would get a chance to use their weapons. Cromwell and Mendez were good at what they did.

He was right. When they entered the dome, they saw burning buildings. Bodies lay on the ground, unmoving.

Cromwell and Mendez appeared in the entrance to the other dome.

"Mission accomplished," Cromwell reported. "No survivors."

"Good." Chelzic sounded cold. His voice displayed no emotion.

They didn't bother to check the buildings.

Once outside, back in the tank, Mendez fired a round into each of the domes, destroying what was left of anything inside. Nobody could have survived the final destruction.

The jungle would do the rest.

For a long time everyone was silent inside the tank. Stonewall had no desire to comment on the incident. It was on Chelzic's conscience, not his. He still didn't believe it was a pirate base. Those destroyed buildings had looked too much like laboratories. But then again, they could have been drug-processing facilities. He could be wrong with his assumption.

They arrived in Epsilon City shortly after noon. Stonewall had been briefed about the city but seeing it in person was different from having it described. Epsilon was not like any city built on other planets. The builders of the city had long moved out and left it abandoned for decades. They had not been Humans but Uur, the giant ants who built it centuries ago.

Stonewall didn't know the history of the giant dome nor the reason why the original inhabitants left it. The Humans found it empty and it was a logical choice to transform it into a suitable habitat for Humans. It offered protection against the perils on an inhospitable planet.

Epsilon City was not the only abandoned hive the Humans remodeled. Star City, three hundred miles northeast of Epsilon City, was another one. The giant dome rose to over a thousand feet into the sky, much taller than the one Stonewall had been held prisoner in on his first encounter with the *Bugeyes*, as they called the giant ants.

An electric fence surrounded the whole complex. The only entrance was closed by a gate. As they approached the gate, an armed guard stepped out of a guardhouse and motioned for them to come out of the tank.

Cromwell stepped outside but left the exit door open. "Commodore Chelzic and company," he said with a crisp voice. "Open the gate!"

The guard shook his head. "I have orders to detain you until the Chief of Security arrives."

"What the hell for?" Chelzic bellowed from inside the tank.

The guard shrugged his shoulders. "I wasn't told." He made a motion with his rifle. "Please, step out of your vehicle."

"We'll do no such thing," Chelzic thundered. "Do you know who I am?"

"No sir, I don't. It doesn't really matter. You won't get into Epsilon City until the Chief clears you."

"I could blast my way in."

"That you could, sir, but I would advise against it. I have two very capable sharpshooters inside the guardhouse. They have their rifles trained at your head, sir. If you make an attempt to close the door they will shoot you."

"This is preposterous," Chelzic blustered. "Someone will pay for this. I will make an example out of you."

"I'm only following orders. Now, please, come out of that vehicle."

"He's a good soldier," Stonewall said. "You should appreciate that, sir."

He didn't wait for Chelzic to answer and climbed out of the tank. He smiled at the guard. "It's a beautiful day."

The guard didn't comment. Stonewall could see the tension in his stance. It wouldn't take much to set him off. Unfortunately for him, he didn't have a ghost of a chance against Cromwell and Mendez should Chelzic decide not to follow his request. The sharpshooters in the guardhouse might be able to get off a shot before Mendez blew up the whole structure. It was probably already marked as a target by the tank's cannon.

When he looked toward the giant cone that was Epsilon City, he could see a vehicle coming out of the entrance to the city and head for the gate.

Chelzic decided to leave the tank after all and joined Stonewall. The two soldiers and Peters stayed in the tank.

"He'd better have a damn good excuse," Chelzic growled.

"Maybe we should have announced our visit," Stonewall said.

"I didn't see any reason to do so. I wanted it to be surprise." Chelzic sounded annoyed at being questioned by Stonewall.

Stonewall couldn't help but say, "Some people don't like surprises."

The vehicle from the city came to a halt and a short, somewhat corpulent man climbed out. Two uniformed and heavily armed security men flanked him as he came through the narrow gate.

"I am Security Chief Moore," the corpulent man introduced himself. "Whoever you are, you are under arrest. Please, don't resist."

"We are under arrest?" Chelzic let out a contemptuous laugh. His six foot six frame loomed over the short Chief of Security. "Obviously, you don't have the faintest idea who you are dealing with. Whatever reason you may have for trying to arrest us, let me tell you this...nobody arrests me or my men. Ever! I am Commodore Chelzic of the Solar Union Space Navy and I am telling you to open the gate so we can drive through."

"And I am telling you that you are under arrest. Surrender peacefully and without fuss. I promise you a fair trial if you co-operate." Chief Moore spoke with authority like a man used to being obeyed.

For a moment Stonewall thought Chelzic may give Mendez the order to take out the guardhouse or even shoot at the city itself and prepared to dive away as soon as the rifles of the security men began firing their lethal bundles of energy. He let out a sigh of relief when Chelzic shrugged. "I am not in the mood for arguing out here in this blistering heat. I'll make you a deal. Open the damn gate and let us drive in. As soon as we're inside the city I will accompany you to your headquarters or office or wherever you spend your days and we'll straighten out this whole thing."

His gray eyes narrowed. "Let me give you a word of caution, Chief Moore. Don't ever threaten me again. We are Union soldiers, trained in warfare. Your men are nothing but glorified watchmen. You wouldn't stand a chance against us."

Without waiting for Chief Moore to answer, he turned and climbed back into the tank. Stonewall looked at the short Chief of Security and shrugged. Then he followed the Commodore.

Glorified watchmen! He seems to find pleasure in saying it.

Chelzic let out a satisfied grunt when the gate opened, and the tank began rolling. "Patch me through to Headquarters, Cromwell."

Stonewall listened with an uneasy feeling as Chelzic ordered a couple of warplanes to be dispatched to Epsilon City.

"It is best to be on the cautious side," he said after he finished talking with his lieutenant at the Outpost. "Sometimes you have to flex your muscles to get results."

When Stonewall looked outside, he saw the vehicle of the security men following them closely. His eyes roamed across the area surrounding the city. In the distance, he saw a habitat near the dome. A number of spaceships were parked on the hard ground, a few of the ships bringing new colonists or visitors. Some were probably freighters delivering goods or taking goods back into space.

———

THEY ENTERED THE CITY THROUGH A GIANT HOLE AND DROVE UP a wide road that led into the interior. The last time Stonewall had been inside a hive the corridors were lit up by light-bugs, but now minisuns attached to the ceiling at regular intervals had replaced the living light source.

Cromwell stopped the tank in the middle of the road. Chelzic turned to Stonewall. "Go and ask him where we can park the tank."

Stonewall climbed out and walked toward the security vehicle. When one of the men asked him what the problem was, he said, "The Commodore wants to know where we can park."

"Just follow us."

The vehicle pulled ahead. After Stonewall was back in the tank, they followed the other vehicle.

Stonewall knew that the road they drove on spiraled all the way up to the top of the hive. Smaller tunnels led away from the main road at every level.

He already felt sorry for Chief Moore. Chelzic would cut him down to size.

He smiled at his thoughts. *If the man reaches a couple of inches over five feet he's tall. He'll disappear after Chelzic gets through with him.*

They took a side tunnel and finally arrived in an area with a number of vehicles parked against one wall. Cromwell stopped the tank. "I guess here is as good a place as any," he said.

Chelzic nodded. "Now, let's see what this is all about. Stay alert. Even these local heroes can be a nuisance. Shoot to kill if it becomes necessary. We have no time to play games."

"Yes, sir."

Cromwell and Mendez carried their flash rifles openly, while Chelzic slung his across his shoulders. Even without displaying any weapons, he presented a formidable force. One look into the Commodore's cold gray eyes was enough to intimidate and convince anyone that the two oversized energy pistols hanging on either side of his hips were not decoration.

The Chief of Security waited for them. His two men stood uncertain, fingering their weapons. Stonewall could see them throwing glances at Cromwell and Mendez. The two Troopers looked grim and determined. Their eyes were hard and didn't miss a thing.

Stonewall turned to look at Peters, who had poked him in the side. "This is going to be interesting," Peters whispered.

Stonewall nodded. "Very."

They hung back as Chelzic and his Troopers entered Epsilon City Security Headquarters. One of the two Security officers motioned with one hand. "You too."

The desk clerk watched them all walk in with questions in his eyes, but when his chief told him that everything was all right, he relaxed.

Chief Moore stopped and cleared his throat. "Only my officers are allowed to carry weapons in these offices. I would like to ask you to leave yours at the desk."

Commodore Chelzic's chuckle sounded like the growling of an enraged beast. "No Union Trooper ever gives up his weapons freely. It won't happen. You'll have to pry them out of our dead hands. Let's get this over with."

Chief Moore's face hardened for a moment. It took on a deeper color, but he controlled his obvious anger. "All right." He looked like a child who had been denied a piece of candy.

Stonewall couldn't help but feel sympathy and a hint of pity for him.

The door beside the desk stood open and the group spilled into the room behind it. Officers and clerks sitting behind desks reacted the same way as the desk clerk, but nobody spoke. Stonewall felt the tension in the air as the group walked past them. They entered another office. There was only one large desk in it. From the size of the office it was clear it belonged to Chief Moore.

The Chief went behind the desk and planted his corpulent body into the chair. He looked at Chelzic for a moment. Sitting behind his desk seemed to instill in him some of the confidence and authority he had displayed by the gate. "This is a matter of extreme gravity," he said with a solemn expression.

"Explain yourself, man," Chelzic barked.

"I have a report on my desk that men fitting your description driving an armored vehicle have committed a serious offence." Chief Moore spoke slowly as if weighing each word before he uttered it.

"Really? And what would this offence be?" Chelzic sounded amused.

"Murder!"

"Murder? And this murder took place where?"

Moore touched a flat shiny screen on his desk. A hologram popped up showing five men standing beside a black vehicle. Three wore camouflage uniforms and two were dressed in the brown uniforms of the Scouts. All five men carried flash rifles.

A cold shiver ran down Stonewall's spine. He didn't have to guess who those five men were.

He watched with horror as the men in the hologram spread out and surrounded the two habitats beside the smoking ruins of a small space shuttle. Then he watched the destruction of the habitats.

The hologram ended with a shot of the armored vehicle disappearing in the jungle.

Chelzic had said nothing. Now he smiled. "Where did you get this?"

"There were survivors of this horrible massacre."

"We destroyed a smuggler's camp. Where is the crime in that? You witnessed the precise execution of a military mission."

"You destroyed a research facility. Those were innocent men and women you murdered, sir! Scientists. Researchers." Chief Moore's voice was hoarse when he spoke the accusation. "I do not care who you are. You will stand trial for murder. You will answer to your superiors. Until then we will hold you in one of our prisons. I am asking you to surrender your weapons...now!"

"You know the answer to that, Chief Moore." Chelzic's voice had dropped to a dangerous level. His hand touched his sidearm. "According to information we received that was a pirate base. If the information was incorrect then we made a mistake. That happens in war. There are always casualties. Unfortunate but unavoidable."

"Unavoidable?" Moore's voice came out in a whisper. "Do you know that my daughter was among the victims?"

"I'm sorry to hear that. It can't be undone. We will have to live with that." Chelzic's voice became hard. "You will tell your officers to remove their weapons and put them on the floor. You, sir, will be suspended from your post if you decide to resist."

"You have no authority over me, sir," Chief Moore straightened his body and stared at Chelzic.

"I have every authority, Chief Moore. I am Commodore Chelzic and the temporary Supreme Commander of Planet Epsilon. I am the representative of the Solar Union Military and I am declaring Marshall Law. If you insist on questioning me you will be removed from office right now and deported to a Union prison, unless I decide to have you executed immediately. Is that clear?"

Moore stared at the energy pistol that had suddenly appeared in Chelzic's hand. Everything happened quickly and with precision after that.

Cromwell and Mendez covered the two security men with their flash rifles and told them to put down their weapons. When they hesitated, Cromwell smashed the butt of his rifle into the nearest man's belly.

The man doubled over and made retching sounds. Cromwell stared at the other man. "You I'll shoot," he growled.

"This is preposterous," Chief Moor shouted. "*You* are the criminals."

Chelzic leveled his weapon at the Chief's head. "One more word and I will charge you with insubordination and execute you right here!"

Moore lifted both hands. "My blood and the blood of my daughter will be on your conscience."

"Disarm him," Chelzic ordered Stonewall. Then he turned to Peters. "Go outside and inform everyone of the situation. Anyone resisting will be shot. At this moment I have two warplanes landing outside Epsilon City. They are bringing twenty heavily armed Troopers who will back up my orders. Go...tell them that."

Peters disappeared through the door. Stonewall walked behind Chief Moore's desk and relieved him of his sidearm. "Do as you're told and no harm will come to you," he murmured. The pit in stomach was a heavy weight. His fears had been realized. They had murdered innocent men and women. The fact that he hadn't fired a shot didn't make it any easier. He was guilty by association.

"Master Scout Stonewall," Commodore Chelzic barked. "I am appointing you temporary mayor and Chief of Security. Can you handle that responsibility?"

Stonewall stared at Chelzic, not quite sure how he should respond. "I am a stranger in Epsilon City, sir. I don't know anything about the regulations..."

"I didn't ask you that, Stonewall. I just want to know if you can handle a responsible job like this."

"Of course I can, but..."

"No buts, Chief Stonewall. Don't disappoint me!"

AFTER CHELZIC LEFT HE WENT INTO THE MAIN OFFICE AND asked for attention. He could see the hostility in the men's eyes and faces and he didn't blame them.

"You are probably aware by now that Chief Moore has been

relieved of his job. I am the man who is replacing him. I don't like it any more than you people do. I didn't volunteer for this job, but since I've been put into this position, I expect everyone to accept me as the new Chief of Security." He paused and cleared his throat. "I came here as Master Scout Stonewall, but you will address me as Chief Stonewall."

He didn't give them any time to respond to his little speech and went in his new office. He barely managed to walk behind the desk and sit down when he heard voices outside his office. He got up again and opened the door to check out what it was all about. "What is going on here?"

The Trooper turned when he heard Stonewall's voice. "This man insists in seeing you, sir."

A wide-shouldered, stocky man stepped around the Trooper, who had been blocking him. "The security of the city, possibly the whole planet, maybe at stake here, Chief Stonewall. It is of utmost urgency that I talk with you...now."

Stonewall hesitated, but then he nodded. "Okay, come into my office." He looked at the Troopers and smiled thinly. "Don't worry about my safety. I can take care of myself if need be. And I don't believe this man came here to assassinate me."

The man followed Stonewall into his office.

"Have a seat." Stonewall pointed to one of the two wooden chairs. "And then tell me what this is all about."

The man took it gratefully and looked at Stonewall. "So you are the new Chief of Epsilon City's Security."

"Yes, I am, but I don't believe you came here to tell me that."

"Of course not. I can tell by your uniform that you are a Scout. Most likely you are not familiar with Epsilon City. Does the name *Tunnel Rats* mean anything to you?"

Stonewall shook his head. "No."

"Well, they are a bunch of criminals. Young men who roam the tunnels of Epsilon City on their scooters and harass innocent citizens." The man paused, cleared his throat and wiped his hand across his face. "A few days ago a young lady by the name of Tara Turner came to me for help. She had just arrived on Epsilon and had no place to go, so I let her stay in my apartment." He made a gesture as if apologizing. "Until she found a more permanent place."

"I understand Mr...?"

"Houston. David Houston." He stared at Stonewall. "I don't believe you do, because there is nothing going on between me and Miss Turner."

"I didn't say that."

"No, you didn't, but I can see in your eyes what you are thinking."

Stonewall smiled. "Are you a mind reader, Mr. Houston?"

"No but it is obvious that you assume...never mind. That is really irrelevant. It doesn't matter what you think. Four days ago we were attacked by the Tunnel Rats. They beat me unconscious and kidnapped Miss Turner. I found their hiding place, but I have no way of getting into it."

"Why did you take this long to report the kidnapping?"

"I needed to recover from my beating and I wanted to find them myself."

"Why? What were you going to do once you found them? One man against how many?"

Houston shrugged. "I never gave it much thought. I just wanted to find her. To be honest...I didn't expect to get much help from Security. So far they haven't done anything about the problem we have with the Tunnel Rats."

"Then why come for help now?"

"Because I found something that defies explanation. In the caverns underneath Epsilon City."

"How about giving me a hint."

"They might possibly be ruins of an ancient civilization."

"Interesting." Stonewall touched his wristband. "Peters, I'd like to see you in my office."

Almost immediately the door opened, and Peters walked in. He threw a passing glance at Houston, and then he looked at Stonewall. "What is it, Chief?"

Stonewall shook his head slightly. A brief smile crossed his lips. "Cut the crap, Peters. You don't have to call me Chief."

"But you are the new Chief of Security. With the position comes the title. Better get used to it." He grinned. "Or would you prefer if I called you Mayor Stonewall?"

"I won't even comment on that," Stonewall said.

Peters planted his lanky frame into the second chair. His eyes rested on Houston. "Who are you?"

"That is Mr. Houston," Stonewall answered the question. "Apparently, he discovered ancient ruins underneath this city."

"Fascinating," Peters said. Then he shrugged. "I think right now we have larger problems than the dead leftovers of an ancient civilization."

"These *leftovers* don't appear to be dead, Scout Peters, and I have reason to believe that a friend of mine is held prisoner behind a wall of metal that seems impenetrable. I think there is a secret door to get into the room behind the wall," Houston said, obviously getting impatient.

"A secret door," Peters mused. "That has such an ominous sound to it."

"Please, do not try to humor me by analyzing what I'm telling you." Houston's face reddened with anger. "There is no time to be lost. A young woman's life is in danger and she needs our help. I promised her protection and I failed her miserably." He rose from his chair and stood wide-legged in front of the desk, clearly agitated and desperate. "If you won't help, I'll have to seek it elsewhere."

Stonewall lifted a hand. "Take it easy, Mr. Houston. We didn't say we weren't going to help you, but you must understand my position. I just inherited a job I never wanted. I am not familiar with this city and the people who inhabit it. So give me some slack, all right? What makes you think those ruins are not dead?"

"Because I saw a man disappear right in front of my eyes. One moment he was there, the next he was gone."

Stonewall threw a look at Peters. "That doesn't sound like whatever Mr. Houston found is dead. Is it possible that the Uur are technically more advanced than they admit?"

"No." Peters shook his head. "The Uur or anyone else on this planet don't have the technology. By that I mean the indigenous population. Whatever is underneath this city belongs to someone else. Either to the Dragons or the Spiders. If it still works, we may have a potential threat." His face and eyes were grim. "I suggest we check it out."

Stonewall nodded. "I agree, but we need to keep it quiet. We don't want to create a panic. You and I and the two Troopers will accompany Mr. Houston."

"When?"

"Now."

Stonewall was aware of Houston's sigh of relief. "We will need transportation," he said. "What are you driving, Mr. Houston?"

"A scooter. Only large enough for two people."

"Security has larger vehicles. We'll have to request one without anyone asking questions."

Peters chuckled. "You don't have to ask for permission. You are the Chief, remember?"

A short time later, they were on their way. Peters drove the vehicle. Stonewall sat in the passenger's seat, while Houston sat in the back. The two Troopers had decided to take another scooter.

They took a tunnel that led underground. The tunnel was not as well lit as the tunnels on the upper floors. After driving through a cavern filled with stalactites and stalagmites they arrived at the mysterious wall. Stonewall stood gazing at the shiny barrier. He put his hand on the smooth surface and said, "It feels warm. You were correct, Mr. Houston, whatever this is it is not dead."

"I believe that the Tunnel Rats are hiding behind this wall. And they have Miss Turner with them," Houston said.

"But how did they get beyond this barrier?"

"They teleported?" Peters suggested, shrugging his shoulders.

"Nobody possesses that technology. Not even the Spiders."

"As far as we know. Even if they did, they would never share it with anyone." Peters walked closer and touched the wall. "I am detecting a slight vibration. Where exactly did you see that man disappear, Mr. Houston?"

"Right about where you are standing, Scout Peters."

Peters took a few steps with his hand still touching the wall. He walked back and forth a few times. "The vibrations seem to be stronger in this area," he said.

"If your theory is correct then that is where the portal must be." Stonewall stroked his chin. "How do you activate it?"

"By sending some kind of a signal?"

"That would suggest a remote device. The man must have carried it on his person."

"I remember he had an ancient looking medallion hanging from a chain around his neck. Could that have been the device?" Houston nodded. "Yes, you could be right. They all wore them around their necks. Each one of those youths who accosted us had one. I assumed they were jewelry."

"Well, we don't have one. Maybe we can blast our way in," Peters suggested.

Stonewall waved to the Troopers. "See if you can cut a hole into this wall."

The Troopers nodded and stepped back. Then they aimed their flash rifles at the wall and washed it with bursts of pure energy.

The wall didn't show any signs that the onslaught produced any results.

Stonewall stopped them. "It is useless. That leaves us with only one option. We will have to intercept either one or all of them. They'll have to come out sooner or later. For now we'll leave in case they have the means to see us." He turned toward the two Troopers. "I want you to guard this door."

"Our job is to protect you and not some wall," one of them protested.

"I appreciate that," he told them. "But my safety comes second to the safety of Epsilon. This whole planet may be threatened by what lies behind this wall."

[5]

STONEWALL RECEIVED A CALL WITHIN BARELY TWO HOURS THAT the Troopers had taken a couple of the Tunnel Rats into custody. He called Peters on the communicator. "We have a couple of live ones. Bring the guy Houston with you and we'll take another trip down below."

He decided to take two Security men with him, just in case they needed reinforcement. They didn't ask any questions when he told them to accompany him, only nodded their willingness.

The two he picked seemed to be the most amiable of the bunch. He knew that most of the men held a grudge against him for ousting Chief Moore.

He, along with Peters and Houston, took the same vehicle they had used before, but this time he told a third Security man to come along as the driver. The other two officers rode their own scooters.

The two Troopers were waiting in the tunnel. The Tunnel Rats with them didn't look happy, but they stared at him in defiance when he approached them. Gaudily dressed and displaying shaved heads, their ears adorned with large rings, their bodies tattooed in many places, they produced in him an instant dislike toward them. He had never been fond of men or women who showed contempt for the society they lived in and displayed it in such utter and obvious fashion.

One of them opened his painted lips and pushed out a split tongue. His eyes were focused on someone behind Stonewall. "You'll never find your beautiful lady, Davy. Are you still so angry, Davy?" He spoke with a singing, mocking voice. His split tongue lent it a ghostly lisping quality.

Houston brushed past Stonewall and stood in front of the man who taunted him, his fists lifted threateningly. "If you harmed her in any way, I swear I'll kill you, you freak!" he said, gnashing his teeth.

"First you'll have to find her, angry Davy."

Stonewall grabbed Houston's arm and pulled him away. "Let us handle this, Mr. Houston." He glared into the youth's laughing face. "We have no time to play games. I'm only going to ask once. What is behind that wall at the end of the cavern and how are we going to get behind it?"

The youth grinned and then he spit into Stonewall's face. "Go fuck a lizard," he sneered.

Stonewall backhanded him and noted with grim satisfaction the split lip his hand left behind. It should go well with his split tongue.

Wiping the blood from his mouth, the youth spat again. Then he pushed out his tongue and made a warbling sound. His friend joined him in his act of defiance.

"Make them talk," Stonewall said calmly to one of the Troopers. He turned to Houston. "Is he one of the ones who kidnapped your friend?"

Houston nodded with a grim expression. "He is one of them. I'll never forget his ugly face. Let me have a go at him."

Stonewall shook his head. "Can't do that. You're a civilian. Let the professionals handle it. It won't be long before they're going to spill their guts. Literally, if necessary."

He turned away from the two Troopers and their prisoners. "Give them a few minutes," he said to his companions. "There is no need for any of us to watch this."

Before long, moaning sounds and then a loud scream, followed by another one, testified to the efficiency of the Union Troopers.

"Are you sure that is necessary?" one of the Security men asked.

"If we want to achieve our objective it is," Stonewall assured him.

"What is our objective?"

"To rescue a young woman and to make certain there are no entities that could be a danger to this planet hiding beneath Epsilon City."

"The Tunnel Rats are nothing but a bunch of over-zealous young men creating a nuisance for the citizens, but they are certainly no danger to Epsilon." The Security officer shook his head when another scream echoed through the tunnel. "There is really no need to torture them."

"They are criminals," Houston said with a loud and angry voice. "The security in this city is at best laughable. You people have no problem harassing an innocent young woman who committed one small oversight, but you won't take these vermin off the street!"

"If they commit an offence, we will arrest them, until then we have no reason to waste valuable recourses chasing unsubstantiated rumors." The officer spoke calmly, hiding his own irritation well.

"We are able to proceed," one of the Troopers said behind Stonewall.

When Stonewall looked, he saw the two youths lying on the ground. They didn't move. The Trooper saw him looking. "They are alive," he said. "But they may need to seek medical help."

"Will they be all right if we leave them here for a while?" Stonewall asked.

"They will be in pain, but otherwise they'll be fine."

"Good. Then let us carry on. Do you have the means to get past the barrier?"

The Trooper held up one of the chains the youths had been wearing around their necks. A medallion momentarily reflected the light from Stonewall's headlamp. "This is the key," he said.

"Did you get instructions how to use it?"

"We did."

Stonewall stared at the Tunnel Rats. "I don't want to leave them here. Put them into the vehicle. Peters and Mr. Houston...hitch a ride with the Security men. We don't have far to go."

They left the dark tunnel behind and entered the large cavern. Getting to the wall didn't seem to take as long as the first time. Stonewall got out of the vehicle and waited with apprehension for one of the Troopers to approach the wall. He touched the medallion in his hand against the smooth surface and disappeared.

When the other Trooper attempted to follow him, Stonewall called him back. "No. We don't know what's on the other side. Let's find out how we all can pass through." He walked to the Security vehicle and peered inside. Both men sat in the backseat and stared at him with dull eyes. Their faces and upper bodies were covered with blood and grime. He didn't have to be a doctor to know they needed medical attention.

He hardened himself against the momentary pity he felt. These men were misfits, criminals. They had kidnapped another person, maybe even more than one. Possibly even committed murder. They didn't deserve sympathy.

"How can you transfer more than one person through that wall?" he asked.

"Fuck you!"

Stonewall glared at the tall youth. Crusted blood covered his ripped earlobes. The rings he had been wearing were gone. "I can have my man work you over a little bit more," he said grimly. "Maybe we can spare us a trip to the hospital."

"I'll tell you," the other youth said.

"All right. I'm waiting."

"If you let me out, I'll show you."

"Traitor," spat the other one.

"I don't want to die. You can do what you want, Trevor. I'm done with this shit anyway." He got off his seat, moving slowly, obviously in pain. Moaning, he stepped out of the car and stood swaying. "I think I'm going to be sick," he said.

Stonewall grabbed his arm. "Save it for later. Now...tell us how it's done."

"It is quite simple. All you have to do is stay in a tight cluster while one of you touches the wall with the medallion." He tried to smile but only managed a pained grimace. "Can you give me something for the pain? Please."

At first Stonewall felt like denying him but then he changed his mind. "What's your name?"

"Sel."

"Okay, Sel. You've been helpful. Maybe not all is lost with you."

"I promise if you help me out of this, I'll quit the Tunnel Rats. They're a bunch of losers anyway." Sel gave him a hopeful look.

Stonewall took a caplet out of a pouch he wore on his belt. "Here, chew on this. It will ease the pain."

The youth took it eagerly and put it into his mouth. "Thank you, sir. I won't forget this. One more thing. If I help you will you go easy on me? Can you promise me that?"

"I'll promise." Stonewall waved to the Security guard who had been driving the vehicle. "Stay with the prisoner and guard him." Then he turned to the other men. "All right let's all stay close together. Keep your eyes open and weapons ready." He glanced at Sel. "You're coming with us. It better work."

As soon as the Trooper touched the medallion to the wall, a slight tingling went through Stonewall and then he found himself in a different location. The others were right beside him.

The Trooper who had stepped through the barrier first, stood nearby, his weapon leveled at a group of men. They stood with arms raised above their heads. One lay on the ground, his body in a heap, a gun in his twisted hand. Stonewall knew he was dead, even without a closer look.

"I was beginning to wonder if you could make it through," the Trooper said.

"We did have a slight holdup, but we are here now." Stonewall appraised the men lined up against one wall like condemned prisoners in front of a firing squad. They were dressed in flashy clothes, with painted eyes and lips and chains around their necks and waists. Their heads were shaved, and he could see tattoos on their exposed skin. "Were you going to shoot them all?" he asked the Trooper.

"Just about. They are unwilling to cooperate." The Trooper waved his weapon at the group in a threatening gesture.

"Where is the girl?"

Stonewall glanced at Houston who had shouted the question. "Take it easy, friend," he said. "One step at a time."

"Every moment we waste puts her in deeper danger," Houston said, his voice urgent.

"It's *Angry Davy*," one of the Tunnel Rats said with a mocking voice.

"Angry Davy...Angry Davy..." all of them sang.

"Tell them to shut up!"

Stonewall couldn't blame Houston for being upset. He stared at the chanting youths. "You heard the man," he said, putting an edge into his voice.

His request only made them laugh. "He's no man. He let us take his girlfriend with his lizard tucked between his legs," one of them shouted.

"That's enough!" Stonewall was getting impatient and angry. "Now I'm asking you the same question. Where is the girl?"

"She's with the others," a youth with a hooked nose said, chuckling. "And the others." His friends thought that was funny and broke into loud laughter.

"I can show you," Sel said behind Stonewall.

One of the Tunnel Rats stepped away from the group. Glaring at Stonewall, he said, "Your ape-man murdered one of my friends. I will take that up with Security. Besides, you are trespassing. This is our domain. Nobody is allowed here without special permission. Our permission." His eyes fell on Sel. With a pointing finger, he said, "We'll deal with you, traitor. You are a dead man!"

"You are in no position to threaten anyone," Stonewall said coldly. "If you have a complaint, you can tell me right now. I am the new Chief of Security. You are all under arrest."

"You can't arrest us," one of the youths said defiantly. "We are citizens of Epsilon city. We have rights like everyone else."

Stonewall glared at him. "The only rights you have are the ones I allow you. You are misfits of society, who prey on upstanding citizens. By being members of a gang makes you criminals in my eyes. I might just decide to have you all shot. It will save us all a lot of trouble and expense." He couldn't believe he said that, but he was angry for being put in this position. He was a Master Scout, not a politician, and certainly not a policeman.

He grimaced. Chelzic would be proud of him. He looked at Sel. "All right. Now earn your freedom. Where is the girl?"

Sel nodded, his face more relaxed. The medication seemed to have taken effect. "Follow me, please."

Stonewall threw another look at the Tunnel Rats. He counted eleven. Plus the dead one on the ground. They'd need a large vehicle to transport them back to Security Headquarters. "Call for a prison wagon," he told one of the two Security men. "Then disarm the prisoners and make sure you get all of the keys. We don't want them escaping. If one resists or tries to make a run for it, shoot him."

He was aware of Peters looking at him and he could guess what he was thinking, but he was beyond caring. When he turned to speak to his friend, he avoided his eyes. "Mr. Peters and Mr. Houston, please accompany us."

When the second Trooper followed them, Stonewall shook his head. "Stay with the prisoners. I don't trust them. They are desperate, with nothing to lose. If I find I need you, I'll call you."

Sel took them to the back of the room, past machines of alien design that made Stonewall's eyes ache when he looked at them too closely. A narrow corridor led to another, larger room, filled with more machines and something that gave Stonewall the shivers. There were shelves stacked with transparent globes. Each globe contained an oval body. There was no doubt what those bodies were.

"Are those what I think they are?" Peters whispered.

Stonewall nodded grimly. "There is no mistake. We are looking at preserved Spider bodies."

"Are you sure they are dead?"

"You're not suggesting they are alive inside those globes?"

"Not alive in that sense. I mean, they could be in stasis. Look at the wires leading to the globes. And those machines, they are still working. Why? For what purpose?"

Stonewall stopped to study the shelves. Then he shook his head. "This doesn't make sense. When did the Spiders build all this?"

"Everything looks almost new, but it can't be. We've been here over twenty years. Somebody was bound to notice Spider activities on Epsilon." Peters touched one of the globes. "It feels awfully cold and there is definitely some kind of power enveloping the whole thing. I can detect a slight vibration, like static electricity."

"Do you know what this is?" Stonewall asked Sel.

The young man shrugged his shoulders. "Like you said, they're Spiders. You'll understand better when you see what I'm going to show you."

They rounded another corner and Stonewall stopped short. Beside him, Peters cursed loudly.

Stonewall stared at the creatures clambering over each other behind a transparent barrier.

"Those are young Spiders," Houston said, voicing Stonewall's thoughts.

White bones littered the ground and a cold shiver ran through Stonewall as he recognized their origin. When he stepped closer to the barrier, the Spiders scuttled toward the transparent wall, sharp mandibles clicking. A small group that had been busy in the back of the enclosure broke apart and rushed to join the others in front of the window to stare at the Humans. Stonewall turned away for a moment when he saw what they had been tearing apart, fearing he would be sick. It was not the first time he saw dead people, but the sight of a bloody, half-eaten human body is not something the human mind can easily digest.

The anguished cry of a man made him look at Houston, who stood, bent over, making retching sounds. Even Peters, who was no stranger to death, stood white-faced, staring at the torn mess of what was clearly the body of a young woman.

"I will kill them for this." Houston's voice came out in choked gasps.

———

THEY ALL TURNED WHEN THEY HEARD THE WEAK VOICE OF A woman calling. Stonewall spotted a young girl standing inside a cage behind the bulk of one of the alien machines. She was naked and appeared emaciated. Her long hair hung in matted strands down to her hips, partially covering her breasts.

"Please, help me," the girl cried, stretching out her thin arms.

"Are you Tara Turner?" Stonewall called to her.

She shook her head. "My name is Sherina."

Stonewall walked slowly toward the cage, still in shock from what he had seen in the other room. Houston rushed by him and grabbed the bars of the cage. "That...that body in there...is that Tara?"

The girl shook her head again. "That is..." she stopped and put her hands over her face, her whole body wracked by a series of loud sobs. Then she wiped her eyes and stared wild-eyed at the three men. "Are you with them?"

"No, we are not with them," Stonewall said softly. "We are from Epsilon Security. We'll get you out of here."

The girl cried openly but no tears came. "I've been praying for a long time," she whispered. "I never thought my prayers would be answered." She smiled bravely. "I'm not really a religious person." Her hands moved down to cover her dark triangle. "I must look a sight and I'm naked..."

"You look beautiful and don't worry about being naked," Peters said. "You can have my shirt."

"Thank you. You are so kind." The girl's smile became contorted and she put one hand against her mouth.

Stonewall noticed her cracked and swollen lips and anger welled up inside him. "Stand back," he told her. "We'll have to cut through the bars."

It didn't take long until they had cut a large enough hole to get the girl out of the cage. She stumbled as she stepped through and Peters caught her. Then he took off his shirt and draped it around her shoulders. She clung to him, sobbing again.

He put an arm around her shoulder. "It's all right. You're safe now." His voice came out hoarse and Stonewall knew how he must feel inside.

"You were trying to tell us who that girl was inside that room," he said.

"Her name is...was Helina," Sherina said with a choking voice. "She was so scared. Like all of us. I'll never forget her screams."

"How many girls were there?"

She shrugged. "I don't really know. When I got here there were five girls in this cage with me. They're all dead now."

"So there could have been more?"

She didn't answer, only nodded.

"Those bastards! They need to be punished," Peters said between clenched teeth.

"They will be," Stonewall said with a grim voice. He felt dead inside, but he was determined not to let emotions cloud his judgment. Yet he knew what he must do.

"I feel cold," the girl said. She gasped when her eyes fell on Sel, who had been silent. Fear showed suddenly in her face and she sobbed, "He is one of them. You said you were Security..."

"We are," Stonewall said soothingly. "Has he harmed you in any way?"

"No, not him. I've never seen him in this room."

"That's right," Sel said, his voice urgent. "I would have never touched her or any of the others."

"Did you know about this?" Stonewall pointed at the transparent wall.

"I did, but I didn't want any part of it. I told them it wasn't right." He stared at Stonewall. "You have to believe me."

"Where is Tara, the last girl you brought here?" Houston asked.

"I don't know. I assumed she was in here?"

"You assumed? Didn't you see her?"

"No. Trevor said he wanted to look after her personally."

"Trevor, that's your friend who we caught with you?"

He nodded. "That's him, but he is not my friend. I never liked him." Sel spat on the floor. "He's the one who came up with the idea how we could feed those...those creatures."

"Well, we'll give him special treatment, I'll promise," Stonewall growled. "Let's go back. Somebody has to know what happened to Miss Turner."

"What about me?" Sel pulled on Stonewall's sleeve. "Are you still going to keep your promise to me?"

Stonewall glared at him. "You helped us getting through that wall, but otherwise you haven't given us much."

"I will testify against them. Just don't shoot me, please. I never felt like one of them, anyway. I'll be a good citizen after this, I swear by my dead mother's name."

"We'll see." Stonewall didn't feel charitable, but he would keep his promise.

The Tunnel Rats sat on the floor, with their backs against a wall, watching sullenly as Stonewall and the other men came back into the room.

Stonewall stared grimly at the group. "Who is the leader of this gang?" he bellowed.

One of the youths lifted a hand. He stared defiantly at Stonewall. "I am the leader. But let me correct you, sir. This is not a gang. We are nothing but a peace-loving Scooter Club."

Peters snorted beside Stonewall and Houston let out a loud growl.

Stonewall pointed at the girl, who hung onto Peters, her green eyes overly large in her thin face. "Explain how this girl ended up in a cage and explain to me the creatures behind the transparent wall. Explain the torn, bloody body that had once been a girl named Helina. Explain the bones!" He spoke slowly, choosing his words carefully, trying to stay calm, and finding it extremely difficult not to scream at them.

The Tunnel Rat shrugged and grinned. "We managed to bring those critters back to life. They needed to be fed. Those girls were trash anyway."

Sherina let out a loud sob and pointed a finger at him. "You murdered my brother!"

The youth shrugged. "He shouldn't have resisted."

"He tried to save me from you. You're not human, you're a beast, an animal. I hate you and if I could I would kill you myself." Her voice had risen and ended in a scream. She put her hands over her face and sobbed loudly.

Stonewall glared at the man who had proclaimed himself as the leader of the Tunnel Rats. "What is your name?"

The youth drew his body erect. "I am Sirus Kidwai. My father is Ali Kidwai, the Advocate. You can't touch me."

"Well, Sirus Kidway, please rise and stand over there against that wall." Stonewall spoke calmly. He was cold inside and determined to see justice done.

Sirus rose and followed his instruction. Leaning against the wall, he stood wide-legged, a mocking grin on his brown face.

"Do you recognize anyone who was present when they took the other girls into that room?" Stonewall asked Sherina.

She lifted her face and looked over the group. Then she pointed at three of them. "Those. They were the ones who dragged Helina away."

"You are certain?"

"Yes, I am. I will never forget their faces and the way they laughed when those creatures tore Helina to bits."

"Thank you." His eyes raked the three she had pointed at. "Join your friend over at that wall," he ordered them. He waited until the three stood beside their leader before he said, "We're looking for the last girl that was brought in here. Her name is Tara Turner. Does anyone know what happened to her?"

Nobody spoke. They all stared at him. A few looked toward the opposite wall, at Sirus.

"Don't look for advice from him and don't let him intimidate you. He is no threat to anyone," Stonewall said.

One of them shifted uneasily, staring first at Sirus and then at Stonewall. He lifted his hand halfway but seemed to change his mind.

Stonewall caught his eye. "You! Do you have anything to tell us?"

The youth coughed into his hand. "You should ask Trevor."

"Trevor? Okay." Stonewall turned to one of the Troopers. "Go, bring in the other prisoner."

The Trooper nodded. He pressed one of the medallions against the wall and disappeared from view. He came back a short moment later, dragging the blood-covered Trevor into the room.

Trevor's face was gray, and he stumbled when the Trooper gave him a shove.

"Hello, Trevor," Stonewall said. "How are you feeling?"

"Fuck you!" the youth cursed and showed his forked tongue. "I demand to see a doctor. I'm dying."

Shaking his head, Stonewall stared at him coldly. "I'm going to ask you a question. If I like your answer, I might just give you something to ease the pain."

Trevor glared at him from bloodshot eyes. "What do you want to know?"

"Where is the girl you kidnapped?"

"She's safe."

"Where?"

82

"I can't tell you. Not until you make this pain go away. She is my trump card."

"All right. I'll give you something."

"Let me at him," Houston growled beside Stonewall. "I'll beat it out of him."

"And kill him in the process." Stonewall shook his head. He groped around in his pouch and took out a pill. He handed it to Trevor and watched him swallow it eagerly. It took only a few moments until the effect was visible.

"Start talking," Stonewall said.

Trevor shrugged. "One more condition. If I tell you I won't be prosecuted. I'll go free."

"That is something I can't promise." Stonewall shook his head. "You committed a crime and need to be punished. Show or tell us where the girl is. If she's safe, then we'll talk again. That's all I can offer you."

"Well, she's not down here."

"Then tell us where she is!" Stonewall's patience was wearing thin.

"In my room."

"He's lying," Houston spat.

"No, I'm not. It's the truth. I didn't want her to become food. You know...like the others."

"That seems like a noble enough reason," Stonewall said sarcastically. "We can easily check out if you're telling the truth. What's your full name and what floor do you live on?"

"Trevor Fullborne. I live on the forty-second floor. Apartment number twenty-seven."

"Anyone else live there?"

He shook his head. "No, I live alone."

Stonewall turned to one of the Security men. "Have someone check it out."

"Aye, aye, sir. I can't get through from here, though. My signals are blocked."

"Try from the other side of the wall." Stonewall thought for a moment. It would be better if Houston didn't witness the coming events. It was strictly a police matter. "There is no reason for you to stay here any longer, Mr. Houston. I know you're anxious to find out if your friend is okay. Go with the officer. Take one of the scooters to get to head office. You can accompany the men to Fullborne's apartment."

Houston seemed to hesitate for a moment, but then he nodded. "Thank you for your help, Chief Stonewall."

The Security man took one of the medallions and waited for Houston to join him by the wall.

After they were gone, Stonewall took a look around the room. He was intrigued by the alien machines. Whenever he looked closer at them, his eyes seemed to play tricks with his mind. The images of the machines became blurry; the outlines twisted into impossible angles. His head hurt after a while and he had to tear his eyes away.

"How did you stumble upon this place?" he asked Sel.

"Pure coincidence, really. Somol found one of the medallions outside. When he leaned against the wall to study it, he found himself in here." Sel allowed himself a little chuckle. "You can imagine he nearly crapped his pants. In his panic he pounded the wall with the medallion and it transported him back to us. It didn't take much to figure out the rest."

"How about those young Spiders in that room behind the window? Who figured out how to hatch them?"

"That was *Genius*. That's not really his name, but we call him that because he can solve puzzles nobody else can. He suggested we hatch those eggs. We freaked out when it worked."

Stonewall looked grim. "Whose idea was it to kidnap young women and let the Spiders eat them?"

"Trevor came up with that idea, but I told you that already."

Stonewall nodded. "I just wanted to make sure I had my facts straight."

At that moment the Security man came back through the wall; he brought with him two additional Security men. "The prison transporter is here," he announced.

"Good." Stonewall cleared his throat. What he had to do was not pleasant, and he hated himself for it, but he knew his hands were tied in the matter. He was the appointed Police Chief of Epsilon City and therefore responsible for the safety of the City. Chelzic had declared Marshall Law, which meant the harsh and swift law of the Military negated any existing laws. Even though he was not a military man, he was aware of military laws. "Trooper Slesky, under Marshall Law what is the penalty for murder?"

Slesky's eyes were cold when he spoke. "According to the code there is only one penalty, Chief Stonewall. I'll recite it if you want…"

Stonewall lifted his hand to stop him. Nodding solemnly, he stared at the small group of Tunnel Rats he had separated from the others. His eyes fell on Trevor, not sure what to do with him. After a moment of deliberating, he said, "Trevor Fullborne, go and join your friends over there." He pointed at the larger group. Trevor would be dealt with later. Even though he had come up with the idea to kidnap young women, it needed to be determined that he took part in the actual killings.

Clearing his throat again, he said, "All of you are members of this criminal gang you call the *Tunnel Rats*, therefore, you are guilty by association. You have committed a crime more hideous than anyone can imagine. You kidnapped young, innocent women and kept them captive in deplorable conditions. Some of you have sent these young women to a horrible death; the rest of you have stood idly by and let it happen."

His eyes raked the four standing against one wall. Sirus, their leader gave him a defying stare, a smug, amused smile playing around his lips.

"Sirus Kidway, step forward, please."

Sirus took one swaggering step and grinned. "I'd like to remind you that my father is a prominent Advocate in Epsilon City."

"So you've told me. He is not here right now and I'm afraid he can't help you. You are on your own." Stonewall felt a heavy stone in his stomach as he delivered his next words.

"Sirus Kidway, as leader of the Tunnel Rats you are responsible for your own acts and those of the members of your gang. I find you guilty of murder. By the power invested in me I am sentencing you to death."

Sirus glared at Stonewall. Then he broke out into a wild laughter. "You are sentencing me to death? You are crazier than a fucking *Moonsnake*! My father will tear you apart with his bare hands."

Stonewall ignored him and addressed the other three. "Your names, please."

"Herm Meeler."

"Phillippi Fander."

The third one made an obscene gesture with his fingers and hissed, "Suck your lizard! I'm not telling you my name."

"That's okay. It doesn't really matter. Herm Meeler, Phillipi Fander, and you without a name...for the murder of a young woman named Helina, and possibly others, I am sentencing you to die."

"You have no right to judge us," Meeler said, his face white. "And besides, she was nothing but a common whore, a Girl of the Night, just like all the others."

"We will appeal." Fander turned to Kidway. "Your father will get us off, won't he, Sirus?"

"My father will make mincemeat out of this crazy upstart dictator," Sirus said with confidence. He spat in Stonewall's direction.

"I'm afraid he won't get the opportunity." Stonewall nodded to the two Troopers. They nodded back and walked up to the four angrily shouting gang members.

"Turn around, your face against the wall, hands behind your back," one of the Troopers ordered them.

They obliged, grumbling as they did so. "I need to go to the bathroom before you cuff me," Sirus said.

The Trooper stepped behind him, put his gun against the back of his head and pulled the trigger. Sirus collapsed without a sound.

Three more times the Trooper used his gun and then it was over.

There was silence from the other Tunnel Rats. Stonewall gave them one last glance and saw the fear and sudden terror in their eyes.

Thank you, Chelzic, for the position you've put me in.

"Load the prisoners into the wagon," he said tonelessly. He felt empty and cold inside.

[6]

STONEWALL STARED AT THE FACE OF THE MAN INSIDE THE hologram on his desk. "Who are you again?" he asked.

"I am High Commissioner Quintana, the CEO of the Trading Commission here on Epsilon. I'm surprised you're not aware of me."

Stonewall detected the irritation in the man's voice. "So far I've had no reason to be. What can I do for you, Commissioner Quintana?"

The man's laugh sounded almost jovial. "Well, for starters you can explain this nonsense that happened in Epsilon City. I've had to hear it from other sources that Chief Moore has been replaced. Why wasn't I notified?"

Stonewall took a deep breath before he answered. He was getting tired of all these nuisance calls from people who believed they had to be kept in the circle of knowledge when it came to everything that happened in Epsilon City. "I wasn't aware that I had to report to anyone, Commissioner. In fact, I only report to Commodore Chelzic, the man who appointed me Chief of Security and Mayor of Epsilon City."

Quintana's expression hardened, and his thick eyebrows pulled together in a deep frown. "Chelzic? Is he the man who put Epsilon under Marshall Law?"

"The very same." Stonewall was becoming impatient. He had better things to do than explain politics to someone who was obviously trying to throw his weight around. "He is a commander in the Solar Union Space Navy. Here in this sector of space he is *The* Commander. He decided to take over Epsilon in the name of the Military. There is no reason for you to be concerned if you are an honest citizen of Epsilon, sir."

Quintana's laugh was anything but pleasant. "I'm not a citizen of Epsilon. I'm a citizen of Earth, therefore immune to the laws on Epsilon. But I am quite concerned about this whole thing. We need to talk. I'll connect you with my secretary and she'll make an appointment for you to come to my office where we can become more acquainted with each other."

Stonewall was taken aback for a moment by the man's pompous attitude and assumption Stonewall would visit him in his office because he commanded it.

"I'm afraid that won't be possible. I'm swamped with work right now. I can't go around wasting my time making social calls. If you have something you want to discuss with me, make an appointment with *my* secretary. I'm sure your secretary knows how to get in touch with my office. Good day, Commissioner Quintana." With that he terminated the connection.

Leaning back in his seat, he allowed himself the luxury of a satisfied smile.

Son-of-a-bitch! Who does the man think he is?

He looked up as the door to his office opened and Peters walked in. "Someone..."

Before he could say more, a tall, dark-skinned man sporting a thick black beard pushed his way past him. "Are you the new Chief?" he barked.

"Yes, I am. And who are you?"

"My name is Ali Kidwai. I am an Advocate and I demand you explain to me what happened to my son Sirus Kidwai."

Stonewall regarded the man silently. Then he spoke slowly, "Your son committed a serious crime for which he was found guilty and punished under the military law of Epsilon."

"You murdered my son without giving him a chance to defend himself in a court of law!" Kidwai thundered.

"Not murdered, sir. He was executed. He died a quick and merciful death, something he denied his victims." Stonewall didn't raise his voice, even though he felt like shouting.

"What gave you the right to judge my son? He was a good man with a promising future." Kidwai glared at Stonewall.

"He was the leader of a criminal gang, sir. A gang that kidnapped young women and used them as fodder. Your good son was a murderer."

"My son may have been a little misguided, like most young men. He and his friends were scooter enthusiasts, that's all. Sure, they were a bit rowdy at times, but murderers? No, they were not murderers. This is all a big misunderstanding. I will initiate an investigation into this affair, and you, sir, will have to answer for your crime." Kidwai pointed a finger at Stonewall, his dark eyes ablaze with anger.

Stonewall glared back at him, suppressing his own anger and distaste for Advocates. "There will be no investigation. Justice has been done. This matter is closed," he said calmly.

"It is far from closed! I will be representing the other young men who are falsely kept in prison. There will be no more executions!"

"Let me remind you, Mr. Kidwai, that as long as Epsilon is under Military Law, civilian Advocates will not represent anyone in a Court of Law. All of the people arrested are members of a criminal gang and therefore automatically guilty of a crime. A prosecutor will determine the level of their guilt and they will be sentenced accordingly. We will not waste taxpayer's money and the court's time to establish something they are not...innocent. Now, good day, Mr. Kidwai. I suggest you leave my office before I have you arrested for obstruction of the Law." He turned away and studied his computer screen.

"I will not..." Kidway fumed but didn't finish his sentence when he was grabbed by the two Troopers who had silently walked in during his tirade. Struggling and cursing, he was dragged out of the door.

"Good riddance," Stonewall murmured, heaving a deep sigh. He hated this whole affair and cursed Chelzic, not for the first time, for putting him into this predicament. He never asked for this job, but he was determined to see it through. It was not an easy thing to hand out death sentences and watch them carried out. To be responsible for the death of anyone, guilty of a crime or not, was a burden he never meant to have on his conscience. It was one of the reasons he became a Scout and not a soldier.

"John Moore to see you, Chief."

Stonewall smiled at Peters. He insisted in calling him *Chief,* even though he had told him to stop doing that. Peters winked and closed the door.

"You wanted to talk to me?" Moore stood in front of Stonewall's desk, *his* desk only a short time ago, looking with an expressionless face at the man who had replaced him.

Stonewall could not blame the former Chief for hating him. He indicated the chair and said, "Please, have a seat."

Moore shook his head. "I prefer to stand."

"Very well." Stonewall blew air across his lips. What he was going to propose was not something sanctioned by Chelzic and the Commodore may not approve of it, but this would be a gesture of good will and, hopefully, make his own job a little easier. He needed every help he could get. "Mr. Moore, I have a proposal and I hope you will give me a favorable answer."

"I don't know if I'm interested."

"I'm not going to make excuses and explanations for the situation we are in right now. It is something that happened, and we will have to make the best of it. As you are fully aware, it was never my idea to become Chief of Epsilon Security, never mind also the mayor. I'm a Master Scout for the Solar Union, not a politician and, frankly, I find this job demanding and stressful. I am offering you the position of Advisor to the Chief."

"Why?"

"Because you are more qualified for this job than I am. It is in the best interest of Epsilon City. I will still be the Chief but in name only. In essence, you will be handling the affairs of this city." Stonewall pointed at the chair again. "Please, don't turn me down. Let's discuss this between two men who are interested only in what's good for the citizens of this city and not worry about Union politics or the ambitions of a madman."

Moore accepted Stonewall's invitation and planted his bulk in the chair. "I'm listening."

———

THE DAY MIGHT HAVE ENDED ON A POSITIVE NOTE HAD IT NOT been for Migual Quintana, the High Commissioner. He stormed into Stonewall's office, seething and red in his face, trying to free himself from the Trooper's iron grip.

"Tell this buffoon to remove his hand from my person!" He glared at Stonewall. "Who the hell do you think you are?"

"I am Chief of Security and also the mayor of Epsilon City. I am the Law and what I say will be done," Stonewall said calmly. He nodded to the Trooper. "Release the man but keep an eye on him. Shoot him if you must." Turning his attention to Quintana, he said, "Now, please, explain this outburst, Commissioner."

"You will address me as High Commissioner, Stonewall!"

"Chief Stonewall, please." Stonewall was determined not to be intimidated by the man. His talk with Moore had been quite revealing, and he knew much more about politics than he had known when he took the job as Chief of Security. He didn't invite Quintana to sit down.

The man was of average height. A little under six feet, Stonewall estimated. Handsome with his curly black hair and naturally brown skin, and arrogant, obviously used to getting his way. Butting heads with him could be a dangerous game. He had connections to high places and money. He was not just a commissioner; he was part owner of the Trading Commission.

The common assumption was that the Trading Commission was another government department, another arm of the Solar Union, but Stonewall knew now that this assumption was wrong.

The Trading Commission was a privately owned company that had been given the monopoly to mine Epsilon. Chief Moore didn't know anything about the other owners, except that some of the members of the Board of Directors had high government positions. He also hinted on drug cartel connections.

Stonewall knew he was walking on thin ice taking on this man, but he hated corruption and favoritism. A man should make his own way to the top, the honest way, and without help from others. He knew his thinking was old-fashioned, naïve, and provincial, as his father used to call it. However, growing up on a farm taught him a lot of basic values and he tried to stick to them.

"This would never have happened with Chief Moore. He knew better than to do anything without conferring with me. Where is Chief Moore?" Quintana said with a demanding voice.

"Mr. Moore is not the Chief anymore. I am."

"I want to talk with Chief Moore." Quinana was ignoring Stonewall's words, clearly trying to get a reaction from Stonewall.

Stonewall leaned forward, giving the impression of being calm and collected, but he was fuming inside. "I understand you brought armed men with you," he stated. The arrival of the High Commissioner with his entourage had not gone unnoticed when he drove into the City complex, and Security had alerted Stonewall to the fact. Stonewall had then ordered his Troopers to intercept the group and disarm the men.

"My personal guards are always with me. Never before have I been treated like this when I came here," Quintana blustered.

"Armed civilians are not allowed in Epsilon City, according to our bylaws. I realize that Security has always been a bit more lenient with certain individuals, but that is changing now. There will be no more exceptions. We are enforcing that law now."

Quintana put his hands on the desk and glared at Stonewall. "Either you really have no idea who I am or you are stupid and have a death wish, Stonewall." He spoke with a low but rough voice, forcing each word through his teeth.

Stonewall returned his stare and said, "I am fully aware who you are, Mister Quintana, and I don't care. From now on there will be no more deliberations with you about anything, unless it involves the Trading Commission. You run your business and we look after the affairs of Epsilon. You are not an arm of the government but a private institution. Right now we have other problems to worry about than what your company does to the honest citizens of this planet, but as soon as we have resolved the current situation, we will have a closer look at your company's involvement in the affairs of Epsilon."

"Is that a threat?"

"Take it any way you want, sir."

Quintana's laugh was anything but pleasant. "Stonewall, Stonewall, you have absolutely no idea what and who you're meddling with. You don't even know who the real movers are on Epsilon. I think this job is going to your head. I have friends in the government and I can promise you one thing...your days as a Scout are numbered."

Stonewall gave the High Commissioner a tight smile. "I see you've been digging around in my past."

"I had a talk with Chief Wallace at the Outpost and he filled me in. You are not even a military man, only a lowly Scout." Quintana's words dripped with contempt.

"I am a Master Scout," Stonewall said proudly.

"When I get through with you, nobody will even remember who you are, Master Scout Stonewall. Your name won't be found in any registers. You and your name will be wiped from existence!"

"Until that happens, I am Chief of Security in Epsilon City, the man who wields all the power in this part of the planet. I suggest you go back to your little empire under the dome outside this City and work on your schemes, High Commissioner Quintana. Let me make a prediction. The day when the Trading Commission is no longer dictating the rules on Epsilon is not far away. Think about that. Good day, sir." He gave the Trooper a sign. "Escort the High Commissioner and his associates out of the City. We will deliver the confiscated weapons to his habitat at a more convenient time."

Quintana shook off the Trooper's hand. "I don't need any help, you idiot." Before he walked out of the door, he turned and said, "This isn't over, Mister. You are a walking dead man."

———

STONEWALL GLARED AT THE CLOSED DOOR, HIS STOMACH IN knots. "Damn you, Chelzic!" he cursed. "You left me here to deal with all this shit. It's easy for you with the might of the military machine behind you, but what about me? I'm lucky if I leave this planet alive."

He had no illusions about what he was playing with. Quintana was a formidable force, a man with powerful connections and he was foolish to have made a man like him his enemy but Stonewall hated corruption at all levels. He hated the way Quintana had waltzed into his office assuming Stonewall would roll over and be the obedient little puppy, jumping through hoops for the man.

He sighed and opened one of the drawers to take out the bottle he had found. He wasn't surprised that Chief Moore had searched solace in that bottle. This job was not for a man with a soft backbone and sympathetic heart. Nor was it for a man with a weak stomach.

He touched the communication's screen on his desk. When the face of his secretary materialized inside the tiny cube, he said, "Miss Sindhu, I'd like to see you in my office, please."

She walked in a few moments later and gave him a questioning look.

He pointed to the chair. "Sit, please."

She sat down, crossing her legs. Her short skirt rose up to expose part of her thighs. She was not that young anymore, in her early thirties, he guessed, but quite attractive with her black hair and bright gray-blue eyes.

"What do people do around here for fun?" he asked.

"Fun?" She raised an eyebrow, clearly surprised by his question.

"Yeah, fun. You know...relaxing, having a good time, blowing off steam..."

She shrugged. "I wouldn't know. I usually stay home and watch old holograms." She smiled. "Not very exiting I admit, but there isn't much opportunity for a single woman to blow off steam, unless you're a *Girl of the Night*."

"I gather you're not married?"

"No. Never found the right man."

"No male friend?"

She shook her head.

"Female friends?"

She smiled, obviously understanding his meaning. "I don't swing that way."

"Can you recommend a place where two lonely people could go to relax and have a nice meal together?"

"You and your wife?"

He laughed. "I'm not married. What sane woman would marry a

guy who jumps from planet to planet? I was thinking you and me. Or am I too forward?"

"A little." She studied him with obvious interest. "I'm not used to being asked out by my boss. What should the answer be?"

"It should be affirmative." Lifting a hand in an apologetic gesture, he added, "Forget I'm your boss. It's only temporary anyway. Just think of me as a lonely man who was forced into a job he didn't want. A man who needs a sympathetic ear and a beautiful woman to keep him company for an evening."

"And you think I'm all that?" Her smile seemed encouraging, so he pressed on.

"I wouldn't have asked if I thought otherwise."

"Okay. I have nothing planned for tonight anyway, except for...you know...old holograms." She uncrossed her legs and rose, smoothing out her skirt. "If we hurry, we can make it to *The Happy Dragon* in time for supper. They serve a great lizard steak, I'm told. Or a delicious medley of steamed tubers and ferns, should you happen to be a vegetarian."

"I'm a meat eater." He got out of his chair, chuckling. "In fact, I'm so hungry right now I could eat a whole dinosaur."

When they walked out of the door, the two Troopers stationed on either side fell in behind them. He wanted to tell them there was no need to tag along, but he knew it would be useless. Their orders were to protect him, and they were good soldiers. Aside from the fact they only took orders from Commodore Chelzic, their real boss. He suspected that their duties also included keeping an eye on him.

The *Happy Dragon* was on the thirty-second floor. Since he didn't have his own vehicle, he asked one of the Security men to drive them. The Troopers followed on their own scooters, which they had appropriated from Security.

Stonewall was surprised at the pleasant atmosphere inside the restaurant. A waiter took them to a table and asked for their orders. The service was quick and efficient. It didn't take long until Stonewall had a plate with a decent-sized steak and boiled tuber in front of him.

His female companion ordered only a small plate with steaming vegetables, no meat, but she did not decline a glass of wine.

"You come here a lot, Miss Sindhu?" Stonewall asked.

Shaking her head, she said, "As I told you, I don't go out much, but I've been here a few times with...someone..." She hesitated and looked away. "It's been a while."

He didn't ask. Her private life was none of his business. "This is very good," he said, slicing off another piece of steak. "I've eaten dinosaur steak before but never as good as this."

"I'm glad you like it." She looked at him over the rim of her glass. "Can I ask you a question?"

"Sure."

"Is it true that you are responsible for the death of Chief Moore's daughter?"

The meat seemed suddenly tasteless at the memory of the destruction Chelzic and his Troopers had caused. Valuable property had been destroyed and innocent people died. Even though he and Peters had not taken part in the horrible act, he couldn't shake a feeling of guilt.

Perhaps he could have stopped it.

However, deep down, he knew that he could have done nothing. He had gone through the same agony when he spoke about the incident with Chief Moore. Moore had tried hard to understand. Upon Stonewall's insistence they had watched the hologram again. It had not made it any easier seeing that his claim of innocence was the truth. Watching the murders for a second time only brought back more pain.

Neither Peters nor he had had killed anyone personally, they were nevertheless guilty by association, as guilty as the Tunnel Rats. Crimes had been committed by both parties...the Tunnel Rats and the Military. The only difference was the fact that the researchers had been killed by agents of the government, which somehow made it all right. Victims of mistaken identity and of false information. Nobody would be punished.

"I was there," he said, tonelessly. "But that is all. I'm not responsible for the death of Chief Moore's daughter. Neither am I guilty of killing anyone that day."

It was the truth. Not that day.

"You were present when she was murdered?"

He nodded slowly. "Not by choice, though. Sometimes we get into situations beyond our control. In defense of the men responsible for the deaths of all those researchers I can only say that we had the wrong information. We were told it was a base set up by smugglers. We didn't know anything about Chief Moore's daughter or how many people were in that habitat. The whole thing was a senseless act. It should never have happened."

Her bright eyes searched his face. "I believe you," she said. "I suppose much of the time we receive incorrect information. There are rumors that you are ruthless and without feelings, and without little respect for human life. I'd like to believe those rumors are wrong."

His smile was painful. "Rumors usually are, even though they sometimes contain some truth. I have a strong sense of what is right or wrong. Life to me is precious and needs to be protected, but there are people who will take a life without blinking an eye. Their only reason may be their desire to take something that is not theirs. There are a host of other reasons; cruelty being one of them or finding pleasure in seeing others suffer. Those criminals lose their right to live and need to be punished. I have no pity for them. Does that make me cruel or without feelings?"

"You remind me very much of my older brother," she said, smiling gently. Reaching across the table she touched his hand for a fleeting moment. Then she pulled back her hand as if afraid he might grab it.

"Your brother?"

"Yes. He was a Security man. He used to talk the same way."

"Used to? What happened to him?"

"He became disillusioned with the politics in Epsilon City and quit Security. He decided to try his luck in the jungle. I haven't heard from him for six years. Apparently, he was killed by smugglers. But that's only a rumor." She ran a finger across her closed eyelids. When she opened them, they were shiny.

"I'm sorry," was all he could say.

"It's okay."

"I don't want to pry into your private life, but I'm curious. How did a beautiful, smart woman like you get stuck on this forsaken planet?"

She sighed deeply and stared into her glass. "I was born on Earth, in New-Delhi. The city is huge and overcrowded, like most cities on

Earth. I was one of nine children. The second youngest." She smiled when she heard his grunt and looked up. "I know, the law requires couples to have no more than two children, but there are ways around that. My parents claimed me and six of my brothers and sisters as foundlings. Abandoned children they took into their home. There are plenty of those because of the rigid birth control."

"There is a reason for that law," he said softly.

"You are right of course. People like my parents are responsible for the overcrowded conditions on Earth. My parents got away with it because they had government connections. Both of my parents were doctors. It was easy for them to falsify birth records. It does not justify their actions and I make no excuses for them. Anyway, my brother and my fiancé, who was also my brother's best friend, they had big dreams. It was their idea to come to Epsilon. As for myself...?" Her gaze dropped, and she spread the fingers of her right hand, pressing it against the tabletop, her fingers drumming against the smooth surface.

"You don't have to explain yourself," he said.

She was still staring into her glass and continued as if she had not heard him. "I had no choice. I loved Sahir, my fiancé. He was a good man, a dreamer, not an adventurer. He was not meant to explore unknown frontiers."

"Did he leave with your brother looking for treasures?"

"No." She shook her head. "He was killed by one of the flying dinosaurs the first month after our arrival. He went out by himself one day to observe a herd of young Apatosaurus. He was very much interested in all the strange animals on Epsilon."

She emptied her glass and said, "That's how I ended up all alone on this freaken planet. Do you mind if I have another glass of wine?"

"Of course not." He waived to the waiter. "Can you bring us another bottle?"

They didn't finish the second bottle, but there was not much left in it when he called the waiter over to settle the bill. When he reached into his pocket, he realized something. "This is embarrassing," he said to the woman, "I have no money."

She giggled and waggled a finger at him. "I think you are trying to take advantage of me, Chief." Her speech was slurred, which was no big surprise, since she had drunk most of the wine.

"You will be reimbursed as soon as we get back to the office tomorrow, Miss Sindhu. As Chief I should get a decent salary." He lifted his shoulders apologetically.

"It's okay, I'm only kidding." She opened her purse and handed the waiter a card.

The waiter ran it through a scanner and handed it back to her. "Have a pleasant evening," he said politely.

The security vehicle that had brought them was not there when they stepped into the corridor outside the restaurant, but the two Troopers were leaning against the wall, their scooters beside them.

Stonewall called Headquarters on his comm. It didn't take long and another vehicle arrived to pick them up.

"My scooter is parked on the second floor," Miss Sindhu said. "Where is yours?"

"I don't have one."

"How do you get to work in the morning?"

"I usually walk. I have a room in one of the hotels on the third floor."

"Oh." She leaned back into her seat while the vehicle took them down to the second floor. After they got out, she came up to him and looked into his face. "I had a nice time, Stonewall, and I don't want it to end yet. Stay with me tonight."

"Are you inviting me into your apartment?"

She nodded. "Yes, I am. No commitment. Just have a cup of coffee with me and keep me company. You asked for mine, now I'm asking for yours."

"Okay."

"My scooter is in the parking lot."

He turned to the Troopers who had been watching. "We'll be all right. Why don't you two call it a day?"

They hesitated but didn't object when he walked away with the woman.

He found it strange sitting behind her while she operated the scooter. She lived on the forty-seventh floor and it took a while to get there. He was a little worried about her ability to control the scooter, since she had been drinking quite a bit, but they arrived at her apartment without any problems.

"It's not much," she said as she opened the door.

"Anything is better than what I'm used to most of the time," he said.

She took off her jacket and threw it on the couch. Then she kicked off her shoes. "Make yourself comfortable while I go and change my clothes." She disappeared through a door.

He took off his own boots and sat on the couch, stretching his legs. Looking around the apartment, he could easily see that it was owned by a woman. It was nice and tidy; everything had its place.

She came out a short time later, dressed in a thin gown. He could see her breasts through the practically sheer material, and when she stood in front of him, the dark triangle below her flat belly was clearly visible.

Lifting up the already short gown, she straddled his legs and sat in his lap, facing him. "Am I too forward?" she asked with a smile.

"A little," he answered. Then he pulled her close and kissed her.

She opened her lips and sucked in his tongue, grazing it with her teeth. He probed the cavity of her mouth, tasting the wine. It turned him on, and he put his hand on her breast, kneading it gently.

With frantic haste, she undid the front of his shirt. Then she fumbled with his pants, trying to open his belt. Breaking the kiss, he said hoarsely, "Let me do it." He slipped out of his shirt and unbuckled his belt. She slid off him and knelt on the floor in front of him. Pushing his pants down to his knees, she exposed his erection.

With a sigh, she bent forward and licked the tip of his penis. Closing her lips around it, she slowly took him into her mouth.

Groaning, he leaned into the cushions and, closing his eyes, he enjoyed the sensation of her warm mouth moving up and down on his hard penis.

He didn't want to come inside her mouth. When he felt the throbbing getting stronger, he eased out of her mouth and pulled her up. "I want you naked," he said.

She grabbed the hem of her gown and pulled it over her head. He studied her for a moment. She had a curvy figure, nicely shaped breasts, a flat belly, and slim thighs and legs. It was obvious that she worked out. "You're beautiful," he said.

She laughed and pushed him onto his back. Then she straddled him and touched his stiff penis. "I haven't been with a man for a while," she whispered. "Let's not hurry. I hope you can last a long time. I want to enjoy you as long as possible. By the way, don't worry about getting me pregnant. I've had my prevention shots. A single working woman cannot afford to get herself pregnant, not here on Epsilon."

Rubbing her thick labia over the tip of his penis, she brought herself to a quick orgasm. When he tried to enter her, she held his mast with her hand. "Not yet," she breathed. "Give me time."

She went crazy after that, moaning and crying out as she experienced a series of orgasms, still not letting him into her. Finally, she took her hand away and opened her thighs wide. He slid into her slippery channel with a loud groan and grabbed her buttocks.

She bucked and squirmed on top of him for a long time, until she collapsed onto his chest. "I'm getting tired," she said.

"Then let me be on top."

She left him and lay down on the carpeted floor. Opening her thighs wide, she waited for him to move between them. With deliberate slowness, he entered her again and fucked her with steady, powerful strokes.

[7]

STONEWALL ACTIVATED THE COMMUNICATOR ON HIS DESK AND watched the viewing cube spring to life. Staring at the three-dimensional image of the guard, he said, "What is it?"

"There is a small delegation of *Bugeyes* asking for an audience with the mayor, sir."

"What do they want?"

"They're not saying, sir."

"I'll send someone."

"Okay."

The image of the guard disappeared. Stonewall pressed one of the symbols on the small screen set into his desktop. The face of Peters took form inside the cube. "Yes, sir?"

"Come into my office, please."

Peters walked in a few moments later. "What's up, Chief?"

Stonewall didn't comment on that. He was getting used to Peters calling him *Chief*. "I have a job for you. You're the liaisons officer between the Uur and the Humans. Apparently the Uur want to discuss something with us. A delegation of them is waiting by the gate. Go, and bring them here."

"Will do, Chief." Peters saluted sloppily, grinned, and walked out of the door.

Stonewall shook his head and smiled. It was good to have at least one friend on this planet.

He busied himself with checking out files in the database, cursing again the day he came back to Epsilon. Actually, it wasn't the day he arrived; it was the day Commodore Chelzic made his appearance.

When the door opened, and Peters walked in, followed by a number of the giant Ants, Stonewall looked with apprehension at the group of natives. He was not surprised, when the body of one of them seemed to undergo a metamorphosis into a different being, knowing that his mind was manipulated into seeing something that wasn't there.

Instead of seeing a black, hard-shelled Insectoid, he saw a beautiful woman, wearing a warrior's kilt and a leather harness to cover up her upper body, looking at him out of large, brown eyes. Her face looked vaguely familiar.

I am Zira, daughter of Zeer.

The words formed inside his mind.

He made a little bow and said, "Welcome, Zira, daughter of Zeer. I am Terrex Stonewall, mayor of Epsilon City. How can I help you?"

We are concerned, Terrex Stonewall. One of your flying small hives has destroyed with its weapons of light a large part of one of our nectar-producing farms. They have broken the pact we have with the Humans.

"I am as concerned as you. I know nothing about the incident, but I will have it investigated. The guilty will be punished." He looked at Peters. "You are the liaison officer, Peters. What do you know about incidents like that?"

"We have had reports about ships landing on Epsilon without permission. They are pirates and some of them are non-Humans. We don't have any control over that."

You have told us so before, Human Peters. You also promised that you would make it stop. You have not kept your promise. We are getting impatient.

"It is not that easy," Peters said. "These things take time." He turned to Stonewall and made a gesture toward the Uur. "You might be interested that she is the daughter of the Queen you met fifteen years ago."

Stonewall nodded. That is why she looked familiar. She probably got the image of a Human woman from her mother's mind. "How is your mother?" he asked, addressing Zira.

Zeer is still the queen of our hive. She remembers a Human by the name of Terrex Stonewall. I am privileged to meet you. I will tell her about your return. She will want to speak with you.

"I would be honored to be invited into your hive and to speak to your mother. I remember her fondly."

I have another request.

"Please, tell me what I can do for you."

We want you to supply us with weapons that kill with light so we can defend our hive against invaders from the stars.

Stonewall didn't know what to tell her. How could he justify giving weapons like that to the indigenous people of Epsilon? They were technologically not far enough advanced to handle weapons capable of causing destruction of such magnitude. "I will bring up your request with my superiors," he said, knowing she had mentally followed his train of thought. He didn't quite know how it worked. She couldn't exactly read his mind, but she received the abstract thought impulses his mind broadcast.

They will deny our request, Terrex Stonewall. You must make the decision. Many of our people will perish if we are not able to defend our hive. That is what our 'longseers' have foretold. You will be responsible for the consequences.

Stonewall thought of Earth's history, of the time when European conquerors invaded the Americas. How the Spaniards destroyed the Empire of the Aztecs, how they murdered thousands upon thousands of innocent people with their superior weapons; how the English and French killed off the natives that roamed the prairies of the North American continent. Perhaps things would have turned out differently had they possessed weapons equal to those of the invaders. The history of the Humans was full of examples like that. The ones with superior weapons always came out the victors.

Perhaps he could prevent such a thing happening on Epsilon. Then again, perhaps it would be a grave mistake with dire consequences arming the indigenous people with weapons they may not be able to handle responsibly.

The Uur in the guise of a human woman watched him with interest.

We will use the weapons only against our enemies.

He smiled grimly. That was not comforting. Friends sometimes turn into enemies. He made a decision.

"I will commit an act I may have to pay for dearly. All of the warriors with you will receive a flash rifle. I'll have someone teach them how to use the weapons."

Thank you. You will not be sorry.

He hesitated. "How long will you stay in our city?"

Her smile lit up her face. It made her appear extremely beautiful and human. It was easy to forget that her real face was immobile, unable to show any emotion.

I will accept your invitation to 'take me out for lunch'. Did I say that correctly?

Her uncanny ability to interpret his thoughts with such accuracy almost made him believe that she could read his mind. He chuckled. "You did, but it was just a thought that popped into my mind. You're not a human woman. I'm afraid it is not possible."

Why not?

"What could I offer you to eat?"

Anything a human woman eats. I promise you the illusion will be perfect. She came around his desk and stood beside him. When she touched his neck, her hand felt warm on his skin. *Nobody will know that I am not human, not even you. I can do anything a human woman can do.*

He looked at Peters, but it seemed Peters had not heard Zira's words, because he didn't show any reaction. Zira's hand moved up his cheek in a gentle caress before she moved away. Turning her head, her eyes threw him a smoldering look. *I am looking forward to tonight. Until then I would like to rest. It is a long walk from our hive to yours.*

"Peters will arrange for quarters where you will be able to rest undisturbed," Stonewall said, wondering about her words. What exactly did she mean by them?

He watched her and her warriors leave his office, feeling uneasy about the promise he made. Chelzic would not be a happy man when he found out that he was arming the natives with flash rifles. He knew it would not end there. Once a process has started, it was nearly impossible to stop it. Things would never be the same again on Epsilon, but he could not sit by idly watching while the Uur might follow in the footsteps of the American Indians and other races that had been eradicated by their conquerors.

Peters came back about thirty minutes later. He didn't look cheerful. "I hope you know what you're doing, Stonewall," he said.

Stonewall knew that even Peters took the plan to supply the Uur with modern weapons as a serious decision. By not calling him *Chief* he showed his great concern.

"I'm not sure if I'm doing the right thing, old friend," he said. "It might earn me a place in front of a firing squad, but deep down I know that it is the only thing to do."

"I hope history will be kind to you," Peters said, sighing. "I don't envy your position."

———

She looked ravishing in her blue, tight dress that showed off her generous curves. She smiled and hooked her arm into his as they walked down the corridor.

Do you find me beautiful and desirable?

"You mean do I find the image you are projecting beautiful?" he asked. "Of course I do."

And desirable?

He glanced at her sideways. "More than desirable. Is it your intention to make me desire you?"

Her laughter sounded silvery in his mind. *You are a male and I am female. Is it not the nature of a female to be desirable to a male?*

"A male and female of the same species, but you and I are too different from each other to even think about that."

She laughed again. *You have been thinking how it would be to join your body to mine, haven't you?*

"How could I not think that? The body you are showing me is of extreme beauty and I can almost feel the pheromones exuding from it. I know it is an illusion. How could it be otherwise?"

She stopped walking and stepped in front of him. Her arms went around his neck. Before he realized it, he felt her lips on his. They were warm and pliable.

She broke the kiss and laughed. *The pheromones are not an illusion. They are real. They are a direct response to the pheromones your body is exuding. I am young and quite susceptible to those emanations. I am ready to mate.*

"I'm afraid we are both going to be disappointed with the outcome of this," he said, inhaling the feminine scent of her warm body in his arms. He wanted her so badly. His penis was a hard piece of wood inside his pants and he cursed when her hand went down to touch it.

My real body has a female organ and is quite capable of accepting your male organ. I feel you are as ready and willing as I am. Let us go into my quarters and follow the demands of our bodies. I promise neither of us will be disappointed. It will be a wonderful way to seal the bargain between our species. She kissed him again with great passion.

Inside her apartment, she lay down on the wide bed, her dress pushed up to expose her genitals. He groaned and undressed with shaking hands. He didn't remember ever feeling this horny.

Naked, he fell between her spread thighs and stabbed frantically. Her hand moved between them and took hold of his hard penis. He let out a loud moan when he slid into the unexpected creamy softness of her vagina. She felt tight, but wet and slippery and he had no problem pushing his penis fully into her. Her arms went around his back and held him close as he moved forcefully on top of her.

She lay silent under him, but her lower body responded to his thrusts. Pushing up against him, she kept his penis prisoner inside her hot sheath, letting her soft inner muscles ripple the length of his hard member.

His mind forgot that this was not a human woman with soft flesh but an alien creature with a chitinous body, a female with no soft breasts, and yet, he could feel them digging into his chest.

He cried out harshly when a tremendous climax took away his clear thinking and made him into a primitive animal bent on only one thing...to shoot his sperm into the clutching organ of the female in his arms.

When his sanity returned, he relaxed into her arms and lay gasping for air on top of her. She stroked his back with soft hands.

That was beautiful. Her thoughts drifted into his mind.

He lifted his head and looked into her smiling face. "Did you enjoy this as much as I did?"

My mind blended with yours at the moment of your release and I felt what you felt. My real body may be hard on the outside, but my flesh is soft inside the outer shell and our minds are much alike. I also feel pain and pleasure, just like you. Females and males of my species enjoy the joining of our bodies, just like you.

"I am glad to hear that. Let me see your real body."

Are you certain?"

"Yes, I am."

The outlines of her body wavered. Suddenly, he could feel her hard upper body under him with her arms still around his back. Her face was cold, immobile, and her eyes large and multifaceted. The soft mouth he had kissed only moments before was a wide slit with thin lips.

Oddly though, her lower body still felt pliable and warm. When he looked, he could see his penis buried inside her sex-organ and he was surprised to see how similar her vagina looked to that of a human woman. Her vagina-lips were thick and soft, bare of any hair or anything similar to hair.

At least that was comforting. It would have disturbed him to find out he had put his penis into a round hole in a hard, unresponsive shell.

Do I repulse you?

"Surprisingly not," he answered truthfully. "Am I repulsive to you?"

No. It is not only your body I see. I perceive you as a combination of your body and mind. She chuckled. *That is why in many ways we are superior to Humans. I do not judge you by your appearance, rather I judge you by what your mind emanates.* She moved her lower body. *I feel your sexual appendix hardening inside me. It seems you find joining with me in my real body as stimulating as when I appear to you as a human female. I find that interesting.*

She was right. Knowing that he was having intercourse with an alien female for some reason turned him on immensely. "Don't change," he gasped, finding his penis hard again inside her clutching vessel. Holding onto her hard upper body, he began thrusting into her, grunting loudly. She responded to his wild thrusts and writhed under him, her soft lower body whipping against him.

He could feel her mind caressing his and it spurned him on to plunge his rampant penis deep into her quivering alien vagina again and again with great enthusiasm.

Barely realizing that her body didn't feel hard anymore but soft and warm beneath him, his mind was clear enough to know that she was manipulating his thoughts again and made him see and feel a human woman in his arms. He looked into her brown eyes and put his lips on hers, kissing her deeply when his climax approached.

Shuddering in her embrace, he let out a hoarse cry as his body was shaken by the force of his eruption. She milked him with powerful sucking motions until he was finished. Then she held him tight, making strange clacking sound.

I am satisfied. She spoke softly in his mind. *Stay with me until morning when our bodies shall become one again.*

"THE UUR DELEGATION HAS LEFT," PETERS TOLD STONEWALL. "Zira told me to thank you for the flash rifles. I admit her warriors are quick learners. They have become quite adapt with their new weapons. I'm still not certain if we did the right thing giving them such powerful weapons. I hope it doesn't bite us in the ass someday."

"There will be consequences, I know," Stonewall admitted. "But I still say we did what needed to be done." He hadn't talked to or seen Zira since he left her apartment the morning before. She had left her mark on him, something he could not deny. They had coupled again one more time in the morning, just as she had told him they would.

He became aware of Peters watching him with curiosity.

"You seem distant," Peters said. "Is everything okay?"

Stonewall rubbed his forehead to ban the memory. "I'm fine," he murmured. "Just a bit tired."

"You should take a few days off," Peters suggested. He grinned. "Maybe get laid or something."

Get laid. If you only knew, my friend.

He couldn't get her out of his mind.

She rode him with fierce passion, displaying her savage but at the same time gentle side. Almost like a lover. He heard loud clacking sounds, the same sounds she had made during their coupling the evening before. Her body swayed above him, fading in and out of her projected human form. He reached up and put his hands on her chest, kneading her breasts one moment and feeling the cool hard exoskeleton of her upper body the next.

"Hey, Terrex, are you feeling okay?"

His eyes came back into focus. "Yes, I'm okay. Listen, I appreciate the suggestion, but I have too much on my mind to think of romancing someone."

"I never said *romance*. I told you to get laid. A good piece of tail can do wonders for a man's psyche."

"Not always." Stonewall slapped Peters on the shoulder. "Don't worry about me, old friend. I'll survive."

Peters grimaced. "There is more to living than just surviving. Oh, something else. Zira also told me that she's planning to set up some kind of trading agreement. She wants to outfit her whole army with weapons, but she understands that she won't be able to get them for free."

Stonewall let out a loud snort. "It seems the Trading Commission is going to get even richer, thanks to me. Obviously, they'll be the only one trading with the natives. Instead of being reprimanded I should get a plaque with my name in golden letters."

He turned when the door to his office was pushed open and Commodore Chelzic walked in.

"Stonewall, get ready. You'll be going on a mission."

"Hello to you too, Commodore," he said, irritated at seeing the big man barging into his office. "What mission?"

"I've had some disturbing reports from the northern communities. I want you to investigate them."

"What kind of reports?"

"It seems our reptilian friends are trying to create chaos on Epsilon. We should have blasted that Anorian ship out of the water," Chelzic barked.

"Why? What are the Anorians doing?" Stonewall nodded to Peters and mouthed *go*.

Peters grinned, winked, and left.

Chelzic didn't even seem to notice him leaving. He planted his bulk into the chair behind Stonewall's desk, something that irritated Stonewall even more. "The reports are sketchy and don't make much sense. That's why I want you to check them out."

"Any particular place?"

"*Raptor's Tooth* is one that sticks in my mind." Chelzic grunted. "What a dumb name to give to a town."

"How was your trip to Star City?" Stonewall asked.

"As well as can be expected. I'm going to set up a base there. It is a perfect location."

"I'm sure they'll all be thrilled." Stonewall couldn't help but put a sarcastic tone into it.

If Chelzic heard it, he didn't react. "My sources tell me that you had to flex the muscles I gave you."

"If you're referring to the incident with the youth gang your information is correct. I'm not proud of what I had to do." Stonewall glared at the big man. "I never asked for this assignment, Chelzic. You put me into a position that forced me to commit acts of violence my conscience doesn't condone."

"Positions of power also carry responsibilities. I must say I am proud of you, Stonewall. Even though your conscience didn't allow it you carried out an act of justice. Criminals have to be punished. There is no room for criminals in a just world."

"Who decides what constitutes a just world?"

"Whoever holds the power. In this case the Military."

"In other words *you*, Chelzic!"

The Commodore's eyebrows pulled together as he studied Stonewall. "You have a rebellious streak in you, Stonewall. Count yourself lucky that, for some reason I can't explain, I have taken a liking to you, or you might face a military court for insubordination."

"I'm not in the Military, Chelzic," Stonewall said, annoyed, and angry.

"That's right, I forgot. You're a Scout." He made a rolling motion with his hand. "What do you call yourself...? Refresh my memory."

Stonewall drew himself erect. "My title is *Master Scout*."

"That's right. Master Scout. How can I forget? Well, let me remind you of *my* title." Chelzic glared at him. "I am *Commodore* Chelzic. Got that?"

"Yes, Commodore." Stonewall made a mock salute. "I got that, *Commodore* Chelzic."

"Good. Now let's talk about your assignment. By the way, you look tired, Stonewall. I think a change in location will do you good."

———

THEY LEFT TWO DAYS LATER. STONEWALL, PETERS, AND TROOPER Mendez. The Trooper drove the tank. He didn't appear too happy about his assignment, but he was a good soldier and followed orders.

"How long will it take to get to Raptor's Tooth?" Stonewall asked.

"Well, we're talking about a thousand miles traveling down an almost groomed road that goes all the way to Desert Hell." Peters chuckled. "As groomed as a road can be on this planet. Vehicles do travel on it on a regular basis. Mainly the Trading Commission buses. If everything goes well, we might make it there in three days."

"Three days," Stonewall mused. "That's not too bad. How long to Raptor's Tooth?"

Peters grinned. "Now that's a different story. The fun will end once we get to Desert Hell. The road to Raptor's Tooth is practically nonexistent. It's a trail, that' about it. Two hundred miles long. The mode of transportation is usually on the back of a Boraz. Or, if you can afford one, on a scooter."

"What's a Boraz?"

"A reptilian creature as large as a small horse, quite docile, easily tamed. Its splayed feet make it an ideal animal to use in swamps. It can even swim in water. What makes it also quite valuable to a prospector is the fact that it does provide some protection against the smaller predators. Even though it is not aggressive, it will defend itself when attacked, using its hard, knobby tail and short horn quite effectively."

"Interesting. Who would have thought there is an animal on Epsilon that can actually be useful." Stonewall watched the jungle outside moving by. It never seemed to change. Everything looked the same mile after mile. Nothing but huge mushroom trees, tall ferns and grasses, and shrubs. And the millions of smaller mushrooms on the ground in between. The tank rolled over the small mushrooms, flattening them under its wide tracks. New ones would replace the destroyed ones within hours. The jungle never slept.

They couldn't hear the sounds of the jungle inside the tank; neither did they smell the odors in the air, some of them pleasant, some of them vile. The air inside the tank was fresh and cool. At least something to be thankful for.

The trip was uneventful. Stonewall did not complain about that and he even managed to sleep a little. They arrived in Star City on schedule after being on the road for a little over six hours. Mendez drove into an artificial habitat near the tall cone that was Star City and parked the tank. An underground tunnel led into the city.

"Quite sophisticated," Stonewall commented.

"Yes, it is. As an alternative to building an electric fence around the city, the local administration decided to put up a habitat for the vehicles instead of parking them inside a fenced-in parking lot. Visitors will be safe from attacks by flying predators, as well as from the ones roaming the jungle," Peters explained. "Apparently, the tunnel was already there. Much of Star City is underground. It seems the original builders used existing natural tunnels in which to live."

"Reminds me of Epsilon City. Remember the grotto underneath the city?"

Peters nodded. "This one is a little different. I don't believe you will find a Spider post here."

"You never know. The one under Epsilon City stayed undiscovered for years. Even the Uur didn't know about it."

"That's true."

Stonewall noticed that quite a few of the citizens they met threw curious glances, not all of them friendly, at the black-clad Trooper Mendez.

"I get the impression you're not a welcome sight, Mendez," Stonewall remarked.

"It looks that way, doesn't it? I wonder why." Mendez didn't seem to be concerned about it.

Peters chuckled. "It can't be your height. You're the shortest man of the three of us. Maybe it's the clothes you're wearing," He looked down at his own brown Scout's uniform. "People usually give me a friendly smile when they see me."

"Must be the clothes *you're* wearing," Mendez said good-humoredly. "I actually don't give a crap what people think of me. I'm here to protect them from the enemy, not to make friends."

"I have a feeling that Commodore Chelzic didn't make many friends, either. I think his visit here stirred up a lot of emotion," Stonewall remarked.

"That reminds me," Mendez said. "I have to deliver a message to the Mayor. His office is on the thirty-second floor. We'll take the express elevator."

"You seem to know your way around here."

Mendez glanced at Stonewall. "I was here with Commodore Chelzic, remember?"

They stepped into one of the elevators. People already inside the large cubicle made room for them, most of them staring at Mendez with unveiled hostility. A few nodded to Stonewall and Peters. Nobody said anything. The elevator made only a few stops. It didn't take long to reach their destination.

The thirty-second floor held a number of private offices and the offices of Star City administration. Nobody stopped them when they strode into the mayor's office. Mendez addressed the woman behind the desk. "Trooper Mendez to see Mayor Garland. Is he in?"

She nodded, throwing him fearful glances. "He's in."

Mendez didn't wait for her to announce him. He just pushed open the door that led into the office and walked in. Stonewall and Peters followed him slowly.

The tall, haggard-looking man behind the desk lifted his head when the door opened. His expression changed from dour to angry. "You could at least knock before you enter my office unannounced," he said harshly.

"I only knock when I'm breaking down a door," Mendez said, his voice level but hard.

"Well, of course. How stupid of me to assume otherwise." Garland glared at Mendez. "I thought you people had moved out. What brings you back so soon?"

"I am here to remind you that even though no Union Troopers are here anymore, Marshall Law still exists in Star City and everywhere else on this planet. You can expect a small unit of Troopers in a few days. Prepare an office for them where they can set up a command post."

"What for?"

"To insure the safety of this city."

"We don't need you for that. Our city is safe." The Mayor spoke with a loud voice, expressing his anger and annoyance.

Mendez leaned across the desk and said with a low voice, "I have the power to arrest you for insubordination and keep you in jail for as long as I desire, Garland. Commodore Chelzic allowed you to keep your job as mayor of this city, but we can easily replace you. Do you understand?"

Garland glanced past him at Stonewall. "I was under the impression that the Scouts are here to protect us, not to rule us. Am I wrong? Tell me, what is the Military doing on Epsilon?"

Stonewall lifted his shoulders. "Apparently we are under siege from the Spiders. That's why Earth sent the Military. We have no control over that, Mayor Garland."

The Mayor stared at his desk for a moment. Lifting his eyes, he looked resigned. "We'll get an office ready," he said.

"I'm glad you are so amiable." Mendez straightened up and rubbed his hands. "Now we would like to have something to eat. I am starved. Can you recommend a good restaurant?"

Garland shook his head, disbelief clearly in his eyes. "Yes, it is called *Hell*. You'll find it in the deepest pit of this planet."

Mendez clucked his tongue. "And here I was beginning to like you, Garland." He looked at Stonewall and grinned. "Seems we are on our own. Perhaps his secretary will be more helpful."

"Let's just get out of here, Mendez," Stonewall growled. Mendez's performance reminded him again why Scouts and Union soldiers didn't get along.

Outside the mayor's office, Peters asked the secretary, "Where is a good place to eat, Ma'am?"

"Most restaurants are on the fifth floor," she told him. "Star's Inn is one of the better ones. They serve great food."

"Thank you." Peters gave her a friendly smile. "We'll mention your name."

"I wish you wouldn't." Her eyes wandered to Mendez and back to Peters. "Besides, I never gave you my name. It is better this way."

"Sure. Thank you, nevertheless."

As they walked back to the elevator, Stonewall said, "I have to hand it to you, Mendez. You sure know how to piss off people. Is that what they teach you in the Military?"

"No, I acquired that all by myself," Mendez said with a belligerent tone. "When you're in the Military as long as I've been, you learn how to protect yourself. With a weapon and with words. You can't afford to get too close to anyone. It only creates grief and heartache. Your best friend might be killed tomorrow. The best thing is to keep to yourself. So, don't criticize me, Stonewall. Just worry about your own skin."

"Wow, Mendez, that was a long speech. I believe I've just discovered a kink in your armor. You *do* care about people," Stonewall said. "We might even become friends some day."

"Go and fuck yourself, Stonewall," Mendez cursed.

It was Stonewall's turn to cluck. "Keep it up, my friend, keep it up."

They found the place easy enough. The secretary had been right...the food was good. Even though the proprietor argued the meals were on the house, Peters insisted on paying for all three of them.

"I'll pay you back some day," Stonewall said. "As soon as I get my first paycheck."

"Don't worry about it," Mendez growled. "The Military will take care of all our expenses."

They took the elevator back down underground and found accommodations in the hostel for travelers. The owner told them that they were in luck and could each have their own room, since most of them were empty. One of the buses had just left a couple of days before and he didn't expect another bus for at least a week.

Stonewall slept well for a change. He was tired but relieved that he had been ousted from his post as mayor and Chief of Security of Epsilon City. He'd rather spend the next few days traveling inside the cramped quarters of a tank than spending another day as a city administrator. He was not a bureaucrat or politician. His life was outdoors not indoors.

They left early the next day. Peters had the foresight to pack a lunch for all three of them, and even Mendez thanked him grudgingly when noon came and their bellies reminded them that they were empty.

"I'm surprised, Mendez," Peters said. "I thought they taught you survival. How can you forget about lunch?"

"I can go without food for days," Mendez growled. "But I do eat it when it's offered."

Suddenly the emotionless voice of the tank's computer interrupted their bantering. "I am intercepting a radio message."

"What?" Stonewall sat up straight. "A radio message? Out here?"

"Computer, play message," Mendez said.

The interior of the tank was suddenly filled with static clatter. Stonewall strained his ears to understand the words of the faint human-sounding voice. "Can you clean that up and amplify the voice?" he asked.

"Computer, eliminate static and amplify," Mendez ordered the Artificial Intelligence.

The voice sounded stronger without the static, but still hard to understand.

"...listening, please help us. We are stranded on Epsilon in the jungle. Few survivors. Food is running low. We are surrounded by giant lizards. If anyone is listening, please help us. We are stranded on Epsilon in the jungle. Few survivors. Food is running low. We are surrounded by..."

"Sounds like a recording. Could be old," Stonewall mused.

"The signal is weak. That can mean distance, but it can also mean that the transmitter is running out of power. I doubt the latter. We'll have to investigate." Peters looked at Mendez. "Can you determine where it originates?"

"I could send out a *Seeker*," Mendez suggested. "It'll follow the signal."

"Do it," Stonewall said.

"Computer, launch a *Seeker* and find location of radio signal."

"Seeker launched," the voice reported a moment later.

"One thing I'm quite certain of...whoever sent or is sending that signal is not a local," Peters mused.

"What makes you assume that?"

"Nobody here would say *giant lizards*. We call those beasts by their names...like Rex or Raps. They also said that they are stranded on Epsilon. That means a ship from the outside. And the thing about food running low...there is plenty of food growing everywhere. Anyone familiar with the jungle knows where to find it."

"Maybe the survivors are injured," Stonewall suggested.

"Maybe, but I still say they are not from here."

"It doesn't really matter, does it? We still have to try to find and rescue them."

The voice of the computer broke into their conversation again. "Origin of message located twelve point three miles north-north-east."

"Computer, display on screen." Mendez spoke crisp and precise.

The computer screen sprang to life and the three men looked at the displayed image.

"I was right," Peters said. "That's a space shuttle."

"Not a shuttle but a small ship," Mendez said.

"All right, a small ship. What I mean it is not one of ours."

"Could be a smuggler," Stonewall suggested. "One thing is obvious...it was designed and built by Humans."

"Smugglers, then," Peters agreed. "A legitimate visitor would not land in the jungle."

Stonewall studied the downed vessel. It reminded him of the first time he came to Epsilon when he and Peters searched for a crashed spaceship. That one had been manned by aliens.

Fifteen years ago.

Who would have known then he'd fall in love with a Tangari girl.

Sheera. I really loved you.

He banned his thoughts before they became too painful. "It doesn't look damaged," he said. "Can you zoom in on it?"

"No. The *Seeker* is not that sophisticated."

"I don't see any of those *giant lizards*," Peters said, chuckling a little.

"Dinosaurs are curious by nature. Their absence means that the novelty has worn off. This ship's been here for a while." Stonewall studied the image, noticing the vegetation growing close to the ship.

"We'll still need to investigate. There could be survivors."

"Computer, show exact location in reference to base," Mendez said.

The display changed. It showed a map with the location of the tank and the crash site as red circles.

"We'll stay on the road until we get to this position." Mendez put his finger on the screen. "Then we'll turn east. This way we won't have to travel for nearly twelve miles through thick jungle. I estimate the ship is only about three miles away from the road at that point."

"Sounds reasonable," Peters said.

"Computer, follow the road to the indicated position then use shortest route through the jungle to get to location beta. Engage automatic pilot." Mendez craned his neck to look into the sky. "I wish we'd have a flier instead of crawling in this tank on the ground. I'm getting sick of seeing nothing but mushroom umbrellas above me."

"I thought you soldiers can adapt to any situation," Stonewall said, not hiding his sarcasm.

"It is not a question of adapting. I'm comfortable in any situation and environment. The question is *do I want to adapt*. I prefer to fight a war where I know my enemy and my surroundings. I'm more comfortable manning a flash-cannon than operating a tank. I'm itching for action."

"Who knows, you might get your wish sooner than expected, Mendez. Those reports about something happening in the northern communities probably have some merit. Unless your commodore finds perverse pleasure in sending us on some hair-brained mission."

"Commodore Chelzic does nothing without a valid reason," Mendez said, annoyance creeping into his voice. "He would never waste valuable manpower on a useless undertaking."

"I don't want to say *I hope so*. I'd rather get there and find we've been sent there for nothing instead of stumbling into an act of aggression that could throw us into a conflict we don't want or need," Stonewall said. "For one thing, I don't believe that the Anorians are behind whatever is happening in Raptor's Tooth. The Anorians are not a warlike race."

"As far as we've been made to believe," Mendez agreed. "I share your opinion, but I've been wrong before." He grinned and touched his sidearm. "I'm ready for anything."

Stonewall stared out of the window and at the mushroom-covered ground ahead of them. He could see the wide tracks of some large vehicle that had come this way before them, even though a new crop of mushrooms and mosses was already beginning to cover up the evidence.

"How often do the buses travel this route?" he asked.

Peters shrugged. "Sometimes once a week, but it depends on the demand. It happens that you might have a second bus go up north during one week."

"I wonder why none of them ever picked up that distress call?"

"I can answer that," Mendez volunteered. "That transmitter uses a frequency that is not common. Perhaps they don't want just anyone responding to their call for help."

"What do you mean?"

"That frequency is used mainly by Pirates. Maybe they were hoping that one of their friends picks up the call and comes to the rescue."

"It confirms my suspicion about smugglers," Peters said.

"I suggest we use extreme caution approaching them," Mendez advised.

Stonewall pulled his brows together in a frown. "Let's not get paranoid now. I don't want a repeat of what happened with that research facility Commodore Chelzic decided to destroy."

"I am suggesting no such thing," Mendez defended his remark. I'm only saying let's be careful. I'd rather destroy than be destroyed."

"Typical soldier mentality." Peters snorted. "Shoot first, ask questions later."

"It's kept me alive this far," Mendez grunted.

The tank rolled across the uneven ground, crushing the newly grown vegetation underneath its wide tracks. A herd of small, scaly lizards busily ripping pieces of meat out of the carcass of a larger reptilian creature near the road, hissed at the tank with open jaws as it rumbled by, but they didn't give up their spot.

We don't belong here, Stonewall thought. We are the invaders. This planet belongs to the reptilian races.

The tank slowed down and made a right turn, winding its way through tall shrubs and massive trunks of mushroom trees. The ground was rougher and overgrown with smaller mushrooms and thick bushes. Mendez disengaged the automatic pilot and took over the controls.

Stonewall recognized a cluster of red-glowing thorny shrubs and was quite happy to be inside the protection of the tank. The shrubs were preferred hiding places of *Fire-spitters*, and he had no desire to walk around outside and become their target for a wad of acid-spit in the face.

The computer screen displayed the progress of the tank and he noticed that they were getting close to their goal.

"We're almost there," Mendez broke into the silence.

The scene on the screen changed, displaying the bird's eye view of the *Seeker*. "Everything still looks the same," Mendez observed.

"That is a good sign...I hope," Peters said.

[8]

THEY COULD SEE THE SMALL CLEARING AHEAD AND PART OF THE alien ship behind a massive mushroom trunk. The clearing was empty of wildlife, confirming the transmission of the spy-eye. Shrubs and newly grown mushrooms as tall as a man surrounded the ship, more evidence that the ship had been there for some time.

At the edge of the clearing lay a pile of bleached bones. Stonewall discovered a few more strewn around the area. He looked at the ship and caught slight movement on the dull surface near the front.

"Stop!" he called out sharply.

Mendez, used to following orders without questioning them first, brought the tank to an abrupt halt. "What's the problem?" he asked quietly, his eyes searching the clearing.

"I believe I figured out why there are so many bones lying around," Stonewall said. "Look at the top of the hull."

"Looks like a small laser cannon."

"Precisely. It's tracking us."

"Not a friendly way to greet potential rescuers," Peters said.

"Is there any way to contact the people inside the ship without us getting out of the tank?"

"Maybe they'll contact us first," Mendez said. "Computer, play message."

"...stranded on Epsilon in the jungle. Few survivors. Food is running low. We are surrounded by giant lizards. If anyone is listening, please help us. We are stranded on Epsilon in the jungle. Few survivors. Food is running low. We are..."

"The same message. I don't think they are aware of us."

"Then why are they tracking us with their laser?" Stonewall stared at the shiny oval object protruding from the hull of the ship. The flat multifaceted eye in its front seemed to watch them like a guard dog, daring them to make their first move.

"I'd like to make an educated guess," Mendez said. "The laser is in automatic sentry mode. It will shoot at anything that comes too close."

"Great!" Peters threw up his hands. "How are we going to get near the ship?"

"We'll have to disable the canon," Mendez said matter-of-factly.

"That might be construed as a hostile gesture by the people inside." Stonewall peered at the ship, almost expecting someone to appear in the visible exit door.

"It is either that or leave without saying *hello*. Or we could let them incinerate us."

"Not much choice is there?" Stonewall mused. He made a decision. "Take out the laser."

Mendez climbed into the backseat and activated the onboard canon. A few moments later a bright light flashed toward the ship. A melted lump of metal was all that was left of what had once been part of a weapon of destruction, useless now.

"I would still suggest a cautious approach," Mendez recommended. "Especially after we committed an aggressive act."

"Can't argue with that," Stonewall said grimly. "There might be other dangers lurking nearby. Let's not forget that."

Mendez chuckled. "I believe there is hope that some day you might even be good soldier material."

Stonewall's smile was tight. "Not a chance. Now, let's go."

The door of the tank opened, and they climbed out into the hot, humid environment. Stonewall gripped his flash rifle tightly, scanning the surrounding mushroom trees and shrubs. He was not too concerned about a hostile welcoming committee from the ship, rather he feared the more ferocious denizens of the jungle who might be lying in wait among the tall ferns, or shrubs, eager to bound on the three intruders into their world.

He almost stumbled over a pile of bones. When he looked down, he saw the bleached broken pieces of what once had been the jawbone of a large dinosaur, probably the jawbone of a Rex, judging by its shape and the few leftover teeth. Tiny teeth marks covered the bones. It wouldn't take long until there would be nothing left of the once giant owner of the powerful jaw. The jungle had a way of taking care of that. Even the largest carnosaur was not immune from being devoured by creatures much smaller, but no less ferocious.

The steps leading up to the door were down, but the door into the ship was closed. When they tried the handle, it wouldn't budge.

"Locked," Mendez said laconically.

Peters banged on the door. They waited for a response, but nothing happened.

"I don't think anyone is home," Peters said.

"It doesn't appear like anyone's been using this door and these steps for a while. The vegetation is undisturbed," Stonewall said, after looking around.

"We can't leave without investigating the inside of the ship." Peters banged on the door again.

"There is only one way in," Mendez leveled his flash rifle at the door and made a few adjustments to the control on the side of its butt. "Of course, after this the ship won't be space worthy until the door is fixed."

Stonewall nodded. "Go ahead. I don't believe this ship will be going anywhere for a while."

A blinding pencil-thin bolt of pure energy bit into the metal of the door. Mendez cut a circle around the handle, causing it to fall out. Then he cut a slot toward the frame of the door, until the bolt was visible. "We'll have to wait until the metal cools," he said.

While they waited, they listened for movement from inside the ship, but everything stayed silent. Stonewall's gaze fell onto an object near the bottom of the steps. It looked like a round ball. When he studied it closer, he could see that it was the remnant of a skull.

A human skull. Somebody had died here.

Mendez put his hand into the opening and pulled. The door began to move outward. He pulled it open completely. The three men entered the ship. To Stonewall's relief the door from the airlock into the interior of the ship stood open.

"What a stench!" Peters exclaimed and pulled his air filter mask over his mouth.

Stonewall had to agree after getting a whiff of the air. It smelled stale with the strong odor of reptile and other unpleasant sources. He and Mendes followed Peters' example. It was dark inside the ship. They turned on their headlamps to light up the corridor. Proceeding carefully, they walked into one of the front cabins. It was furnished with a couple of couches and a few chairs. A large screen in one wall told Stonewall that this room had been used by the crew and passengers for relaxation.

"Let's check out the ship's controls," Mendez suggested.

They walked to the front of the ship onto the bridge. It was empty. Mendez looked over the controls. "Nothing seems to be out of place, although somebody did some damage to these controls. Power is on standby. The ship must have powered down for some reason. That's why there are no lights anywhere. The life-support is still working but only partially."

"Don't touch anything until we know more," Stonewall warned.

"Okay. We'll check out the rest of the ship."

They left the bridge and proceeded to walk down the corridor on the main floor. All of the doors leading into the cabins stood open. They didn't find anyone in any of the cabins.

"I wouldn't mind having a look at the storage area," Stonewall said. He headed for the stairs leading into the bowels of the ship.

"What the Hell!" Peters exclaimed when they came to the first storage room.

Stonewall peered into it and cursed loudly.

The room was filled with blue-shimmering oval objects.

"What are those?" Mendez asked.

"It seems our friends were collecting dinosaur eggs."

"Why?"

Peters gave a barking laugh. "Probably to introduce dinosaurs onto other planets. This is a serious situation we've stumbled upon. These are the eggs of a species of Deinonychos, rather nasty critters.

You don't want to have these hatching and growing up on any planet."

The next room held more of the same, or nearly the same. The eggs were of about the same size, only brownish in color, with large black spots.

Some of the eggs in the other rooms had been slashed open and the insides spilled onto the polished floor. Peters closed the doors quickly to keep the stench inside.

A scraping sound made Stonewall freeze and reach for his flash rifles.

Peters made a motion with his hand, pointing to one of the storage rooms. Stonewall nodded and walked on cautiously, his weapon held in front of him.

Mendez was the first one to spot the creature that charged out of the room, hissing angrily. He fired his flash rifle once and, cursing, swung it around to fire it a second time. Stonewall and Peters discharged their weapons almost simultaneously, killing two more of the dark shapes.

It was suddenly silent in the corridor. Bright spots of light still flashed in front of Stonewall's eyes. He tried to focus them on the four carcasses on the floor. Recognizing them, he cursed loudly.

"Raptors," Peters said. "They must have hatched only recently."

"Lucky for us. Had they been larger we would not have stood a chance. Not here in the confinements of the ship's corridor." Stonewall shuddered, his eyes and ears open, his finger on the firing stud of his rifle. He could feel his heart pounding against his chest and his breath coming fast.

"Stay back. There might be more inside." Mendes pointed his rifle at the open door. Cautiously, he walked forward. Peeking inside the room, he lifted his hand. "Clear. Nothing but empty egg casings and a few small bones. They must have started eating each other."

Stonewall turned his head and listened when he heard noise coming from a room further down the corridor. He almost fired his weapon when a shape appeared in the darkness ahead of them, but for some reason he controlled the urge.

"Oh, my god," a voice cried out. Then the figure disappeared.

"Sounded like a woman," Peters said.

"Be careful," Stonewall warned. "She might come back with a weapon."

They waited, but she didn't come back.

"I guess we'll go and investigate," Mendez said, walking forward.

When they reached the open door to the cabin the woman disappeared into, they stopped without getting too close.

"We picked up your distress call," Stonewall said loudly. "Whoever you are, you have nothing to fear. We came to rescue you. If you have any weapons, put them down."

"I don't have a weapon," the voice answered.

"How many of you are left on the ship?" Stonewall asked.

"There's three of us."

"All right. We're coming in." Stonewall was the first to enter the room. By the light of his headlamp, he saw a figure crouching in the corner. A woman, judging by the long hair and soft face.

"Don't be afraid," he said soothingly.

"Are you Humans?" she asked with a trembling voice.

"Yes. Are you?"

"Yes, I am." The figure rose and came forward. Stonewall saw that it was indeed a woman. She was naked.

"Where are the other two you mentioned?"

"Upstairs."

Stonewall held out a hand. "Let's go and find them."

The woman nodded. "Follow me."

They walked behind her to the end of the corridor, up a flight of stairs. Another set of stairs led to the upper deck. For some reason emergency lights on the walls were still working and made it possible to see. The woman led them to one of the rooms.

"I'm bringing company," she called into the room before she entered it.

As the woman had told them, there were two people in the room. They came out of the shadows and walked into the light that fell in through the open door. Both were also naked. One was a woman, older than the first one. The other one was a man. It was impossible to determine his age because of his unkempt wild beard and hair.

"How long have you been here?" Stonewall asked.

"I don't know. A long time," the man said. His voice sounded weak.

Stonewall studied the three people. They looked emaciated, like people who had been starving for weeks.

The man held his hand over his eyes to protect them from the light. "Do you mind shining that somewhere else," he said.

"I'm sorry," Stonewall said, switching off the light. "What happened to you?" he asked.

"Do you have anything to eat?" one of the women asked.

Stonewall shook his head. "Not here, but we can find something for you later. Where are the rest of the crew and passengers?"

"Dead. They're all dead."

"How?"

"We found dinosaur eggs in the storage rooms," Peters injected. "It is against the law to remove dinosaur eggs from Epsilon."

"We know."

"Then what is the purpose of collecting them?"

"Money," the man said.

"In other words you people are smugglers, criminals," Mendez said.

"Can we discuss that later," the older woman pleaded. "We need food and fresh water. We ran out of food weeks ago."

"What did you eat since then?" Stonewall asked.

"We ate from those eggs. We had no choice."

"Is that why you were on the lower deck? To get some of those eggs?" Stonewall looked at the younger woman.

She nodded. "Yes, but then I heard a noise and I hid inside the room where you found me."

"Count yourself lucky. If we hadn't come along when we did, you'd probably be dead by now. Ripped apart by the hatched Raptors we killed."

Her dark eyes were large, and she looked scared for a moment. "They weren't supposed to hatch. Not in the ship anyway. The rooms were designed to keep the temperature cool inside."

"Well, I guess something went wrong." Stonewall studied her thin body. "Why are you naked?"

"Our clothes became too filthy to wear, aside from the fact that it is too hot in here. We were more comfortable going naked." She threw a quick glance at the man. "There was nobody else around except for Xander, and he didn't mind."

"I bet he didn't. How did everyone else die?"

"Most of them were killed when they were attacked by a pack of lizards. And the others? Three committed suicide by eating poisonous mushrooms. One died when he was bitten by a poisonous snake. Another one fell into a flesh-eating plant. All of them suffered a horrible death. That's when we stopped going outside...the three of us. We're all that's left from fifteen."

"Couldn't you just leave? There is nothing wrong with the ship," Mendez said.

"Our pilot and our engineer were among the first ones to be killed. Nobody knew how to operate the ship."

"Didn't anybody know how to turn on the lights at least?"

"No, we didn't." The older woman shrugged. "I'm a nurse. Sariha is a biologist, and Xander..." she shrugged again. "He is...Xander, the guard. He's good with guns and a good storyteller. Anyway, one day the lights went out, the air began to turn stale, and the food processor stopped working. We didn't know how to turn them back on."

Stonewall found it difficult to believe anyone could be so ignorant. "You are lucky those eggs didn't hatch earlier, otherwise you wouldn't have survived even this long." His eyes lingered on the man.

Xander, the guard. He's good with guns and a good storyteller. In other words he has no special trade. Of course, smugglers don't need much of a trade. Anyone can do it. He probably did more than just telling stories with these two women. Can't really blame him. A man alone with two naked women. Nothing else to do...

He turned to Mendez. "Can you power-up the ship so they can get cleaned up, maybe take a shower? I'm sure we can find some clean clothes for them somewhere." He removed his air filter mask and nearly gagged. "Maybe we can freshen-up the air at the same time."

"I'll try," Mendez said. He walked away toward the front of the ship.

A few minutes later the lights lit up. Suddenly things didn't look so gloomy anymore. Stonewall looked at the two women. They were skinny, undernourished, but both had nice breasts, not large but firm and well-formed. He'd always preferred women with smaller breasts. They saw his eyes studying them and almost simultaneously their hands moved down to cover their genitals.

"We are naked in front of strangers," Demi, the older woman, said, her face flushed.

Stonewall smiled. "I've seen naked women before."

"We are also filthy," Sariha added to Demi's comment.

"Perhaps the showers are working now. Why don't you check them out?"

Both women left, leaving Stonewall and Peters with the bearded man. He looked even grubbier in the light.

Running his fingers through his beard, the man watched the women walking away. Sighing, he said, "I believe I need a shave badly. And perhaps a haircut. I hope they like me still without my beard. It makes me look more sophisticated, don't you think so?" He lifted his chin and turned to give them a view of his profile.

Even though the situation was grim, Stonewall almost burst out laughing. Peters snorted beside him and coughed. "A shave and a shower won't hurt you, Mr. Xander," Stonewall said, smiling.

"Oh, it's not *Mister* Xander. Xander is my given name. My last name is Safire."

"Well, all right Mr. Safire, go and join the ladies." Stonewall chuckled. "Not in the same shower though." He waved it off with one hand, still chuckling. "Do whatever you want, just go and get cleaned up."

Peters laughed. "I'm curious what Mr. Sophistication looks like underneath that beard."

"At least he's kept his sense of humor. That is a good sign. These people lived through a lot of trauma." He removed his air filter mask and sniffed. "The air is beginning to clear. At least we won't pass out from the stench. Let's go and see what Mendez is doing."

———

WHEN THEY WALKED ONTO THE BRIDGE, THEY FOUND MENDEZ standing in front of the giant screen that displayed the jungle outside.

"Holy crap!" Peters exclaimed. "I'm glad I'm safe inside this ship."

Stonewall had to agree as he looked into the open maw of the giant carnosaur towering above them on the screen. The three-dimensional picture created an almost instant feeling of dread, and he had to suppress the sudden urge to aim and discharge his flash rifle at the terrifying image, even though he knew the large reptile couldn't see them.

"It's a big boy," Mendez commented. "He walked out of the jungle a few minutes ago and it seems he is in no hurry to leave."

Stonewall looked at his watch. "Neither are we. It is too late to travel on. We'll never make it to Camp Diamond before dark. I suggest we stay the night and leave early tomorrow morning."

"I won't argue," Mendez said. "Not with that outside." He lifted his chin to indicate the huge lizard glaring at them from the screen.

Stonewall noticed that Mendez didn't wear his air filter mask anymore either. Taking a deep breath, he found the air smelling almost normal and the temperature seemed to be dropping also, making it quite comfortable. He seated himself in the pilot's chair. Watching the behemoth stomping around under the giant mushrooms, he almost wished they would blast off into space and leave the alien jungle with all its inhabitants behind.

He closed his eyes for a moment, his mind drifting back to his childhood, to his early dreams. Maybe he should have become a space pilot, traveling from one planetary system to another, never having to spend much time on a planet, never to worry about poisonous plants or animals, never to dodge giant lizards...

"Hey, Stonewall, are you sleeping?"

He opened his eyes and looked at Peters. "I wish I could," he said. "Sometimes I wish this were just a bad dream." He grinned when Peters rolled his eyes. "Looking at your ugly mug confirms that this *is* just a bad dream. Maybe I'll wake up soon and find myself in bed with Lucinda, my first great love."

"Didn't you tell me she was the reason you joined the Scouts and left Earth in the first place?"

"I did tell you that, didn't I? Maybe I'm also wishing she would have never cheated on me with her own cousin. That's when this whole nightmare began. I did love her, you know."

"You also loved that Tangari girl. What was her name?"

"Sheera." Stonewall stared at the viewing screen. "Yeah, I loved her too. She was quite beautiful."

"Was she part of your nightmare?"

Stonewall sighed. "If she was, I'm not sorry I met her. I was happy for a while."

Peters slapped him on the shoulder. "Snap out of it, my melancholic friend. I hear footsteps heading this way. Our new companions are probably looking for us. They should have made themselves presentable by now."

Stonewall could hear the sound of boots on the hard, metallic floor of the corridor.

At least they won't be naked...I hope.

When the women walked onto the bridge, Peters let out a little whistle, an action that brought a smile to their lips. They wore clothes that didn't quite fit. Sariha's, the younger of the two, seemed a bit too tight, which accentuated her breasts, making them appear larger than they actually were.

Even though he had seen her naked, Stonewall had to admit that the clothes and high boots made her look more attractive. *Funny, what clothes and a shower can do to a woman.*

Demi had put on clothes a trifle too large for her, but her combed hair and cleaned-up face made her no less appealing. In fact, Stonewall noted that she had the most delicate features.

"I've lost some weight," she said, chuckling. "I'm not complaining. I used to be a bit on the frumpy side."

Sariha seemed suddenly self-conscious when she saw the men staring at her. She looked down at her revealing garment. "Maybe I should have looked for some different clothes. These belonged to Mara. She was a little smaller than me." She let out a giggle. "Everywhere."

"These look fine to me," Peters said.

"I'm curious. Didn't you have any clothes of your own?" Stonewall asked. "Not that it matters to me."

"Sure, but they don't fit at all. I must have lost about forty pounds. I haven't been this thin for years. Not to mention the fact that they were soiled beyond cleaning."

"All right. As long as you're happy for the moment."

Demi stared at the giant carnosaur on the screen. The terror she felt inside was clearly displayed in her eyes. "Why hasn't the laser-cannon killed it?" she asked.

"Because we had to destroy the cannon so we could get close to the ship," Mendes explained.

"I'm not going out there with that...that thing loose," she said, a loud sob escaping her lips.

"You won't have to," Stonewall said soothingly. "Not today anyway. We won't be leaving until morning. Hopefully, by then it'll be gone."

"What if it isn't?"

"Then we'll take care of it. Don't worry. Have you by any chance checked out the Food Processor to see if it's working?"

"No, we haven't, but I'm sure Xander has."

As if on cue, he walked through the door. "I heard my name spoken," he said.

If Stonewall hadn't known the man to be Xander, he would not have recognized him. He had shaved off his beard except for the mustache, which was thick but trimmed. The uniform he wore hung a bit on his thin frame, but it made him look official and proper.

Grinning from ear to ear, he struck a pose. "Well, do I pass inspection?"

"With flying colors," Stonewall said. "I'm glad you found some clothes to wear."

"They're my own. I was employed as a guard on this ship." He patted the gun on his hip. "I hope you don't mind that I armed myself. If we have to go out there..." he indicated the screen, "...then I want to be prepared."

"I'm afraid a handgun won't be adequate," Mendez remarked. "You'll need something more powerful than that against our nosy visitor." His thumb pointed at the image on the screen.

"I know but not all lizards are that huge. Also, it lends me confidence knowing that I am not completely defenseless." He looked at Stonewall. "If you want to go outside and put that monster down, I'd like to come with you. There are flash rifles in the armory and I am quite good with weapons."

"You might get a chance to show off your skills tomorrow, Mr.

Safire. We won't be leaving today. It is getting too late for that. Speaking of late, my stomach is reminding me that I haven't had anything to eat for a while. Is the Food Processor operational?"

"It is. I already ate a small sandwich." He shrugged in an apologetic gesture. "I was hungry, sorry."

"Well, we'll forgive you. As long as you left a few sandwiches for us."

"I believe we can offer you more than sandwiches. We have quite a sophisticated Food Processor. It produces pretty much anything you desire. Let's go into the dining room."

Safire was right about the menu. On a whim, Stonewall ordered duck and rice, with steamed asparagus. The meat even tasted like duck. They found cases with bottled wine and life was suddenly good again.

"Whoever outfitted this ship didn't skimp on luxuries," he commented as he sipped from the wine. "Who actually owns this ship?"

"It belongs to the *Starburst Cartel*," Safire explained. "The company who hired us."

"I've heard of the *Starburst Cartel*," Peters said. "When we searched for the raiders who murdered my family we ran into one of their ships. The Cartel seems legit at first, but it is owned by War Lords who are into all kinds of shady businesses. It seems collecting dinosaur eggs is one of them."

Safire shrugged. "I didn't ask about their ethics. They offered me a job and I took it. What is so bad about collecting dinosaur eggs anyway? There are plenty of those critters on this planet. Who will miss a few eggs?"

"Nobody will miss them. The problem is much deeper than just a few missing eggs. If those eggs are introduced on a planet where the hatched dinosaurs can thrive, they will dominate the local fauna of that planet in time, since they won't have any natural enemies. Anyone living there might as well kiss their home good-bye and move somewhere else, unless they want to change their whole way of living. It won't be long until their world is as hostile as Epsilon."

"I never thought of that," Safire mused.

"But *you* should have," Peters said, addressing Sariha. "You said you're a biologist. You should know about the consequences when you introduce animals or plants into an ecosystem that is not their own."

"You are right, I should know." Sariha's dark eyes challenged Peters. "When you come from a world where there is nothing but famine and misery, you don't care what kind of job you do, as long as you have enough to eat and a comfortable place to stay. You don't ask too many questions when someone offers you just that."

"Sariha has a point," Stonewall said. "Sometimes we have to do things we don't approve of, but we still do them. The eggs on this ship won't leave Epsilon, but I'd suggest we carry them out of the ship. Most of them are probably spoiled anyway. We'll do that later, for now let's enjoy the food and wine. We may not have a chance to dine like this again for a long time."

"I'll drink to that," Safire said, lifting his glass. He seemed happy and full of energy. Stonewall suspected he was running on pure adrenalin, and he couldn't blame the man. Watching his colleagues die violently, stranded on an alien planet populated with ferocious beasts, living in fear and the almost certain knowledge that he probably would not survive much longer he had a right to be euphoric.

Stonewall couldn't make up his mind about the man. He acted jovial, making jokes and telling stories about his adventures, but deep down he seemed sad about something. Stonewall estimated his age to be around thirty-eight. Old enough to have experienced the things he talked about, but still young enough to look forward to a happier life than the one he seemed to have lived. If the stories he told were true.

Stonewall had the impression that Sariha was fond of Safire, but that could change once the three were back among other people. Tragedy and shared dangers usually bound people together in ways that would never happen under different circumstances.

After dinner they sat in the lounge and talked. Stonewall couldn't help but notice Demi throwing glances at him. When it was time to go to sleep, she offered to show him the cabin that had been used by the pilot of the ship.

"Perhaps you can show me the shower stalls first," he said. "I'd like to take a shower."

"Of course, just follow me." She giggled and hooked her arm into his. "Maybe just walk with me. I have a little trouble keeping my balance. Too much wine."

He chuckled. "I think we both had too much wine."

He was surprised by the luxurious cubicles. They were larger than the ones he was used to on the Scout ships.

When Demi didn't make any moves to leave, he began to undress. She watched him with a little smile on her face. "Do you want me to scrub your back?" she asked.

He shrugged. "Sure, why not?"

He undressed fully and, naked, he stepped into the cubicle. It didn't come as a great surprise, when Demi joined him a few moments later, stark naked. She held a bar of soap in her hand and began to apply foam to his back.

Closing his eyes, he enjoyed the warm water and her soft hands on his skin. Her hand moved across his back, down to his buttocks and his thighs. Then she moved in front of him and rubbed his chest with slow movements.

"You have a deep chest and hard muscles," she whispered. Her hand moved in circles on his belly and slowly crept down to his genitals. He felt his body reacting to her nearness and when her fingers curled around his stiff penis, he groaned and opened his eyes.

"Don't start something you are not prepared to finish," he said, his voice coming out in a hoarse whisper.

She laughed softly and put her other hand behind his neck to pull him down. Her lips closed over his and she kissed him with unexpected hunger. He tasted the alcohol when she opened her mouth to let in his tongue. Letting go of his penis, she wrapped her arms around his neck and pressed her body against his, trapping his hard shaft between her thighs. He took her buttocks into his hands and pulled her up. She opened her thighs, and, with a loud sigh, she sheathed her moist and warm pussy over his straining member.

Pressing her against the plastic wall of the shower stall, he fucked her with vigorous strokes. She cried out sharply when she experienced her first orgasm, but he never stopped moving.

He didn't climax. Somehow, he knew that this was not the end of it. She needed a man to comfort her for the night and he needed her to remind him that there was more to living than just adventure and saving people's lives.

"Spend the night with me," he said when she sagged against him.

She nodded and said, "I was hoping you'd ask." She giggled. "You never came."

"I wanted to save it for later," he grinned.

They dried their wet bodies in silence under the hot air stream and didn't even bother to get dressed. There was nobody in the corridor when they walked to the sleeping quarters of the pilot.

The bed was made. Stonewall smiled. People used to discipline, and order never leave their beds unmade, no matter where they are.

Demi pulled away the covers and slipped underneath. She smiled up at Stonewall. "Are you ready to play some more?" she asked.

He joined her and took her into his arms, kissing her gently. He didn't want this to be just a quick encounter where two lonely people fuck each other until they drop from exhaustion. Stroking her thin body and squeezing her breasts, he let his fingers travel down to her puffy vulva and put his finger between her slippery labia. She squirmed and caught her breath when he touched her clitoris.

"Don't let me wait," she breathed. "Put your big boy deep into me. I'm still slippery from the shower and more than ready."

He chuckled softly and slipped between her opening thighs. She gave a cry of satisfaction when he entered her and began to move underneath him.

They didn't stop for a long time and when his time finally came, he suppressed his joyful shouts of contentment. Afterwards they lay in each other's arms, enjoying this moment of happiness, oblivious of what waited for them outside the safety and security of the ship.

When he awoke, he looked at his watch, and in the dim glow of the nightlight he saw that it was a few minutes before six a.m. Almost time to get up. He turned on the light and found that Demi was still asleep. Her face looked serene, like someone who has finally found peace after enduring much hardship and danger. He studied the delicate features of her thin face, the curve of her lips, the classic lines of her nose, and realized how beautiful she actually was. Even without makeup.

She stirred and moved. Her eyelids fluttered open and she looked at him with a slightly bewildered expression. Then she smiled. "Am I awake or am I still dreaming?"

"You're awake."

"How can I be? I dreamed you and I made love? Did that really happen?"

"It happened."

"It must have, because you are still here and you say I'm not dreaming." She put her hand on her forehead. "I think I drank too much last night and I'm still tired. You wore me out. Is it time to get up?"

"We still have a few minutes." He laughed and put a kiss on the tip of her nose.

"Enough time to make love again?" Her arms reached for him.

He shook his head. "As much as I would like to, I'm afraid we don't have that much time."

She pulled her lips into a pout. "Too bad. You made me very happy last night. I wish we could make all this go away and spend the rest of our days making love. Forever."

"It's a wonderful thought, but reality is right outside this room." He pulled away the covers to expose her nude body. He grinned hugely, staring at her with a leering expression. "Perhaps this was a mistake. You *do* look tempting."

She put her hands over her breasts, chuckling softly. "No free show, unless you mean business. Besides, it is chilly in this room. Either cover me up with the blanket or your body, but don't let me lie here freezing."

He bent over her, pulled away her hands and planted a kiss on one of her nipples. "Come on and get dressed. We have to move on. We've already wasted a whole day rescuing you." He swung his feet off the bed, sat at the edge, looking down at her.

She pinched his naked buttock and sat up. Then she snuggled up to him and leaned against his back. "Thank you for last night. It was wonderful and made me forget everything." She kissed his neck.

"I also had a great time," he said with a gentle voice. "It is good to enjoy the comfort and love of another person once in a while, especially in a world as this one." He rose and dressed. Then he waited for her until she was dressed.

"I'll go and wash up," she said.

"I'll come with you." He held the door open for her.

As they walked down the corridor, she said, "It is best the others don't know about us, if that is okay with you."

"If you so wish," he said, not caring either way. "Are you worried Xander might take offense?"

"Xander means nothing to me. Whatever happened between us is a thing of the past. We were three people in distress, sharing a common bond when we thought we may not survive our ordeal. That has all changed now." She squeezed his hand. "Even what happened last night was not a major event. Don't get me wrong. I will always cherish our lovemaking, but I don't want you to read too much into it. You understand, don't you?"

"Fully." He let out a silent breath of relief. She put it into better words than he could have. When he held her in his arms at the peak of his passion, he loved her unconditionally for the pleasure she gave him, but they were still strangers to each other. He didn't love her, neither did she love him. And that was as it should be. There was no room in his life right now for a woman. He wondered if there ever would be.

"It was the wine and the loneliness," she said.

"I understand." He squeezed her hand in return, dropping it when he heard voices in the bathroom. When they entered it, they saw Peters and Sariha standing by the counter. Sariha was just splashing water into her face from one of the three small sinks.

"Good morning." Glancing at Demi for a quick moment, Peters gave Stonewall a little smile. "Had a good sleep."

"The best in a long time," Demi answered instead of Stonewall.

"Well, that's good, because you'll need your strength when we leave here. I've been thinking about how we can explain your presence on Epsilon. If you go to Epsilon City you may be arrested for illegal entry."

Demi shrugged. "I won't go to Epsilon City."

"Where will you go?"

"I don't know. It never came up. We were too busy worrying about surviving." She looked at Stonewall. "What do you suggest we do?"

"There are not many choices. Peters is right, you are here illegally.

Even though there is no real local government on Epsilon, there are laws. People visiting here need some kind of a visa. Since there is only one spaceport for regular ships, which is located in Epsilon City, visitors have to report to immigration there. The only way to disappear is to go to the frontier towns."

"Then that's where I'll go."

"It won't be a picnic," Stonewall warned. "Nothing but hardship, perhaps even death, awaits you."

"Hardship? Death?" She laughed. "*Hardship* is my middle name. *Death* is my destination."

"What's this talk about death?" Sariha said. "I still have a lot of living to do and I'm not afraid of facing a little hardship. I'll try one of the frontier towns."

"Well then you're in luck. That's exactly where we're heading." Peters drew a little water from the tap and let it form a small pool in the sink. He pointed at it. "This cupful of water probably means little to you, but out there it is a different story. Not knowing if it is safe to drink or if it will turn your intestines into a factory of deathly bacteria that will eat you up from the inside could mean the difference between living another day or dying a horrible death. The delicious looking fruit growing in abundance on a shrub might contain a poison so potent it will kill you instantly the moment you bite into it. Those are only a couple of dangers that you will encounter. I don't have to mention the lizards and other nasty life forms."

"You can't scare me with your horror stories," Demi said. "I'm thirty-six years old. I've seen and done enough to know life is not a walk on the clouds. At least it has never been for me. I'm ready to challenge this planet."

"So am I," Sariha echoed Demi's words.

[9]

STONEWALL THREW ONE LAST LOOK AT THE STRANDED SHIP. THEY had closed the airlock to keep out unwanted intruders. There wasn't much they could do about the hole in the outer door. Mendez had powered down the ship and killed the transmitter that broadcast the distress signal. There was no point luring others who might pick up the signal to check it out. The three survivors were safe inside the tank on their way to one of the northern communities, unless they changed their mind. In that case they would have to find transportation to Epsilon City where they would probably be arrested by Immigration for landing illegally on a restricted planet.

Either way, it didn't really matter to Stonewall. There were other things on his mind than the welfare of three people he didn't really know. He corrected his thoughts. Two people he didn't really know. He did get to know Demi, the older of the two women, quite intimately, but that encounter meant nothing to either of them; Demi had made that clear. Two lonely people had consoled each other for one night, satisfying the urges of their bodies while trying to fill a void in their hearts.

Stonewall sighed. He might have managed to satisfy his desire for sex for a while but the emptiness in his spirit was still there.

Once they were back on the main road, Mendez increased their speed and put the tank on autopilot.

"So...you're a Union Trooper," Sariha said to Mendez.

He threw her a condescending look. "Congratulations for figuring that one out so fast, Missy."

"My name is Sariha, Trooper. Don't call me Missy. I hate that. It sounds so impersonal. What can I call you?"

"You can call me Mendez," the Trooper growled. "If you have to."

"Mendez. Is that your first or last name?"

"*Mendez* is all you need to know."

"Hey, Mendez, you're not very friendly. Don't you like women?" She fluttered her eyelids.

"I like women just fine. But now, if you don't mind, I'd like you to shut up."

"Wow. That's telling me. Okay, I will shut up talking to you, but you can't stop me from talking to your friends," she said defiantly.

"They are not my friends."

"Thanks for letting us in on that secret," Peters said with a sarcastic voice. "Next time I won't pay for your meal."

"I told you the Military will reimburse you. Don't make such a big deal out of it."

"What's your problem, Mendez?" Stonewall asked, annoyed with the Trooper's behavior.

"I think he needs to get laid," Demi said from the backseat.

Sariha laughed. "Demi, what language! But you are probably right. Any man can be calmed down by a woman's pussy."

"Ladies, come on now," Peters said. "You are in the company of gentlemen. Let's keep it civil."

Sariha sat up straight. "You called me a lady. I like that. I don't remember ever being called a lady by any man before. From now on I will behave like a lady." She giggled. Then she suddenly broke into tears and put her face into her hands. "I'm scared. I don't know what is going to happen to me. I'm stranded on a hostile planet with no friends and no place to go."

"I'm your friend," Demi said.

"So am I." Safire put his arm around her shoulder. "We're all in the same boat and we will stick together. Somehow, we'll make it. We've survived so far. From now on it will be a picnic."

Mendez laughed sourly. "I don't want to burst your balloon, but nothing on this planet is ever going to be a picnic. Better steel yourself for an unpleasant journey."

"Hey, look, there is one of those bubbles," Demi said suddenly, pointing out of the window. "Is this how people live out here?"

"That is an outpost of the Scouts," Peters explained. He turned to Mendez. "We should stop and let them know about the spaceship."

"And perhaps we can unload our passengers here," Mendez said.

Demi looked at Stonewall. "Would this be a good place to stay?"

He shook his head. "This is only an outpost. There is nothing here."

Mendez took over the controls of the tank and changed direction, heading straight for the habitat. Everything seemed quiet and peaceful but Stonewall knew that was an illusion. Nothing was ever peaceful here, not the lake, and certainly not the jungle. Mendez had to maneuver the tank between wild-growing shrubs and mushrooms of all sizes to get close to the habitat. The habitat itself sat on top of a rocky hill. Nothing grew near the large bubble.

"It looks beautiful in a way. The tall mushroom trees and that lake make a perfect setting for a fairytale," Sariha said, dreamily. "When I was a child my mother used to tell me fairytales about tiny men and fantasy creatures living under mushrooms. There were handsome princes and beautiful girls in her stories. I can almost see a handsome prince riding out of that forest after having slain an evil dragon."

"The only thing you might see coming out of that forest will be the evil dragon in the form of a Rex or a bunch of Raptors ready to tear you apart," Mendez said.

"Oh, you! You have to spoil everything." Sariha looked at Stonewall. "How can you stand this miserable man?"

"Who says I can stand him?" Stonewall laughed, trying to defuse the tension inside the tank. Maybe a short stay in the habitat might do everyone some good.

A crackling in the tank's speakers announced they had been spotted by the people inside the habitat.

"Approaching vehicle, state your business."

Before Mendez could reply, Peters said, "This is Scout Peters. We are on our way to Raptor's Tooth. Permission to enter habitat."

"Scout Peters, permission granted. We will open the airlock for you. Beware when you leave your vehicle. We've had an incident here a few days ago. There may be Raptors around."

When they climbed out of the tank, Stonewall kept his eyes open for any danger signs. He saw a pack of small scavengers tearing at something on the ground not far away near the lake. Looking closer he noticed a pile of large bones.

A door opened in the skin of the bubble and they hurried through into the interior of the habitat. Demi was the first to enter and she exclaimed loudly, "This is like stepping into another world. They have a garden here. It almost looks like some place on Earth."

Stonewall had to agree. His first arrival on Epsilon had produced the same reaction in him. The illusion was spoiled though when one looked up into the alien sky and the giant mushrooms overshadowing the habitat.

A couple of men wearing the uniform of the Scouts came out of one of the two buildings. The buildings were nothing but rectangular cubes put together from readymade plasteel walls and roofs. Scouts didn't live in fancy homes. Not on frontier planets.

The first man nodded to Stonewall and Peters and put his open hand over his heart, acknowledging them as fellow Scouts. He threw a questioning glance at Trooper Mendez and frowned. "Welcome to Outpost Beta. I'm Supervisor Mofred Brandon. My partner here is Al Schriemer. Which one of you is Scout Peters?"

"I am." Peters pointed at Stonewall. "This is Master Scout Stonewall, and this is Trooper Mendez." Turning to the women, he smiled and said, "And these two lovely ladies are Demi and Sariha, and last but not least Mr. Xander Safire."

Brandon gave the others a little bow and looked at Stonewall. "Master Scout Stonewall, we are honored by your presence. What is your purpose of visiting our modest Outpost?"

"As Scout Peters already said we are on our way to Raptor's Tooth," Stonewall said. "We have discovered a stranded spaceship not far from here and we want to report its location. Perhaps you can relay a message to Outpost Epsilon and suggest they send a crew to salvage the ship. It is considered contraband."

Brandon lifted an eyebrow. "Contraband? Interesting." His gaze fell on Mendez. "I'm curious. Why are you in the company of a Union Trooper and why are you traveling in a military tank?"

Stonewall chuckled. "I guess you're out of the loop in your outpost here. Epsilon has been put under Marshall Law by the Military. We have a Spider battleship at our doorstep and might be at the brink of war with the Spiders."

"Marshall Law? What the hell! The Military can't just come in and take over. How are you even going to enforce Marshall Law on Epsilon? This is insane." Brandon glared at Mendez.

The Trooper glared back at him. "We are here because you Scouts are not capable of defending this planet. You are watchmen, not soldiers."

"We've done quite well so far, thank you," Al Schriemer cut in on the conversation. "Why would we start a war with the Spiders in the first place?"

"The Spiders are the aggressors...not us," Mendez growled.

"What is your purpose of going to Raptor's Tooth?" Brandon asked. "Are the Spiders there?"

"We don't know what is happening there. We've had disturbing reports and we're on our way to investigate them," Stonewall explained. He looked at the first building when he saw a woman in Scouts uniform stepping out and coming toward them.

"Hi," she said when she came closer. "Aren't you people coming in?"

"I was just about to ask them to join us," Brandon said. "By the way, this is Sue Yang. She's our nurse."

Sue smiled and nodded. "I'm not really a nurse, but I have some knowledge in basic medicines and treating injured people. You might call me a 'First-Aid-nurse'."

Safire cleared his throat behind Stonewall. He stepped forward and held out a hand. "I'm happy to make your acquaintance, Miss Yang. Xander Safire at your service, Ma'am. By the way, this young lady," he pointed at Demi, "She is a qualified nurse."

"That's wonderful," Sue said. "Perhaps you can have a look at our patient. We have a woman here who has been bitten by a Rooworm."

"I'm afraid I don't even know what a Rooworm is," Demi said.

"A nasty critter you don't ever want to meet," Sue explained.

"Unfortunately, the area around here has an abundance of them. One bite and it leaves you paralyzed...if you're lucky. I'd appreciate it if you would examine that woman. She should have come out of her coma by now."

"I can have a look but don't expect any miracles from me." Demi smiled apologetically.

"Fine, but first you must all come in and share a cup of tea with us." She laughed. "We don't get too many visitors these days."

They followed the two men and the woman into the building.

"It's not fancy in here," Sue said, "but it is our sanctuary from the violent world out there." She shrugged. "Let's put it this way...we are quite safe in this bubble we're living in but bored as hell. Any disruption in our routine is welcome." Her gaze flicked to Mendez. "Even if our visitors are Union soldiers."

"I'm overwhelmed to hear that," Mendez said, allowing his lips to curl into a small grin. "Usually Scouts don't exhibit much hospitality toward us."

"Well, rest assured, you are welcome here. Not all Scouts are hostiles, you know."

They walked into a room filled with screens and instruments. An older man sat in front of one of the screens, studying it. He lifted his hand in greeting when they walked in and turned his attention toward the visitors.

"That's Marvin Klonski," Sue said. "He is our biologist."

"What exactly are you doing on this outpost?" Stonewall asked.

"We observe and study," Klonski said.

"Study what?"

"The fauna and flora around us. If Humans want to survive on Epsilon, we must understand it. It is a fascinating and exciting place."

"A little too exciting for me," Safire said. "I'd rather be on some exotic planet with less dangerous animals running around trying to eat me."

"Then why did you come to Epsilon, Mr...?"

"Safire. Xander Safire." He chuckled. "I'm here for the same reason most people come here...to become rich."

"To become rich?" Klonski broke into loud laughter. "You've been suckered in, my friend. Nobody ever got rich on Epsilon except for the Trading Commission."

Safire grinned. "We tried to cut out the middleman, so to speak, but we failed because we didn't count on the local fauna and flora."

Klonski threw him a questioning look. "I don't quite follow you."

"This man is a smuggler," Mendez said. "Most of his smuggler-friends were killed off because they didn't understand this planet. We rescued him and these two women from certain death."

"Smugglers," Klonski said. "Where are you taking them?"

"If it were up to me, I'd leave them in the jungle, but my companions here think otherwise."

"We're taking them up north where they can join the rest of the fortune hunters," Peters said. "Maybe they'll get lucky."

"Shouldn't you take them to Star City?"

"Where they'll be arrested and thrown in prison," Stonewall said. "They've been through enough. We'll give them a break and a chance to redeem themselves." His chuckle was without malice when he added, "Who knows they might wish they had gone to Star City instead."

"If you're a nurse you could stay here," Sue said to Demi. "We sure could use someone with more medical knowledge than mine. Now, let's go into the lounge and have that cup of tea. You too, Marvin. Those computer screens will be here when you get back."

The lounge turned out to be more comfortable than Stonewall had expected. A large window in one wall allowed a spectacular view of the lake. A blond woman sat in front of the window, staring at the whitecaps on the water. She turned to look at the newcomers. Stonewall was surprised when he noted her age. She couldn't have been more than nineteen or twenty. She was not a Scout. He deducted it from the clothes she wore.

"That is Millie," Sue explained. "She's a guest here. The woman in a coma is her friend."

"Hello," Millie said with a shy smile. "Who are you people?"

"They're just passing through," Sue said. "Can you make tea for everybody, please?"

"Sure," Millie said eagerly and rose from her seat. She disappeared through a door.

"What a view!" Sariha walked to the window and stared outside. "How can you say it is boring here? I'd give a lot to stay here for a while."

"Really? What is it you do, young woman, except smuggling stuff?" Sue asked.

"I'm a biologist and I'm not really a smuggler. The people I work for hired me to do a job. It was better than starving," Sariha said defensively.

"You don't have to explain yourself," Sue said gently. "We all do what we must do to survive. God knows, I have."

Brandon sat down on one of the couches. "As supervisor of this post I give everyone the day off," he said jovially. "Since it's close to noon, perhaps we should do something more than just have tea. We have an excellent Food Processor and it can prepare wonderful foods." His laugh was cheerful. "The Food Processor alone makes up for all the other shit we have to endure. We also have fresh greens which we grow in the garden. How can you beat that?"

"I'll second that," Schriemer said. He sat down beside the other man.

Peters looked at Stonewall. "What do you think, Chief?"

"I'm not the Chief anymore," Stonewall said.

"Sorry, I got so used to calling you that. What do you say? I'm ready for a nice dinner."

Stonewall nodded his agreement. "I think we can spare the time." He didn't even bother discussing it with Mendez.

The Trooper growled something but didn't object.

When Millie came back with a tray full of empty cups and a large pot of tea, Sue said, "Be a good girl and get the Food Processor going. We'll have lunch after this. And prepare a large bowl of lettuce."

The young woman handed everyone a cup and filled it from the pot.

Stonewall smelled the dark liquid in the cup and found it pleasant. It was hot so he put the cup onto a small plastic table beside his chair.

"Don't you like it?" Sue, who obviously had been watching him, asked.

"I don't like to burn my lips," Stonewall said, laughing softly.

"It's not made by the Food Processor. We make it from leaves we collect from a vine that grows on the mushroom trees. You'll find it tastes a lot like peppermint."

"It does smell like peppermint," Stonewall said. "Listen, who exactly is this Millie, besides being the friend of the woman in a coma?" Stonewall asked. "Furthermore, who is the woman in a coma?"

"Her name is Alitia. She and Millie came with the bus a few days ago. We've had a bit of a mishap here. There was another woman with them. She was killed by a Rex. Outside our habitat. There was nothing anyone could do about it." Sue shrugged. "Another example of what can happen when people disregard the dangers that lurk everywhere on this planet." Her eyes rested on Sariha. "I have a feeling you have your own story to tell."

"I sure have," Sariha agreed.

"Epsilon is a hostile world." Stonewall got up and walked over to the large window. Looking at the lake, he watched the waves crashing against the rocks dotting the shore. A huge black hump rose partially above the water to sink back under the foaming surface. The lake was huge. The shore on the other side was hidden in thick fog.

His thoughts took him back to the Anorian ship hidden in a lake such as this one. Could it be that their ship was not the only one hiding on Epsilon? How many others were there?

Epsilon's environment is not friendly toward Humans and yet we insist on taming this planet. Why? There are other planets out there much more suited for settlement by Humans.

Of course, he knew the answer to his own question. One of the reasons for Humans being here was greed...greed for the treasures hiding under the soil and a need for the medicinal substances produced by the different species of fungus growing in abundance on the planet's surface. But mainly, Epsilon's strategic location in this part of the Galaxy was of utmost importance to the Humans. Or more precisely to Earth's military powers.

Earth could not allow an alien race to set up a military base on Epsilon. That was the main reason Humans were struggling to survive on a planet hostile to anything remotely human.

The Union was willing to risk a war with the Spiders and possibly others who challenged Earth's presence in this system. Men like Commodore Chelzic didn't care about human or material losses. They only cared about power and military might. As long as they could flex their military muscles and play with their destructive weapons, they would do anything regardless of the consequences. It was the history of the human race.

———

STONEWALL TURNED AWAY FROM THE WINDOW AND CASUALLY studied Demi. She was in deep conversation with Sue. Probably discussing some medical stuff. He remembered their lovemaking the night before, her passion and hunger, and he wondered how she would survive in the brutal environment of the frontier towns. Perhaps she'd make herself useful with her knowledge of medicine or perhaps she would find it easier to use her body to make her fortune. She either ended up marrying some prospector or get herself killed by a jealous one. She was still a beautiful woman, but her years were ticking.

His eyes wandered over to Sariha. Much younger than Demi and just as attractive; she would have no trouble finding someone who'd take care of her...for a while. According to her, she was a biologist. If she was adventurous enough, she'd join a group of prospectors in their search for gems and might even become successful in accumulating enough money to live out her life in comparative comfort. Unless one of the carnosaurs cut her life short, something that was a good possibility.

She noticed his eyes on her and got out of her chair to join him by the window. Giving him a friendly smile, she said, "I haven't really thanked you yet for rescuing us. Without you we would have died there."

"Probably," he agreed. "You were lucky we picked up your transmission."

"Yes, we were lucky. Doubly lucky that you didn't ignore it."

"I'm a Scout. My mission is to save people in distress, among other duties."

"Sure, that is your mission but what about that Trooper? He probably would have left us to rot. I don't like him."

"Trooper Mendez?" Stonewall chuckled. "He has his issues. He's a soldier. What do you expect? His mission is not to save lives but to fight his and your enemies. That's what he is good at. That's what he is trained for. So in a way he does save lives."

"I still don't like him." She pouted. "Even though he is handsome in his rough way." She giggled. "Maybe Demi is right. He needs to get laid." Her dark eyes searched his face. "How about you? Don't you have need for a woman?"

"Why do you ask?"

"You're a man. A Scout. Not married I assume. Men have needs just like women. I have needs."

"I'm thirty-eight years old and you are...I guess about twenty-two?"

"Twenty-four." She smiled coyly. "Old enough."

"Save yourself for a younger man."

She pouted again. "Xander is your age."

"Yeah, well, I'm not Xander. Besides, he was the only man around and you were vulnerable. Do you have feelings for him?"

She shook her head in negation. "None. Not anymore anyway. I was thinking...I'm not sure if I want to go to the frontier towns. This is a nice place, safe, and the people seem friendly. Do you think they would let me stay with them?"

"I don't know. Ask them and you'll find out."

At that moment Millie came out of the other room and announced, "If anyone is interested, the Food Processor is finished with the meals. I've ordered pasta and meatballs. I hope that is okay with everyone. Please, come into the kitchen and pick up your plates."

"We've been summoned. I guess we should go," Stonewall said.

They sat down at a table in the eating area beside the kitchen. It was a bit crowded, but they managed to fit around the table. Brandon and Schriemer went to get a couple of stools to sit on. The food was great, as Brandon had promised, and Stonewall, like everyone else, enjoyed the fresh salad.

"I have to admit," he said, spearing a meatball onto his fork, "this tastes excellent. What are you using as raw materials?"

"Mushrooms, tubers, vines, and tree bark. I believe it's the bark that gives it a bit more flavor," Schriemer said.

"How do you collect that stuff without being attacked by those beasts?" Demi asked. "I'd be afraid to go out there?"

"We have a remote controlled robot. It doesn't give out any smell that can be detected by the predators and is impervious to insect stings or anything else that might take an interest in it," Klonski explained. "I'm usually the one controlling it." He laughed. "It's my little pet."

As Stonewall looked around the kitchen, he saw something that piqued his interest in an alarming way. He got up from his chair and went over to the shelf on the wall and picked up one of the black, round objects resting on it. "Where did you find these?"

"Interesting, isn't it?" Brandon said. "We found them in the caves below us."

"Do you know what these are?" Stonewall asked.

Brandon shrugged. "We have no idea. It's not metal, but it isn't stone either. We tried to crack one open, unsuccessfully though. Even a laser doesn't scratch it. It seems there is some kind of energy barrier around it that prevents anything from actually touching the surface of the sphere."

"This is a Spider egg," Stonewall said, putting emphasis on *Spider*.

"Brandon gaped at him. "Are you sure? How do you know? No one's ever seen a Spider egg."

"I have. We have." Stonewall looked at Peters, who nodded.

"We've discovered a whole bunch of them under Epsilon City," Peters said. "In fact, some of them hatched."

"Hatched?" Brandon exclaimed, giving Stonewall a look that spelled *Impossible*.

"These eggs are in suspended animation. The Spiders have discovered a method to somehow bend the time-energy around them and keep them indefinitely frozen in time until someone *unfreezes* them. We don't know exactly how it works." He walked back to the table and rolled the black ball onto its surface.

Sue caught it and held it in her hand. "Amazing! We've always wondered why we felt a tiny tingling sensation when we touched these balls. That explains it." She stared at Stonewall. "How can you hatch them?"

"They can't be hatched without the machines that were designed by the ancient Spiders for that purpose. By the way, these eggs are probably thousands of years old."

"Thousands of years?" Sue asked, her expression one of disbelief.

"What are they doing on Epsilon?"

"We have no idea. I wouldn't mind having a look at the location where you found them."

"Sure. No problem. The entrance to the caves is right here in one of the storage rooms. We had this building put on top of it, so we could use the caves for additional storage. It is always cool down there."

Everyone seemed suddenly eager to finish the meal, even Trooper Mendez showed some interest. Once they were finished, nobody bothered to clean up the table. They all followed Brandon to the storage room where a flight of stairs led into a small room below the building. There was barely enough space in the room to hold them all. A closed door in one wall obviously led into the caves.

"This room is watertight. We had it built in case water seeped into the caves, but until now we've never had any problems with that," Brandon explained. He opened the door to reveal another flight of stairs, which took them deep underground into a large cave.

Stonewall became aware of a somewhat musty smell, but he was surprised not to find any mold or moisture on the walls or ceiling. "This is not a natural cave," he said, running his hand over the smooth surface of one of the walls. "Haven't you ever wondered why it is so dry down here?"

"Actually not," Schriemer admitted. "We were extremely happy to have found additional room to store some of the stuff we didn't want cluttering up the rooms upstairs. Now that you mention it, yes, the air is dry, and the temperature seems to stay the same at all times."

Stonewall walked over to one of the other walls and moved a couple of boxes out of the way. He put his hand on the wall's surface. After a few moments he nodded. "I was right. Unless I'm jittery at the moment and it's just my tingling nerves I'm feeling, there is something behind this wall."

Peters, who had followed him, touched the same wall and said, "I can feel the vibration. Just like in the grotto under Star City."

"So what are you saying?" Brandon asked.

"If my guess is right, there are machines behind this wall that are thousands of years old and they are still working," Stonewall said.

"There's much more than just machinery behind this wall." Peters banged his fist against the smooth material. "Things you might want to leave undisturbed."

"Where did you find those eggs?" Stonewall asked.

"Over there." Schriemer pointed. "In fact, I was the one who found them. There is a round hole in that wall. We covered it up with boxes, because it leads into a cave too small to be of any use. I found them inside that cave."

Stonewall went to check out the cave. Peters and Brandon helped him to move the boxes out of the way. The others in the party just stood by and watched.

"I feel creepy all over," Sariha whispered.

"Me too," another woman whispered back. "This is so exciting."

Stonewall stuck his head into the cave but couldn't see anything because of the darkness. "Anyone have a torch?" he asked.

Brandon pulled a small pencil-shaped object out of his pocket and handed it to Stonewall. "Here."

The little torch threw enough light to illuminate the interior of the tiny cave. Small rocks and pebbles littered the floor. When Stonewall shone the light into a corner, he noticed that the corner was not solid. A narrow crack ran from top to bottom. He climbed through the hole into the cave and knelt on the floor to check the bottom of the wall and discovered that the wall did not rest on the floor but seemed suspended about an eighth of an inch above it.

Shining his light along the wall, he almost missed the tiny crack in the center of the wall. Following a hunch, he pressed his hand against the wall and was not greatly surprised when it moved. Half the wall swiveled away from him to reveal a wide tunnel.

He heard someone curse softly behind him and turned to see Brandon sticking his head through the hole. "This must be one of the tunnels made by the primitive ants who built this mound thousands of years ago. I'm surprised you never investigated this cave," he said.

"We never had reason to do so." Brandon sounded almost apologetic.

"Now you may have a good reason." Stonewall shone the beam of the light into the tunnel, but it was swallowed up by darkness. "You'll need a more powerful torchlight," he said. "I wouldn't mind exploring this place but I'm afraid we have to move on. Orders, you know.

Perhaps on the way back we can stop by and help you check out this place. It may be wise to ask for assistance. You'll never know what you will find."

"I suggest you don't do any exploring until the Military comes here," Mendez said while he pushed Brandon aside to step through the opening. "I will have to report this to Commodore Chelzic. He will send Union Troopers to protect this habitat."

"You can't do this," Brandon protested. "This habitat is the property of the Scouts. The Military has no jurisdiction here."

"You are wrong. This location is now under military command."

"You don't have the power to do that." Brandon looked for help to Stonewall. "Does he?"

"I'm afraid he does," Stonewall said. "The whole planet has been put under Marshall Law. It is out of my control."

Brandon threw up his hands. "What insanity! The last thing we need here is a bunch of Union Troopers trampling on our garden, in this building, possibly tearing up everything to get into these caves. I might as well quit and hand everything over to this Trooper."

"It won't be that bad." Stonewall tried to soothe the man's negative mindset. "There are only two hundred Troopers on Epsilon. Commodore Chelzic will be able to spare only a few of his men to handle this matter. He might even decide not to send anyone. Look at is this way...it is for your own protection. We'll have to make certain that there is no danger to this place and you and eliminate any potential threat that might lie waiting beneath the surface. Please, don't blow this into a tragedy."

"I've been here now for nearly four years and never had any cause to worry about anything attacking us from underground. Why suddenly such urgency to worry about that?"

"We found something similar in the caves under Epsilon City. In fact, somebody managed to hatch a few of the Spider eggs. Now you understand the concern?"

"Those eggs have been there for thousands of years," Brandon said defiantly. "Why is this happening now?"

"We don't know. All we know for sure is that the Spiders are showing a sudden interest in Epsilon. That is the reason for the Military being here." Stonewall didn't know if he should divulge more information and decided it wouldn't do any harm. "The Dragons are also interested. Apparently, somebody found ruins from an ancient reptilian civilization."

"I've heard rumors about such ruins near Desert Hell and another site about three hundred miles east of Emerald Lake. I'm also aware of the so-called ruins of an ancient Spider race. A company that calls itself *Alpha-Epsilon Conglomerate* has set up a base on the other side of the planet where they dug up something. They are quite tightlipped about it. You know how these private giant companies operate. It is a wonder any information leaked out at all." Brandon smiled thinly. "I see you are surprised that I'm aware of this. We are not so isolated in our bubble that rumors don't reach us."

"Well, then you should not act so surprised to find out that the Spiders and Dragons are at our doorsteps and that the Union's armed forces have decided to take an interest in Epsilon also. We have to protect our real estate in this neck of the woods." Stonewall cringed inside saying those words. They did not reflect his opinions. *We should accept our losses, pull up stakes, and look for better properties. The Galaxy is a large playground.*

"I'm glad we all agree," Mendez said. "It is time for everyone now to go upstairs and lock up this place until the Military gets here."

"We can't just lock up," Brandon protested. "We are storing stuff down here which we have to have access to."

"Take whatever you need now. I'll give you one hour. After that this cave and everything in it is off-limits," Mendez said with an authoritative voice that left no room for arguments. He looked at Stonewall, "We'll leave in an hour. I want to get to Camp Diamond still today. We've wasted enough time."

Stonewall couldn't help but grin when he said, "How are you going to enforce your command about anyone not coming down here if you are not here?"

"Don't be so ignorant, Stonewall," Chelzic said, contempt in his voice. "I'll put a lock on the door. Any unauthorized personnel attempting to open it will only succeed in being blown into tiny atoms, along with this whole building. It would be a shame."

"I'm not surprised that you will go to such extremes, Mendez," Stonewall said. "As Scout Brandon already said, these eggs, if we find more of them, have been here for thousands of years. Unless somebody disturbs them they won't hatch by themselves. There is no more danger now than there was before we arrived here."

"It is only your opinion that those eggs won't hatch. What if the machines have been programmed to start hatching the eggs right now? Why have the Spiders sent a battle ship at this time? Why not last year or the year before?" Mendez stared at Stonewall with cold eyes. "You should leave battle strategies to the experts, *Master Scout* Stonewall. Stick to exploring the jungle and rescuing stranded colonists."

Stonewall glared back at the Trooper. "Keep that up and I'll shove those strategies down your throat. Maybe I'll let you find out what Scouts are capable of."

Mendez put a hand on his sidearm and took a step toward Stonewall. "Are you threatening a Union Trooper, Scout?" The scar on his left cheek throbbed visibly as his eyes bored into Stonewall's.

Stonewall didn't flinch and stood his ground. He was a couple of inches taller than Mendez and outweighed the Trooper by at least twenty pounds. He was confident in his own combat skills should it come to that. He noticed that the others were moving out of the way, but he also noticed Peters' hand hovering close to his gun. Even though he fumed inside, he kept his voice even when he spoke, "I am sick and tired of you Troopers putting down us Scouts and your superior attitude. We provide a service just like you. I'm not threatening you but I'm warning you to change your way of behaving toward me and Peters."

"Or else?"

"Don't try to find out, Trooper Mendez," Stonewall said coldly. He became aware of his hand resting on the butt of his gun.

Mendez kept on staring, the scar on his cheek ticking rapidly. Then he suddenly relaxed and grinned. "I have to admit, I didn't think you had it in you, Stonewall. You actually showed some backbone. I respect that. I know you don't like me very much, but I'm willing to call a truce between us. I'll be civil if you are. There is no need for us to quarrel." He held out his hand. "Agree?"

Stonewall hesitated, still too angry about this whole incident, but then he took the offered hand. "Agree. One condition though...no lock on the door."

"All right. As long as nobody tries to go exploring."

Stonewall looked at Brandon. "You heard the man. Are we in agreement?"

"I see no reason why we should start exploring after all this time. We have not much interest in old so-called Spider eggs."

"Good. Then let's go upstairs. Maybe we can all have a stiff drink and unwind for an hour or so." He could almost hear as the others let out their breaths.

"I'm ready for something stiff," Sariha said louder than she probably intended.

Demi and Millie giggled. Sue laughed. "Young women these days are so bold," she said. "I'll opt for the stiff drink. I think we must have something somewhere."

Klonski did manage to find a couple of bottles containing a stronger spirit than the wine the Food Processor produced. Sue and Demi left the group after half an hour to look in on the woman in a coma, who was in the second building.

Sariha sat down beside Stonewall and said, "I've made up my mind. I'm not coming with you. I want to stay here. I'm a biologist and they can use my help here."

"Have you talked to anyone about it?"

"Yes, Millie. In fact, she wants to come with you. She is bored here. So, in a way, it's an even trade."

"I have no problem with that. If they let you stay with them that is okay with me. It's your decision not mine. And if Millie wants to come with us she is welcome to do so. I hope she knows what she is doing." Stonewall looked over to Millie, who seemed to have been watching. As soon as he looked at her, she got up and came over.

"I assume Sariha told you about me?"

He hadn't really looked at her too closely before. Only now did he notice her bright blue eyes. "Are you sure you want to do this?" he asked. "Life in the frontier towns is hard."

"I know all about it, but I don't care. I have nothing else I can do. I want to do this. It's been my goal all along."

"Okay." He nodded. "Pack your bags. We'll be leaving within the hour."

[10]

THEY MADE IT TO CAMP DIAMOND BY NIGHTFALL. AFTER parking the tank in the parking lot inside the dome, they all went to find rooms in the hostel, which was located in the second dome. Millie looked wide-eyed at the park she saw in an adjacent habitat. "Those are real trees," she exclaimed. "Do you think we can walk around in that park later?"

"I'm not sure," Stonewall said. "It might be for residents only."

Even Demi was impressed by the little shops and stores. "I grew up on one of the frontier worlds. It was a rough world but not as wild as this one. It shows again how adaptable the human race is. Being in here one can forget that death waits everywhere outside. If this is one of the frontier towns, then life can't be that bad."

Peters grunted at her remark. "The frontier towns are nothing like this."

"Maybe I should stay here," Demi said.

"I don't think it's that simple," Stonewall said. "You'd need a place to stay. The homes in these habitats are designated for somebody already. Before you stay here, you'll probably have to register your name and your purpose for being here. I'm afraid that idea is not a good one. I can guarantee you that you'll be transported to Epsilon City."

"Too bad." She sighed. "I think I would like it here. How about you, Millie?"

"I'm going all the way to the end of the road," Millie said. "I'm running away from civilization."

"And you, Xander?"

Xander looked past the buildings at the outside world visible through the transparent walls. "It does look daunting. The desire to stay here in this safe haven is great, but as Scout Stonewall says, we won't be allowed to stay. I'll take my chances and move on."

They checked into the hostel. The men had to sleep in one common room, but the women were lucky to get a separate room. After supper, Demi and Millie decided to go and check out the park. It might be their last chance to experience a civilized place where it was safe to walk around without fear of being attacked by some hungry lizard.

Stonewall and Peters stayed in the hostel's lounge and relaxed, while Mendez went to search out the only bar to have a drink. Xander spent his time walking through the habitat to enjoy one more evening in civilization by himself.

Peters stared into his glass. "I wish the women would have chosen to go to Epsilon City. This whole business makes me feel uneasy, especially with what might be happening in the northern communities."

"What do you think is happening?"

"I'm afraid to make a guess. We have a Spider ship waiting at the edge of our system. Waiting for what? It seems so coincidental that it should be here during the time we discover ancient Spider eggs ready to be hatched. We have Anorians spying on us and who knows how many others. The Union sends a battle cruiser with a power-hungry commander, who might be crazy enough to start a war we don't need." Peters shook his head. "I fear we are in for unpleasant changes."

"I can't believe that the Anorians would to anything to our communities," Stonewall said. "They are not an aggressive species."

"How aggressive can a bunch of females who run around naked all the time actually be?" Peters laughed. "We should have taken them up on their offer and stayed a while. That captain...what was her name? I wouldn't have minded..."

160

"Her name was Norgana," Stonewall said. *Your leader is a complicated man with many issues. I hoped I could put a few suggestions into his mind.* Norgana's words echoed inside his thoughts. ... *put a few suggestions into his mind!* Did that sound like someone who was not aggressive? She seduced him through manipulating his mind to have sexual intercourse with her. The act itself didn't bother him, in fact, it had been a pleasurable experience, but it was the way it happened that left him wondering. Perhaps the Anorians weren't as peaceful as they claimed.

"Come to think of it, she was the one who gave us the information about the base we destroyed, the one with the alleged smugglers. That turned out to be a false lead. I'm beginning to wonder about those peaceful Anorians." Peters emptied his glass. "This wine isn't bad," he said. "Hard to believe it is artificial."

"Artificial," Stonewall mused. "Here we are sitting in an artificial environment, safe from the real world around us. What are we doing here, Peters?"

"Relaxing." Peters chuckled. "And drinking wine. I'm having a good time."

"That's not what I am talking about. Why are Humans trying to tame a world that obviously was never meant for us? This is a world for lizards and their relatives...not for Humans. There aren't even any monkeys here. Who are we kidding, Will?"

Peters looked at him sharply. "Are you feeling all right, Stonewall? You called me by my first name. You only do that when you're down in the dumps. Or had too much to drink. What brings this up?"

Stonewall shrugged. "I never told you this. I had sex with Norgana."

"With the Anorian Captain? Whoa! That's news to me." Peters eyed him skeptically. "When did that happen? I was there all the time, remember?"

"She has a dangerous ability. She told me she is a true telepath. She can influence minds and make others see and do things. Who knows what she might have done to our minds had we accepted her offer to stay on the ship for the night."

"Wow!" Peters scratched his head, a far-away smile on his lips.

"Those females...they were beautiful. All of them. I can just image what they might have done to our bodies."

"Not only to our bodies, Will. Look what she did to me in the short time we were there. Imagine giving her a whole night to work on our minds, especially Chelzic's. I don't trust her. Their ship was in that lake for a reason. The Spiders aren't the only ones who want Epsilon."

"It's a sobering thought, but I hope you are wrong. We have enough problems with the Spiders. We don't need any with the Dragons." Peters filled his glass from the jug. "I believe I need another drink. How about you, old friend who worries too much?"

———

THE NEXT DAY THEY LEFT AT DAWN AND TRAVELED UNTIL DARK, not stopping in Heaven's Hope. The trip went smoothly without any mishaps. A tall tree which had fallen across the road before they reached Heaven's Hope caused them a bit of trouble, especially since the bus that came from Desert Hell was stuck on the other side. The three drivers and a couple of miners, who were on their way back to Epsilon City, had already managed to cut out part of it. With the help of Stonewall and the others it didn't take long to open the road again.

When they asked the men on the bus about any disturbing news from Desert Hell, they shook their heads. "Nothing but the usual stuff," one of them said.

They arrived in Lizard's Tongue shortly after seven at night. It was still light enough to see the few habitats that contained the shops and stores. The largest habitat was the one housing the office and warehouses of the Trading Commission, as far as Stonewall knew from his briefing.

"So this is what it's like in the frontier towns?" Millie looked around wide-eyed. "What is that huge mound over there?"

"The citizens of Lizard's Tongue live inside that mountain of rocks," Peters explained. "In caves."

"Who built it?"

"The primitive forbearers of the intelligent giant ants who inhabit Epsilon. This hive is not as sophisticated in design as Epsilon City and Star City."

"Interesting," Stonewall said. He was nearly as ignorant of the way people lived in this town as Millie.

"It seems the people living here are quite safe. I thought they might live in..." Millie screwed up her face. "Actually, I never thought about that. This doesn't seem so bad."

"This is only a taste, little girl," Peters said. "It gets worse the further you travel north. You might be wise to stay here. Both of you." He looked at Demi. "You said you are a nurse. I understand there is a small hospital here...at least there used to be. I suggest if you are interested you should go there and ask if they need someone to help them out." He lifted his hands. "Only a suggestion. I'm not trying to tell you what you should do. The choice is yours."

Demi nodded. "I think it's a good idea."

"How about me?" Millie asked.

"They might hire you also. It wouldn't hurt to go with her."

"I think I'll do that." Millie laughed. Then she gave the surprised Peters a hug and a kiss on the cheek. "Thank you for your help." She turned to Demi. "Shall we go?"

"We don't even know where the hospital is?"

"We can ask the clerk in the Trading Commission."

As it turned out, the office of the Trading Commission was closed, so they headed for the second bubble. Stonewall was a bit surprised to see the well-kept street running through the center of the habitat and the stores on each side. "There is a place where we can find something to eat," he said, pointing in the direction of a sign above one of the places. "The Gourmet Bar and Grill. Sounds interesting."

When they walked into the eatery, the woman behind the counter asked, "Are you all together?"

Peters nodded. "That's right. All six of us."

"There is a table free in the back," she said and directed them to a round table, large enough to accommodate them. Waiting for them to sit down, she asked, "We have some fresh Raptor steaks."

Stonewall nodded. "We'll have those."

"Not for me, please," Millie said. "I don't eat meat."

"How about steamed mushrooms and boiled Fernapple cubes?"

"Fine. Sounds good."

The waitress left to get their food.

"She looks tired," Demi said, looking around in the room. "I'm surprised at the number of people in here. It can't be easy to wait on them if it's like this every day."

"This is probably the only eatery in Lizard's Tongue. People like to unwind after working hard all day. There can't be much to do around here after dark," Stonewall commented. "I can't get over it how much has changed on this planet in the thirteen years I was gone. I would never have guessed the population on Epsilon would explode like this."

"I've noticed other shops in this habitat," Demi said. "I saw a barbershop and a tailor shop. There was another sign, but I didn't read it. I wonder where the hospital is."

"You could ask the waitress. She'll know," Peters said.

Stonewall noticed some of the people in the room throwing glances at them, probably wondering about their presence here. Mendez in his Union Trooper uniform sporting his large military sidearm would definitely be cause for much speculation, as were Stonewall and Peters, who were dressed in their Scouts outfits.

The waitress came back with their food and put it in front of them. "Are you staying long in Lizard's Tongue?" she asked, looking at Peters.

"No. We're just passing through. We're on our way to Raptor's Tooth," Peters said.

"All of you?" She looked at Demi.

"Not really," Demi answered. "In fact, I heard there is a hospital here that might be looking for a nurse. I'm a nurse."

The waitress shook her head. "I'm afraid you're out of luck. Doc Holland and his wife can handle everything by themselves." She gave Demi a calculating look. "If you're interested in working as a waitress, we could sure use some help. My old bones are telling me to slow down and take it easy."

"I'm a nurse. I would rather treat sick people," Demi said after a short pause. "but thank you for the offer."

"How about you, young lady?" She looked at Millie.

"Me?" Millie seemed surprised. She threw a glance at Stonewall and then at Peters. "What do you think?"

"I think here is your chance," Peters said.

164

"I think so too." She clapped her hands together. "I'll take the offer. When can I start?"

The waitress smiled at Millie's enthusiasm. "You can start as soon as you're finished eating. We have plenty of dishes to wash. I assume you have no place to stay?"

"No, I don't."

"You can sleep in the back. We have an empty room. It's not fancy but safe and private. No one will bother you there."

Millie stood up and threw her arms around the older woman. "Oh, thank you so much. You won't be sorry."

"I hope it is you who won't be sorry. I don't know where you come from and what you're used to, but life in Lizard's Tongue can be lonely. I can't pay you much either, however, your room and food will be free."

Millie beamed at her. "That is more than I'd hoped for." She took her place at the table again and attacked her food with great enthusiasm.

"I'm glad you found what you were looking for," Demi said after the waitress walked away.

Millie gave her a thoughtful look. "It is the best thing that has happened to me for quite some time. I've lost two good friends. One was killed by a Rex and the other one lies in a coma from which she might never recover. If she recovers, she will find me again, but in the meantime, I have to survive. Was it my life's ambition to work in a bar at the bottom of the world? No, but this is all fate has given me. I'll take it."

"You are so young and already so cynical," Demi said. "You must have led a hard life."

"I have but I'd like to take a guess that your life hasn't exactly been wonderful, otherwise you would not be here. I wish you good luck wherever you end up. How far will you go?"

Demi laughed softly. "You called this the bottom of the world. Perhaps it isn't the bottom yet. There has to be a worse place than this one. That's where I'll go."

"Well, at least you won't be alone. You still have your friend." Millie's eyes rested on Safire. "I assume you're going with her?"

Safire gave his head a slow shake. "I don't know what waits for me.

I've always been the master of my own destiny, but it seems I've run out of options. Perhaps I'll make my fortune here, who knows. There has to be a reason why fate brought me here to this desolate place. Nothing happens without a reason."

His contemplation extracted a laugh from Demi. "I didn't know you were such a philosopher, Xander. Maybe I was wrong about you and there is more to you than just that large piece of flesh in your pants."

Safire looked around the room as if her remark embarrassed him. "No need to advertise my...endowment," he said with a low voice. "There wasn't much room for deep thoughts in the last few weeks. I'd like to think there is more to me than just my physical appearance and my manhood. I have feelings too, you know."

Mendez burst out laughing. "I hope you don't start crying to display your feelings. I don't think I could stand that."

"I wouldn't expect you to, Trooper. Are you certain you are even human?" Safire glared at Mendez.

"I control my emotions," Mendez countered. "That doesn't make me inhuman."

"No, but it makes you like one of those reptiles out there...cold and uncaring. All you think about are your weapons and your killing machines. I've dealt with your type all of my life. My father was a soldier. I never really knew him, and I never loved him. He didn't give me any reason to love him or to even care about him. When he died fighting in a useless border skirmish, I couldn't even cry." Safire emptied his cup and slammed it back on the table with an angry gesture. "I swore I would never end up like him."

"You are an angry man, Safire. Perhaps you will find an opportunity on this planet to get that anger out of your system. Maybe that is the reason you are here." Mendez emptied his own cup, shaking his head.

"Well, I'm so glad we are having this uplifting discussion," Peters said. "We might all get a chance to get rid of our frustration soon. I wish I'd know what we'll be facing. I'm surprised we haven't heard anything from anyone. Perhaps when we get to Desert Hell, we'll get some news of what is happening further up north."

"Why are they calling that place Desert Hell?" Demi asked.

"You'll find out. I haven't been there for a couple of years and I'm sure things have changed, hopefully for the better. The last time I visited that place I was not impressed. It's hotter than here because of its proximity to the desert and living there is much harder than even in Lizard's Tongue." He smiled almost evilly. "But Desert Hell is still Heaven compared with what comes after that." With a look at Demi, he said, "Let's hope you won't find your destiny there."

"Don't try to scare me," she said. "I've made up my mind. If others live there so can I."

"I hate to break up this party," Stonewall said, "but I think we should go and get our rooms in the hostel."

The hostel was empty and each of them got their own room.

Stonewall undressed and, naked, he crawled under the thin covers. A knock on the door made him wonder who it could be, and he was surprised to see Demi standing in the doorway.

"Would you like some company?" she asked.

He hadn't bothered to get dressed or turn on the light when he answered the door. She giggled when she saw that he was naked. "I feel lonely and I thought you might want someone to share your bed with."

He hesitated, not quite sure what the best decision would be, but then he shrugged and said, "As long as it doesn't bother you to share it with a naked man."

She closed the door behind her and slipped out of her clothes. Then she came up to him. Her hand traveled up his chest. "I have nothing to wear at night either. I hope you don't mind sharing your bed with a naked woman." She lifted up on tiptoes and kissed him.

He picked her up and carried her to bed. "I thought you didn't want anything to do with me anymore," he said.

She laughed softly. "Then you misunderstood. I said I didn't want you to put too much into what happened between us. I'm still saying that, but right now I need to feel your body on top of mine and your big pole inside me. I have an itch that needs to be scratched and you're just the one who can do it so well." She pulled him down on top of her.

He took her into his arms and kissed her gently. Then he moved his hands over her body down to her womanhood. She was already wet, and he didn't lose too much time with foreplay. Sliding between her spreading thighs, he eased his erection into her with a deep, satisfied sigh. She responded immediately by thrusting up against him.

"This is what I needed," she moaned. "You feel good inside me."

They moved in silence for a long time, the only sounds their heavy breathing and loud moans of pleasure.

She stayed with him until morning. When Stonewall woke up, she lay in his arms, a happy smile on her full lips. He trailed their outline with his finger. Soft light falling through the window brushed her face, and he studied her delicate features, wondering what would happen to her in the rough environment that lay ahead of her.

Her eyelids fluttered open and she looked at him with sleepy eyes. "Is it already time to get up?" she whispered.

"I'm afraid so," he said, bending over her to kiss her lips.

She flung her arms around his neck, kissing him back and pulling him against her. Her breasts felt soft on his chest and he reacted to her warm body. She laughed and caught his erection between her thighs, moving back and forth to tease him.

"The last time you said we didn't have time," she crooned. "Don't deny me today. This might be the last time I will have the opportunity to feel a man inside me for a while."

He groaned and rolled onto his back, taking her with him. Lying on top of him, she rubbed her pussy over the length of his penis. Then, with a loud moan, she sheathed him and moved her pelvis frantically in his lap.

Worried that Peters might show up at his door, he didn't drag it out and, after she had her orgasm, he gave in to his body's craving.

"That was wonderful," she said while she was getting dressed. "Thank you for not rejecting me last night."

He laughed and took her into his arms. "I'd be a fool to refuse a beautiful woman like you, Demi? I wish some day you'll find a man who appreciates you, a man you want to spend the rest of your life with. You deserve better than all this."

She stroked his cheek. "You could be that man," she said softly, "but I know you are not. Your destiny is with the Scouts and mine is somewhere out there. These encounters mean nothing in the scope of things, except for letting us taste a life that could be ours but was never meant to be ours. Let's be satisfied with that."

She slipped out of his room to go back to hers before the others woke up and saw her coming out of Stonewall's room. There was nothing to be gained by broadcasting her sexual encounter with Stonewall. They both had agreed to keep it a secret.

At breakfast, Demi hardly looked at him. When their eyes met by chance, he thought that they were extremely shiny, but that could have been an illusion or the reflection of the sunlight illuminating the room through the large window facing east.

He looked out at the tall mushroom trees visible some distance away. All of the trees in the vicinity of the habitats and the *Mound* had been cut down for security reasons, but he knew that danger still lurked everywhere. He worried about Demi's future but realized that it was not up to him to keep her safe.

Before they left Lizard's Tongue, Stonewall and Mendez went to talk to the clerk in the Trading Commission's office.

———

THE REDHEADED WOMAN BEHIND THE DESK LOOKED FIRST AT Mendez and then at Stonewall. "A Trooper and a Scout. Together. Very unsusual. What brings you to Lizard's Tongue?"

"We've received some information about a disturbance in one of the mining camps...Raptor's Tooth. Can you tell us more about that?" Mendez asked.

She shrugged. "Not much. We haven't heard from them since that last message. The message was short and garbled. It seems it was sent from one of the small personal communicators the miners carry with them. They don't broadcast too far. Too much interference in the jungle from all the crystals and other metals. Heller, my colleague, believes it didn't even come from Raptor's Tooth but from one of the closer camps. Whoever sent it just relayed the message, but the sender must have been interrupted before the message could be sent completely."

"What did the message say?"

"Just a minute. I'll find out from Heller." She walked away, heading for another counter. Conversing with the man who had been busy looking at his computer screen, she came back a couple of minutes later. "The message said...*been destroyed...aircraft...attacked by half...reptilian... They are...*That's all we got. Sorry. We sent it to the office in Star City. What do you think it means?"

Stonewall saw the curiosity in her green eyes and said, "We don't know, Ma'am. That's why we are here to find out."

The gaze of her eyes brushed Mendez. "You must know something. Why else send the Military?"

"We have our suspicion..." Stonewall started to say.

"She doesn't have clearance to know that," Mendez said harshly.

"Oh, come on, Trooper!" The woman spoke with an annoyed tone. "I am an employee of the Trading Commission and therefore entitled to any information pertaining to the affairs of Epsilon. You are lucky I gave you my information since you're not in the employ of the Commission."

Mendez made a sound deep in his throat, like a Rex getting ready to attack. "It seems you unaware that Epsilon has been put under Marshal Law, Ma'am."

"That's news to me. What the hell does that mean?"

"It means that the Military has taken over the affairs of Epsilon. That includes everything on this planet, even your little hiding place here. Any information that could endanger the security of this planet is to be forwarded to the Military Command. Since I represent the Military here in Lizard's Tongue, I am considered the Military Command. So anything you know has to be relayed to me. Is that understood?" Mendez glared at her.

The woman glared back at him. "You know what you are? You're full of crap! You think you can come here with your fancy uniform and bristling with all kinds of weapons and shiny badges and intimidate me or anyone else? Well, you're wrong. We are living here in miserable conditions most of the time. We can't go outside without wondering when one of those giant lizards will tear us apart. We can't go for a long walk in the park or go swimming in the gentle waters of a lake. Shall I go on? Well, you go about your business but don't expect any help from us. Unless you ask politely. Is that understood?"

Her gaze swept over Stonewall. "Are you with this pompous idiot?"

He shrugged. "I have been ordered to investigate this transmission, Ma'am, just like Trooper Mendez. We're just following orders and we thank you for your co-operation." He winked with his left eye, trying to suppress a grin. This was one feisty woman, and good-looking to boot.

Wouldn't mind tangling with her. What passion!

He noticed that Mendez was about to say more, but Stonewall turned to him and said, "We've learned all we can, Trooper Mendez. Let's go."

They left Lizard's Tongue an hour later. It was only about one hundred fifty miles to Desert Hell and they should be arriving there in the early afternoon. Stonewall leaned back into his seat and closed his eyes, not caring about the jungle outside or the road they traveled on. He knew they were relatively well protected inside the tank and he trusted Mendez to get them safely to their destination. Besides, there was nothing for him to do in any case and worrying about anything didn't help.

He felt tired and weary, and his sexual escapade with Demi was only partially to blame. He smiled, recalling the passion she had displayed in his arms. It was a shame fate had dealt her a bad hand. The harsh life in the frontiers of a planet like Epsilon was not a place for a woman like her. Of course, his thinking could be wrong. Men had a tendency to underestimate women. They were tougher than most men believed.

Just because she is beautiful and looks soft...

"You're awfully quiet this morning," Peters said, cutting into Stonewall's thoughts.

Stonewall chuckled. "Sometimes a man needs to reflect on things, my inquisitive friend. It would do you some good to do that once in a while."

"You've been reflecting on things a lot lately," Peters said. "Must have something to do with your age."

"I'm a year younger than you as I recall. So that theory doesn't hold." He emitted a small sigh. "Maybe I've done too many things and seen too much misery and it is getting to me. Perhaps it's Epsilon. I don't know."

"You'll probably need a vacation," Safire said from the back.

"Yeah, right. Where would I go? Backpacking into the jungle?"

Safire laughed. "From what I've seen not a good idea. This planet must be one of the most inhospitable ones in the Galaxy. Once I was on a planet that could have been Paradise. The weather was great, the plants mostly harmless, the animals friendly...it had everything."

"I'm sure there is a *but* somewhere," Demi said.

"The indigenous population wasn't friendly. I don't believe I've ever met a race so warlike and vicious. We barely managed to escape with our lives." He exhaled noisily. "And the women! They were so beautiful it made your head spin just looking at them. There were rumors they killed their mates after copulating and ate them, but that could have been only rumors. We weren't there long enough to find out. But if it were true, it would prove again that nothing is ever perfect."

"Speak for yourself, Xander," Demi said, laughing.

"You seem to be in good spirits this morning," he said. "That is usually only the case after you had a good piece of tail." He eyed her suspiciously. "Who have you been banging, Demi? Did you meet some lonely prospector who fell for your charms?"

"You have a one-track mind, Xander," Demi said. "I'm just happy to be alive. Isn't that a good enough reason to lift your spirit?"

"I suppose it is." He leaned back and stared outside.

Stonewall watched him in the rearview mirror that was mounted above the instrument panel. It seemed to be floating in the air since the dome of the tank was transparent from the inside. He had finally gotten used to the fact that what seemed like no barrier between the passengers inside the tank and the outside world was actually a solid, impenetrable, yet invisible partition. It was still a bit unnerving though to have the illusion they were traveling without a protective roof above them.

The mushroom trees in this area were of a variety with small umbrellas, and he could see much of the sky. A flock of Dactyls sailed just underneath the few clouds looking for food or maybe just enjoying the warm air currents.

So far, they had been lucky and not encountered any large carnosaurs. Thinking about that brought back the image of the huge Rex that had attacked them on the way to Epsilon City. Even though Chelzic had given the assurance that nothing could touch them inside the tank, the thought of being rolled into a swamp or swallowed up by a sinkhole didn't instill any feelings of complete safety.

"What was that?" Safire called out, interrupting his contemplation.

Stonewall scanned the area outside. "What was what?" he asked.

"Something just zoomed by close to the treetops," Safire said, his voice thick with excitement. "It didn't look like a bird, or whatever qualifies as a bird on this planet. It moved quite fast. I didn't get a good look at it."

"Anyone else saw it?"

"No," Peters and Demis said almost at the same time.

"Maybe I can find out more," Mendez said. "Computer, provide surveillance data for the last two minutes. Disregard any naturally occurring objects on the ground and in the sky."

"One object passed overhead at ten-thirty-eight hours forty-three seconds. Speed of object was one hundred fifty-seven miles per hour," the voice of the computer informed them.

"Computer. Was it a naturally occurring phenomenon?"

"Negative."

"Computer, supply more details about object. Was it an aircraft? If so was it of known origin?"

"Aircraft of unknown origin."

"Computer, can you supply more details? A picture maybe?" Peters asked.

"Insufficient data."

"Well, at least now we know I wasn't dreaming," Safire said.

"I wonder who has the nerve to be so bold to fly around in this part of the planet. This is the most populated stretch on all of Epsilon," Peters pondered. "You'd think anyone trying to land illegally would choose a less settled area."

"Safire and his friends dropped in unannounced and undetected," Mendez said.

"You're correct, we did, but we are Humans. We have a right to be here."

"Not according to the laws of the Solar Union," Mendez objected. "You are trespassing like everyone else who doesn't ask for permission."

Safire made a mocking sound. "You mean according to the laws of the Trading Commission. Don't think we don't know who really owns Epsilon."

"Who is *we?*"

"The Belters, the Colonies of Bernard's Star and Alpha Centauri, and other members of the High Senate."

Mendez threw Safire a sharp look. "You seem to know more than you let on. What was your other reason for coming to Epsilon besides collecting Dinosaur eggs?"

Safire shrugged. "Why should there be another reason? I'm only repeating what I've heard. Don't think for a minute we in the colonies are oblivious of what goes on in the rest of the Galaxy."

"You should leave politics alone and worry about your survival right now," Mendez suggested.

"What he said isn't far from the truth," Stonewall couldn't help injecting.

"I don't really care," Mendez growled. "I'm not interested in politics. I'm here to uphold the law and to defend what belongs to the Solar Union. You should do the same thing, Stonewall. Don't you have some kind of motto you have to swear allegiance to?"

"We do."

"Well, then stick to it and don't meddle in things you know nothing about. Leave that to the professionals."

Stonewall was ready to retort but then he decided it would be a waste of his breath to discuss anything with Mendez.

You can't reason with an automaton, damn it.

"I wouldn't be surprised if what Safire saw has something to do with the disturbance in Raptor's Tooth?" Peters wondered.

"I guess we'll find out," Stonewall said. *...aircraft...attacked...reptilian...*Much could be read into that message. Nothing about it sounded good.

They pulled into Desert Hell a couple of hours later and Stonewall was none too happy to leave the cramped interior of the tank and smell some natural air, even if it was hot and humid.

His gaze wandered from the habitat of the Trading Commission to the mounds growing out of the stony ground and then to the desert that stretched away into the hazy distance behind the town. He noticed a few men dressed in the brown-yellow outfits most prospectors wore, holding flash rifles, and pulling green-scaled animals behind them, walking between the mounds.

"I think I know now why they call this place Desert Hell," Demi said softly beside him. She wiped her forehead with her sleeve. "It is hot."

"Are you changing your mind already?" Stonewall asked.

She shook her head. "No. I've experienced worse than this. I'm staying."

"Here?"

"Not necessarily. I'll probably go with you as far as you're going. Wherever that is."

"Raptor's Tooth. That's as far as we can go. There is nothing beyond that place," Peters, who had come up beside them, said.

"Then Raptor's Tooth it is," she said with conviction. "They'll probably have need for a nurse there. If not, I will go searching for gems."

"Let's go and search for a place to spend the night," Stonewall said. "I hope they have a hostel here."

"They do. It is in the habitat." Peters turned to walk away.

"Good. I hoped we didn't have to move into one of those trailers." Stonewall followed him after having one last look at the desert and then back at the jungle that was too close to feel secure. Lizards moved fast and they could cross the distance between the tall ferns and the town quickly. He reminded himself to be on the alert at all times when outside.

After entering the habitat, the group walked past the office of the Trading Commission toward the second building which was obviously the hostel. It was not as large as the one in Lizard's Tongue or the other places. The pudgy man, who ran the hostel, told them they'd have to share rooms.

"I have only two rooms left. Sorry. The third one is already occupied by a young couple," he said, apologizing. "We don't get many visitors, you know. This is the busiest I've been for a while."

"I'll share my room with Stonewall," Demi said, to which Safire raised an eyebrow. He gave Stonewall a penetrating stare. "Are you...?" Then he shrugged and shook his head. "Never mind, it's not my business."

"I didn't say I'll share my bed," Demis said, her face flushed. "I said I'll share my room."

"And I said that it isn't my business," Sarfire returned hotly.

"You are right," Stonewall said, "It isn't your business." He smiled at Demi. "I promise I'll be a gentleman."

"I know. That's why I picked you," she said, but her eyes gave a little twinkle when she looked at him.

They took their personal luggage to their rooms and stowed it away.

"No need to open the second bed," Demi said matter-of-factly.

"It never entered my mind," Stonewall said, chuckling. Why waste an opportunity. It may never present itself again.

The hostel manager met them on their way back to the lobby. "If you are hungry, we serve food here also. Not fancy but nourishing."

"Are you serving something now?" Stonewall asked.

"Sure. The other couple is in there now. You are welcome to join them. It will make it easier for me to serve everyone at the same time."

Stonewall walked behind Demi when they walked into the dining room. He barely glanced at the man and woman sitting at one of the three tables, but Demi stopped and said, "Hello there. It is nice to see fellow strangers in this place." Curious, he turned his head and looked at the two people.

———

Keep reading to enjoy a preview of the next novel in
The Stonewall Chronicles
EPSILON CITY

———

Don't miss out on your next favorite book!

Join the Melange Books mailing list at
www.melange-books.com/mail.html

"EPSILON CITY"
THE STONEWALL CHRONICLES, BOOK 2

When David Houston agrees to help visitor Tara Turner to Epsilon he is smitten by the girl's beauty and innocence. Traveling with her through a jungle populated by giant lizards is only part of his troubles. Will the sexual tension between them cause actions that cannot be undone?

"Epsilon City is different from any city on other planets populated by Humans because Humans did not build it. The dome was built by giant ants centuries ago. They abandoned it after parasites invaded the hive and killed off the majority of the ant population. It stood empty for over a century until some enterprising settlers decided the honeycombed structure would make a safe place for Humans to live in. The ants, they call their race *Uur*, are ingenious engineers and builders. The air inside the dome is cool and dry compared to the outside air and stays at a constant twenty-three degrees Celsius."

Houston took a sip from the bottle in his hand. Looking across his audience in the bus he smiled. "Of course, some of our guests, usually of non-human species, of which we don't get too many, find it too cold and we had to install heaters in their apartments."

"What happened to the parasites?" a young woman asked from the rear of the transporter.

"They eventually moved out and died of starvation after their hosts left."

The woman shook her red hair and gave a sigh of relief. "I'm sure glad to hear that. Wouldn't want any creepy-crawlies all over my body."

Houston studied her more closely. His eyes lingered for a moment on her generous display of breasts. *Wouldn't mind roaming my hands all over your body.* Smiling, he said, "As far as I know there would have been no danger of that. Apparently, the parasites were as large as housecats on Earth. Rest assured, when Humans arrived on Epsilon, the dome was empty of life."

"Why didn't the original owners move back?" another passenger asked.

"They built another dome about fifty miles west of here. The area around their new hive is mostly desert and rocks, which gives them more control of who moves in with them."

"How do you know that? Or are you just making this up?" The redheaded woman seemed to challenge him.

Houston frowned, but then he laughed. "We do communicate with the indigenous people. Others have asked that question before, you know."

"Thank you. I guess you should know what you're talking about, after all…you live here." She hesitated slightly before asking, "Are you living in the dome?"

"Yes, I am."

"How large is the dome?"

Houston turned his attention toward the man who asked. Then he looked out of the transporter's window. They were still far enough away to see the top of the huge cone. "It rises about one thousand two-hundred feet into the sky," he said, almost proudly. "From its apex one can see the first hive of the Uur nation to the west. The giant mushrooms of the jungle seem almost small when viewed from the top of Epsilon City. It is a marvelous view."

"How many people live in the city now?"

"According to the latest count nearly ten thousand call Epsilon City their home."

"That's a lot of people."

Houston chuckled. "Believe it or not, there is room for twenty thousand more."

"How do you keep the dinosaurs from entering the area around the city?" another man asked.

"The whole compound is surrounded by a tall electric fence. It keeps out anything trying to invade us." He smiled. "Except for the ones roaming the sky. The larger ones we shoot down with missiles, the smaller ones with flash rifles."

The transporter neared the huge structure and headed for a gaping hole at the base. As the transporter drove through the opening, a large tunnel appeared ahead, winding its way into the dome's interior.

"This tunnel leads all the way up to the top," Houston explained.

Artificial mini-suns lit up the smooth road surface and the walls. In their light, smaller tunnels could be seen leading away from the main road.

"First-time visitors may find everything a bit confusing, but in reality this whole city is well planned. The tunnels leading away on every level split into an apparent maze, but after exploring them, one finds order in the layout. As I said before, the dome is a marvel of engineering. Our own engineers have taken great care not to interfere with the basic design."

The transporter entered one of the side tunnels and came to a halt in a large cavern-like room. Bright light flooded in from a huge opening in one wall. The giant umbrellas of the nearby mushroom jungle could be seen in the distance, which meant this room was still in the lower half of the dome.

"Ladies and gentlemen, we have arrived. I hope you all have a pleasant stay." Houston smiled and made a little bow when a few people applauded. Then he turned and stepped off the transporter.

He walked toward the opening and stood close to the edge. Looking out, he could see the bubble that housed the offices of the Trading Commission. Far to the right rested the spaceship that brought the latest wave of newcomers to Epsilon. Near the Trading Commission's habitat stood two large ships...freighters who delivered supplies from Earth and would take back goods destined for trade with other planets. The group in his transporter was composed mainly of merchants and scientists, who wouldn't stay long. From his vantage point he could see other transporters being loaded with the ones who planned to stay; some for a limited time, maybe a few years, some forever. Fortune hunters, gamblers, prospectors, and farmers with their families. Possibly even one or two con men. A few of them might realize their dream, most would be disappointed, finding nothing but misery, some even death.

Thinking about his own ambitions and disappointments, he stared at the distant clouds hovering above the brown blanket of mushroom umbrellas. A lone *Dactyl* glided into view from the east but was lost again in the mist rising from *Death Valley*, a giant swamp bordering the *Purple Sea*.

"Excuse me…"

He turned around at the sound of the voice. His eyebrows lifted slightly when he recognized the redheaded woman who had been so inquisitive. "Yes?"

She gave him a shy smile. "I don't mean to bother you, but I think I need your help."

"You think?" He returned her smile. "I'm not sure if I can or want to help you. It depends what it is you want from me," he said cautiously.

She shouldered her duffle bag. Then she shrugged and put it on the floor. "Damn thing is getting heavy," she said, smiling uncertainly.

"Well?" Houston stared at her, getting impatient. He studied her casually but with some interest. Attractive women like her didn't usually come to Epsilon, at least not alone. And none of them would approach him and ask for help.

The woman held out a hand. "My name is Tara Turner. This is my first time on Epsilon."

He shook her hand, chuckled. "I would have never guessed, Miss Turner."

She didn't smile, only lifted the corners of her lips. "I…" Her shoulders slumped a little. "Never mind, I'll find help somewhere else." She took her duffle bag and turned to walk away.

On an impulse, he grabbed her arm. "I never said I wouldn't help you."

She looked at him over her shoulder. "No, but you didn't offer it either."

Looking into her green eyes, he felt compelled to ask, "Where are you staying?"

She shrugged. "I was told there are shelters for people like me. I can't afford the exuberant prices of the luxury hotels."

"You can stay at my place." He said it only to be polite, not really expecting her to accept.

To his surprise, she said, "I will if your offer is sincere."

He had committed himself. There was no turning back. "It is," he said.

"I don't even know your name."

"David Houston. Dave to my friends."

"I guess I'll have to call you David?"

"Nobody does." He chuckled. "Call me Dave. The only person who ever called me David is dead."

"Who?"

"My mother." He threw one last look out of the huge window. The clouds seemed darker and closer. It looked like a storm was moving in. "Come on. My scooter is one level up."

She followed him in silence as he walked back to the main road. The rest oft the passengers had already disappeared. Houston walked briskly. The woman seemed to be struggling with her duffle bag as she tried to keep up with him climbing the incline of the road.

"Is it far?" she called.

He stopped and waited for her to catch up. "I guess you're not a mountain climber," he said.

"I've climbed mountains. It is part of my job," she said when she reached him.

"What do you do?"

"I'm a geologist."

"Give me your bag. I'll carry it," he offered.

She seemed hesitant, but then she shrugged and gave it to him. "I'm willing to follow you to your place, even though I don't know you. Might as well trust you with my stuff."

He threw the duffle bag across his broad shoulders. "I've never robbed anyone," he growled. "I'm not going to start now." He turned and trudged on.

"Thank you," she said. "Just so you know...I don't have much money."

"I haven't asked for any."

"No, you haven't." She paused, struggling with her next words. "I...I could pay you in other ways...if that's okay."

"I've never asked a woman to pay me that way, either." He glanced at her. "But with you I might make an exception."

She stumbled and almost fell. He reached out to steady her. When he looked into her face, he thought he saw a small tear in one corner of her eye. "I'm sorry," he said soothingly. "It was a joke. You have nothing to fear from me. I would never ask you to do anything you are not willing to give freely. And this would not be given freely. I don't rape women."

She smiled bravely, swallowing. "Thank you. I guess I'm not such a bad judge of character after all."

"This time. Next time you may not be so lucky. Epsilon is a frontier world. You're quite safe in this city. On the rest of the planet..." He shook his head. "Totally different story. Take my advice. Don't trust anyone. A woman with your looks shouldn't be traveling alone."

"You're not the first person to tell me that," she said, sighing. "All of my friends warned me against this trip."

"You said you're a geologist. Shouldn't you be with a group? I mean, scientists usually travel together as a team."

"I'm not here professionally."

"Why are you here?"

"To find my brother."

"Your brother? He is on Epsilon?"

She nodded. "He came here five years ago. He's a geologist, like me. Wanted to make his fortune."

Houston laughed dryly. "Don't we all?"

"What do you mean?"

He turned into another tunnel. "We're almost there."

"What did you mean with your last remark?" She insisted on hearing his answer.

"I spent two years in that insect-infected jungle dodging lizards and chasing my dream, digging for gemstones. Sure, I found plenty, but they're worthless here and you're not allowed to take them off planet. Nobody tells you that until you find some and try to cash them in." He chuckled humorlessly. "They let you trade them in for equipment so you can keep on digging."

"I don't understand. Who are *they*?"

"The Solar Union. Everything here is controlled by the Union. The Trading Commission will take the gems off your hands for a pittance.

Welcome to *Hell*, pretty innocent lady. With all the riches buried in the ground of this forsaken ball, nobody is able to earn enough money to ever leave again. The Solar Union sees to that."

She gave him an inquiring look. "Is that what happened to you?"

Without answering her question, he stopped in front of a small scooter. "Hop on. I'm living on the fifty-sixth floor. We are on floor twenty-three." He mounted the two-seater, waited until she climbed behind him. "Put your arms around my chest," he instructed. "I don't want you falling off."

The scooter floated on a thin cushion of air. It began moving without making a sound. Houston switched on the low-level siren to alert others of his approach as they moved on the wide road. The tunnel spiraled with a steady incline toward the apex of the cone-city.

When they reached floor fifty-six, Houston slowed the speed of his scooter and took a side tunnel. Stopping in front of a door, he said, "This is my humble place." He parked the scooter beside the door and, pressing his hand on a plate in its center and entering his password into the tiny keyboard, he waited until the door swung open.

"Enter the lair of the Spider," he said, smiling.

She hesitated for a moment.

When he saw the sudden fear in her eyes, he chuckled. "Forgive my sense of humor. I'm probably as apprehensive as you. This is the first time I've invited a woman into my apartment."

"I guess I should feel honored," she said, rewarding him with a smile. "As long as you don't think of me as a fly." She followed him into the room and looked around. "It's nice," she said.

He laughed. "It may not be fancy, but, as the saying goes, it is home. A tiny kitchen, a small living room, and a smaller bedroom. Oh, the bath-cubicle is over there. It has a toilet and a sink. No shower or tub. We have to use the community washrooms for that. They allow us only so much water. You can go right in if you want to freshen up."

"I would. Thank you." She reached for her duffle bag. "I won't use up all your water. I promise." Smiling, she headed for the indicated door.

He watched her disappear into the bath-cubicle. Then he went to the small fridge and took out a can of beer. A luxury he allowed himself only once a week, usually on weekends, but somehow he figured he needed it.

————

TARA TURNER RAN HER FINGERS THROUGH HER HAIR AND SHOOK a few carrot-red strands out of her face. "I don't know how to thank you for your kindness," she said.

Houston smiled and dismissed her concern with a wave of his hand. "You'll get the opportunity sooner or later, don't worry about it. I couldn't let a helpless girl loose on a strange planet and wonder for the rest of my life what kind of trouble she might have fallen into."

She pulled her lips into a mock pout and her eyes flashed green. "I'm not exactly a helpless little girl. I'm twenty-five years old."

He laughed, studying her without being too obvious. He had to admit, she was a beauty. She changed her traveling clothes for a pair of shorts and a blouse that molded itself around her breasts. It was evident she didn't wear any support under the thin material. Not that they needed support.

She noticed his scrutinizing looks and blushed lightly. He looked away. "How long are you planning to stay?" he asked, trying to hide his embarrassment.

She shrugged. "Until I find my brother or..." she hesitated, "or until I find out what happened to him."

"That could take some time."

"I know, but don't worry, I'm not going to stay long in Epsilon City if he isn't here. I might have to go searching for him."

"In the jungle? All by yourself?" He eyed her, his expression skeptical. "Epsilon is a large planet. The jungle seems endless and the deserts stretch forever. Your brother might be anywhere, and there is danger everywhere. This is not a place for a young woman. Especially one who is alone."

She gave him a calculating look. "Would you be willing to help me looking for him?"

"I don't think so. I have no problem giving you a place to stay and trying to keep you out of trouble, but going into that lizard-infected jungle?" He shook his head vehemently. "I have no such desires. Not anymore."

Her green eyes looked thoughtful. "Are you happy here, Dave?"

"Am I happy here?" He chuckled grimly. "What kind of question is that? Of course I'm not happy here. I'd give anything to get off this stinking planet."

"Maybe I can help you."

"You?" He couldn't help but laugh. "It seems to me you need my help more than I need yours."

"I was under the impression you hated the Union."

"I never said that." He wondered where she was heading. Maybe she was a Union-spy trying to trip him up. He didn't trust anyone, not in Epsilon City...or anywhere else on this planet.

"Not in so many words." She tilted her head. "Didn't you tell me the Union controls the gem trade?"

"Yes, I did, because it is true." No harm in admitting that. "Actually, it isn't the Union, it's the Trading Commission."

"Isn't that the same thing?"

"Some people seem to think so." He didn't say any more.

She bent forward and looked into his eyes. "I am going to trust you, Dave. With my life, my future. I need a friend badly and you seem like a nice and descent guy. Yes, I need you but I know you need me too, because I can help you get off this planet."

"If you can somehow miraculously conjure up ten-thousand credits and put them into my hand, I would believe you. But you can't, so please stop playing with my mind." He was annoyed at her for even suggesting she could help him get off Epsilon when it was clear she couldn't.

"You are right, I don't have that kind of money, but I know some people who have."

"Who?"

"The Belter's Consortium."

"What?" He threw back his head and laughed.

She waited until he finished laughing before she said, "It is not a joke. I am deadly serious."

"Why would the Belters help me? I'm an Earthman, a surface crawler. Most Belters hate us because we are able to walk in the sun, walk under trees, swim in big lakes, or the ocean, breathe natural air, while they hide inside hollowed out asteroids and have to breathe artificially created air. They never see the sun except on viewing screens, never smell the fresh, crisp air in spring or run naked in the rain." He laughed again. "I don't know any Belters and I have no reason to expect help from them."

"I'm a Belter," she said softly.

"You don't look like one."

"How should I look?" she asked, an impish smile playing around her lips. "I know you've been scrutinizing me."

"Only because you're so beautiful."

"I shouldn't be beautiful to be a Belter?"

"You should be taller and thinner."

"I guess you don't know much about the Belt and the people who live in it. I am five foot two and I weigh fifty-three kilograms. I was born on Dawson, an asteroid almost two hundred miles in diameter. The surface is dotted with huge habitats where we grow trees, shrubs, flowers, and grass. We even have small lakes. We can do most of the things Earth people can do. As for my height, well, all of the habitats have artificial gravity generators to create one g. Does that answer your question?"

"I guess it does. And more."

"There are tall people on Earth. Some of them are taller than people born on an asteroid." Her smile seemed to mock him. "You're not one of the tall people, though. What happened?"

"Nothing happened. There are plenty of people my height on Earth. I'm happy with my five eight."

"Good for you. Another thing, contrary to what most of you Earthers believe, Belters don't hate you and we don't envy you, either. Earth is overcrowded, depleted of most of its resources. The water is polluted, as is the air, and the weather is unpredictable. Believe me when I tell you we are happy where we are. I'd almost say the opposite is true…Earthers hate us." Her words were proud and her eyes flashed angrily.

He found her incredibly attractive. "You've made your point, but you still haven't answered my question. Why would the Belter's Consortium want to help me?"

"In exchange for *your* help."

"*My* help?" he repeated, giving her a thoughtful look. "Who are you, actually, Miss Tara Turner? If that is your real name."

"It is my name, and what I told you is true." She spoke rapidly, sounding urgent. "I am here to find my brother. At least that is part of my mission. You see, he was sent here five years ago to report on the conditions of this planet, to find out if rumors are true that the Solar Union is preventing gems and drugs to be traded freely. Many Belters who live on asteroids with no or very little gravity suffer from many deficiencies, for instance loss of bone density. Most old Belters have osteoporosis. We need some of the drugs found on Epsilon. We need to have free access to them."

When she stopped to take a deep breath, he interrupted her, "Are you telling me you're a spy?"

She nodded. "You could say that."

"Who are you working for?"

"The PIA."

"Never heard of them?"

"It is short for Planetary Intelligence Agency, the secret service of the Belter's Consortium." Her facial expression was anxious and her eyes studied his reaction.

He sat silent for a long time, staring at the forgotten drink in his hand. "You don't look and act like a spy," he finally said.

She chuckled. "Isn't that the idea? Did you expect a sign around my neck saying *I am a spy?*"

"Of course not. What I mean is you don't come across like a tough, hardboiled, cold-eyed crime fighter. You know…the characters they show in the entertainment holograms."

"You don't really believe those characters actually exist, do you?" Her laugh seemed strained. "Even if they did, I'm not that kind of a spy. When I said I was a geologist I spoke the truth. The Agency hired me to search for my brother and possibly find out more about Epsilon. Of all the colonists and fortune hunters coming here, none have returned. Sure, casual visitors and dignitaries come back after getting the supervised tour, but people who came to stay for a while haven't. People are beginning to wonder what happened to them."

"I can tell you. The same thing that happened to me. They are stuck here. Every day here is a fight for survival. If the jungle or the native wildlife doesn't swallow you up, the laws of the Solar Union and the restrictions put upon every citizen and immigrant make certain you stay buried here." His words sounded bitter in his own ears. Was it possible that this young woman could actually help him to finally leave this hell behind? He hardly dared hope.

She put a hand on his. The touch of her soft, warm hand sent tiny shivers through his body. "Help me and you don't need to stay buried any longer. This could be your chance to escape. You don't have to go back to Earth. There are plenty of asteroid communities who would welcome you with open arms. They need fresh blood. Life in the Belt is not bad."

He shook his head. "I don't know. I can't organize an expedition and search party into the jungle. It takes money to pay for equipment, guards, weapons…"

"How do the new colonists get to their designated areas?"

"The Trading Commission provides them with a transporter, but only to their destination. After that they are on their own. They are stuck wherever they are sent until they can bring back things of value to trade in for equipment. Many of them die within the first few months, unless they can join up with an established community."

"People live in those communities. How do they get around in the jungle?"

"On armored vehicles and local pack animals, which they have to catch and domesticate, or just plain old walking on their own two legs.

Life in those frontier towns is hard, be it a farming community or a place where fortune hunters and prospectors dwell." Acutely aware of her touch, he pulled his hand away, feeling uneasy by her sudden intimate gesture.

She seemed to notice his discomfort and smiled, rosy color creeping into her cheeks. "Sorry," she said, "Don't read me wrong. I'm not trying to seduce you or anything like that to entice you to help me."

You being here is seduction enough. He grinned lopsidedly. "Having a woman touch me makes me uncomfortable."

"You don't like women?"

That made him chuckle. "Of course I like women. It's just…I

haven't been close to anyone for a long time. Living here isolates you from others, especially when all you think of is survival. Believe me, I would like nothing more than take you into my arms and kiss you, hold you tight and…" He didn't finish the sentence, suddenly embarrassed.

Her eyes were large when she looked at him. "I might just let you do that."

Her words shocked him a little. "You surprise me," he said slowly. "Yesterday when I made a joke after you offered to pay me with…you know…"

"With sex?"

"Well…yes, with sex, you acted afraid as if I might take you up on it. Now you tell me…" He shook his head. "You don't mean it. Maybe you are trying to seduce me after all, but with an ulterior motive."

"Isn't that what women do? Seducing a man they like?"

"Under different circumstances I would believe you are sincere, but I know right now you are desperate and willing to do almost anything to get someone to help you. As I told you yesterday, I don't rape women."

Her smile was warm and her eyes grateful. She reached out and touched his hand again. "You are a good person," she whispered, her eyes suddenly filling with tears. "You are right, I am desperate. I need someone to help me find my brother."

This time he didn't pull his hand away. "I'll see what I can do," he said softly. "But no promises, okay?"

She nodded bravely. "Okay. Thank you, Dave."

"Don't thank me yet."

She delicately dabbed at her eyes. "Sorry about that. I don't usually cry. You must think I'm a weak little girl. Please, don't pity me. I can take care of myself, but maybe this time I've taken on too much." She took a small handkerchief from her pocket and wiped her nose. "You mentioned frontier towns. How do the prospectors travel between Epsilon City and their towns?"

"The Trading Commission has an armored bus traveling back and forth from Epsilon City to Lizard's Tongue. They might give you permission to use it if you have a legitimate reason…one that suits their purpose. Of course, there are other ways. Apparently, there are a couple of airplanes being operated out of Star City, but traveling in the air is dangerous. Too many flying predators prowling the airways. They might decide to attack the plane, mistaking it for a rival. Some travelers use armored land vehicles to brave the jungle. It is a treacherous journey. You never know when a carnosaur is hungry enough to challenge your presence. The only way to be relatively safe is in a huge armored and armed bus."

"How about using a scooter?"

"Only a fool or someone with a death wish would use a scooter to travel through the thick jungle and swamp. Especially not for a long trek like you're proposing."

"How far is it anyway to the next frontier town?"

He lifted his shoulder. "Star City is about three hundred miles north of here, but it is not considered a frontier town anymore. It has grown these last five years. The next one is Emerald Lake, three hundred miles northeast of Star City. There are large farming communities within five hundred miles north of Star City. I have no idea how many frontier towns and camps actually exist. They are spread over a large area to the north."

"What's to the south?"

"Desert. Endless hot and dry desert. No sane man would go into that." Houston looked up when someone pounded against the door to his apartment. "I wonder who that is."

He got up and opened the door.

Two men dressed in the uniform of Security confronted him. "Are you David Houston?"

"Yes, I am. What can I do for you?"

"You have a woman by the name of Tara Turner with you?"

"Yes, she's with me. What about her?"

One of the security men pushed Houston aside and forced his way past him into the apartment.

Tara had left her seat at the table and faced the men by the door.

"Miss Tara Turner? Epsilon City Security. Please, come with us." He spoke with a harsh, authoritative voice that left no room for arguments.

HOUSTON SAT IN THE BACK OF THE SECURITY VEHICLE. He sensed Tara's uneasiness and reached over to touch her arm. "Things will be all right," he said, soothingly.

She shook her head. "I'm scared," she whispered. Then she said aloud, addressing the Security men in the front seat, "Why won't you tell me what this is all about?"

"You will be told," one of them said with a harsh voice.

"I did nothing wrong," she insisted. "I'm a visitor here and I demand the respect I deserve." She looked at Houston when none of the men responded. "Can't you do something?"

He shrugged. "There is nothing to do but wait until we get to the Security office. I'm sure this is just a misunderstanding."

The vehicle glided silently down the corridor. No one traveling from the opposite direction could miss the bright flashing lights in the front and back of the vehicle. They finally took a side tunnel on the second floor and halted in front of a brightly lit barred window. Beside it, a steel door led into the room that was visible through the window. Above the door a sign proclaimed this as *Epsilon City Security Headquarters.*

The guard in the passenger seat got out of the vehicle and opened the rear door. "Please, go through that door," he instructed Tara. He looked at Houston. "You can accompany the lady if you so wish."

Houston smiled grimly. "Don't worry, I will." He got out on the other side and walked around the vehicle. Tara waited until he stood beside her and let him open the door for her.

A guard stood on the other side of the door, a flash rifle in his hand. He pointed at the counter across the room. "Please, register at the desk."

Houston walked beside the woman, who held on to his sleeve. She seemed scared and helpless.

She certainly doesn't act like a spy. Unless she's such a good actress.

The uniformed Security man behind the desk looked up as Houston and Tara approached. His eyes fixed on Tara. "Are you Miss Turner?" he asked.

She nodded. "Yes, I am."

"One moment." The man ran his hand across his computer screen in front of him and nodded. "You've been expected," he said. "Have a seat." He looked at Houston. "You too, Mr. Houston!"

"I wasn't told to come here. I came because I wanted to. How am I suddenly involved?"

The man glared at him. "You involved yourself, Mr. Houston. Now, have a seat and wait!"

Houston looked around and found a bench at the end of the room. "Come on," he said to Tara. "Don't worry, we'll straighten this out. Somebody screwed up somewhere."

They waited possibly ten minutes, when a door beside the front desk opened and another uniformed man came out. "Please, accompany me," he told them.

Houston noticed that the man was armed, but his weapon was holstered. That was a good sign. There was a good chance they would not be shot the moment they walked through the door. At least, that's what he hoped. He didn't trust Security men or soldiers. You never knew when they wanted to try out their weapons on an unsuspecting victim.

The man walked ahead of them. Also a good sign.

He smiled at Tara. "I think everything is going to turn out okay," he said softly.

She smiled bravely. "I trust you," she whispered. Grabbing his hand, she squeezed it tightly. He noted her sweaty palm.

This girl isn't acting, he thought. She really is scared.

The Security man took them through a couple of rooms filled with desks occupied by men and women. None of them paid them any attention as they walked past them. They ended up in a small room with only one desk in it and a couple of chairs.

Behind the desk sat a fat, bald man. One look into his face told Houston he was going to be trouble.

"They are all yours," the Security man said, turned and left. The door closed behind him with an audible click.

The fat man studied them silently. Houston couldn't tell the color of his eyes. They were hidden behind fatty tissues that looked like tiny sausages on either side of his surprisingly thin, hooked nose. His nose surely looked out of place above his thick lips. Enormous bushy eyebrows made him look fierce, like an angry Swamp Dragon about to attack. He had no chin and no neck. His jowls hung across rolls of fat that sat on his bulky shoulders where his neck should have been.

"Tara Turner and David Houston," he said at last. It wasn't a question but a statement. His voice sounded like the grating of a pair of hinges screaming to be oiled.

Houston sank into one of the chairs without asking for permission. He was beginning to get annoyed and angry. "Why are we here?" he asked.

"I will be asking the questions," the fat man told him.

"All right. Go ahead. What do you want to know," Houston said belligerently.

"What is your relationship with Miss Turner?"

"My relationship?"

The man's hidden eyes bored into Houston's. "Yes, your relationship?"

"There is no relationship."

"And yet you offered her a place to stay in your unit. Why?"

"Because she had no other place to go. Besides, what makes you think I asked her to stay in my unit?"

The chair the fat man sat in creaked when he moved his bulk. Bending across the desk, he said, "Don't deny anything. Our security cameras recorded your encounter from the moment she stepped off the transporter until you and Miss Turner entered your unit."

"I see. I guess I forgot that every move we honest citizens are making is recorded by Security. It seems you have your spy-cameras hidden in every corner of Epsilon City."

"A necessary precaution to keep law and order." His bushy eyebrows drew together into one straight hairy bar. "Why did Miss Turner come to you, Mr. Houston?"

"Why did she come to me?"

"That's what I asked. Am I speaking in an alien language?"

"You might as well, because I don't understand the question."

Their interrogator heaved a big sigh. It sounded like the hissing of a Firespitter. "Let me rephrase it then…why did Miss Turner turn to you for help?"

"I told you that already. She had no other place to stay."

"You did tell me that didn't you?" He looked at Tara. "There are hostels in Epsilon City, Miss Turner. What is the purpose of your visit?"

"I'm a geologist. I came to Epsilon looking for rare gems. Is that a crime?" She spoke haughtily, almost defiant.

The man actually smiled. "It is not a crime, unless you plan to smuggle them off Epsilon."

"Why would I want to do that?"

"You'd be surprised what people do around here. Why did you not report to Immigration as soon as you arrived, Miss Turner?"

"Immigration? I'm not planning to emigrate to Epsilon. I have no wish to stay here for a long time." She let out a forced little laugh. "If I had any inkling of the welcome I'd be receiving I may not have come here at all."

The interrogator didn't seem to find any humor in her remark. "Most visitors don't plan to stay here but many do. Are you any relation to Gilbert Turner?"

The sudden question seemed to take Tara by surprise. She gasped and said, "You know of him?"

"I know of everyone who comes to Epsilon, Miss Turner, but you didn't answer my question."

"He is my brother."

"Your brother? Hmm." He leaned back into his chair. Houston almost hoped it would break apart under the man's weight. He would have liked to see the fat man sprawl onto the floor.

"Yes, my brother. Do you know where he is?"

"No. He left for one of the mining towns. That was five years ago. We haven't heard from him since. He either changed his name or he is dead," the man said bluntly. "Epsilon is an unforgiving place. There is no room for mistakes once you enter its domain. Either you adapt or you perish. Not everyone is cut out to live here. Not outside." He eyed her with suspicion. "It seems you didn't tell me quite the whole truth about your reason for coming to Epsilon. What else did you keep from me?"

She shook her head with a defiant gesture. "I didn't lie when I said I was a geologist and that I came here looking for gems. That is my profession. I only left out the part that I'm also looking for my brother. Are you going to punish me for that?"

"You are not here to be punished for anything. We are merely trying to establish a valid reason for letting you leave Epsilon City, should you decide to do so. You were supposed to register with Immigration after your arrival and you didn't. That raised a red flag. Why didn't you report?"

"I came in a spaceship. When I boarded the ship, I registered my name and my reason for coming here. Before we landed on Epsilon, I filed all the necessary information with the ship's destination log. I wasn't informed I had to report again after landing. I didn't drop from the sky, you know." Her voice had risen slightly as she spoke, clearly signaling her annoyance.

Seems she's got some fire after all. I find that extremely attractive. Houston glanced at her sideways. *I hope she knows how to control that fire.*

The fat man wasn't impressed by her show of bravado. "You wouldn't be the first person who comes to Epsilon City without proper clearance making up some story how they got lost in space, how they finally found this planet but didn't know its name, and how their private spaceship crash-landed in the jungle." Tiny points of reflected light appeared between the thick folds around his eyes as he regarded Tara. "May I see your ID card, please?"

She lifted the bottom of her blouse a little, revealing a thin traveling belt strapped around her narrow waist. She pulled out a plastic card and handed it to the fat man. He took it without a word and pushed it into a scanner on his desk. Studying the computer screen in the desk's surface, he nodded. "It seems you are indeed who you say you are." He pulled the card out and gave it back. "I hope you have a nice stay, Miss Turner."

She put her card away and rose from her chair. "Is that it?"

He nodded. "You are free to go. Sorry for the inconvenience. Oh, one more word of advice…before you decide to go looking for gems you need to get a permit from the Trading Commission's office." He looked at Houston. "Next time, be more careful whom you choose as your bed companion, Mr. Houston. She might have turned out to be a spy, possibly even murdered you while you slept."

"There is nothing going on between Miss Turner and me. She is not my bed companion, sir," Houston said, annoyed by the man's assumption.

The fat man chuckled, suddenly jovial. "Not yet, but she will be. You'd be a fool to turn away a beautiful woman like that."

Houston grunted and opened the door. A Security man stood outside, guarding it. "Can you direct us to the exit?" Houston asked him.

The guard nodded and said, "Follow me."

When they stepped into the corridor, Houston said to the guard, "We were brought here in a Security vehicle. How are we going to get home?"

The guard shrugged. "It seems that is your problem." He closed the door and left Houston and Tara standing in the corridor.

THANK YOU FOR READING

Did you enjoy this book?

We invite you to leave a review at the website of your choice, such as Goodreads, Amazon, Barnes & Noble, etc.

DID YOU KNOW THAT LEAVING A REVIEW...

- Helps other readers find books they may enjoy.
- Gives you a chance to let your voice be heard.
- Gives authors recognition for their hard work.
- Doesn't have to be long. A sentence or two about why you liked the book will do.

ABOUT THE AUTHOR

Herbert lives near Winnipeg, Canada. He spends his free time spinning tales about imaginary worlds and the strange creatures inhabiting them. His first published story `The Anniversary Gift' appeared in `Sweet Revenge' published by Midnight Showcase. Even though he writes in other genres, his love is Science Fiction. He enjoys building alien worlds and societies. Most of his stories contain an element of Erotica. All of his books are available from Melange Books.

Website: www.fictitioustales.weebly.com
Blog: hegro.blogspot.com
Blog: hergros.blogspot.com
Email: hegro@shaw.ca

Tarnished Valor